W9-BKF-855

WILDLAND

WILDLAND

A Novel

REBECCA HODGE

CROOKED
LANE

NEW YORK

Copyright © 2020 by Rebecca Hodge

Published in the United States by Crooked Lane Books, an imprint of The Quick Brown Fox & Company LLC.

Crooked Lane Books and its logo are trademarks of The Quick Brown Fox & Company LLC.

Library of Congress Catalog-in-Publication data available upon request.

ISBN (hardcover): 978-1-64385-292-8
ISBN (ebook): 978-1-64385-313-0

Cover design by Mimi Bark
Book design by Jennifer Canzone

Printed in the United States.

www.crookedlanebooks.com

Crooked Lane Books
34 West 27th St., 10th Floor
New York, NY 10001

First Edition: February 2020

10 9 8 7 6 5 4 3 2 1

To my parents, Tom and Ann Elleman, who always encouraged me to reach for new challenges.

CHAPTER ONE

Kat forced the last thumbtack through the yellow bedsheet and adjusted the fabric to make sure the bedroom mirror was covered. Facing her future was the goal of this trip to the southern Blue Ridge, but that didn't mean she had to face her reflection. Cowardly, perhaps, but no one would know. She lifted her empty suitcase off the bed and put it in the closet. A shame the rest of her life wouldn't tidy up so easily.

Lunch was next on her agenda, but the unexpected roar of a car struggling up the mountainous gravel road drew her to the front door, curious and a bit wary. This cottage sat by itself on a dead end. Someone must be lost.

She stepped onto the porch, ready to give directions, as a dust-covered 4Runner with dark-tinted windows came into view, dodging potholes and spitting pebbles in wide arcs. A robin and a pair of towhees took flight in a flurry.

Not someone lost—her daughter, Sara. They had made plans to meet for lunch in Franklin in two weeks to mark the halfway point of her stay, so Kat couldn't think of any reason Sara would drive an hour and a half to visit on her first day here.

A wide patch of gravel in front of the cottage ended at a stone bench that perched at the edge of a steep mountain drop-off. Sara parked, climbed out of the SUV, and waved. "Hi, Mom." She rooted around in the back seat and emerged with a bulging canvas bag and a bouquet of yellow daffodils and blue cornflowers. "I brought you some welcome-to-the-mountains gifts."

A nice gesture, but flowers didn't explain her daughter's arrival. Sara always had a master plan—something else was up. Regardless, it was nice to have her here. "Hi. You've come a long way. I've only been here a few hours."

"It's a nice day for a drive. I wanted to make sure you'd be okay up here." Sara turned and surveyed the view to the east—already Kat's favorite, a panorama that could have sold a thousand postcards. Broad, protective mountains. Gently rolling hills. A long crescent lake, sunlit and spangled, stretching across the valley floor far below.

"Wow. Pretty spectacular." Sara crunched through the band of drought-stricken grass that edged the house and joined her mother on the porch. "You and Dad came up here when I was doing junior year abroad, right? He must have loved it, away from it all."

"He did. This is the same cottage, too. He went hiking every day." Jim was the one who had gone out exploring while Kat enjoyed the view from the front porch. She had seen this forest, these mountains, through his enthusiasm—a landscape

2

of nuance and mystery, waiting to be embraced. She wasn't all that outdoorsy herself. Now, here on her own, she found herself focusing on practical details she hadn't fully considered—how isolated she was, how long it was going to take to drive to the nearest grocery, how much hassle it was going to be to live up here with no phone.

Kat gave Sara a quick hug and wrinkled her nose. Her daughter smelled like a mixture of citrus shampoo and wet dog, her consistent perfume. Between her job as a dog trainer, working with everything from police dogs to agility competitors, and her volunteer work at the Asheville animal shelter, Sara was never far from a four-legged companion. She preferred dogs to dates, and any hopes Kat had for grandchildren had proven wildly unrealistic.

Kat took a deep breath and let a wave of sadness roll past. Now, more than ever, it mattered that she would leave so little behind.

"Not a bad drive," Sara said. "But could you rent a place any harder to find? I passed the last house at least a mile back." She frowned at the fluttering strips of peeling paint that hung from the cottage siding. "I can't believe you'd rather be here than back home."

Kat bit back an illogical urge to defend the house. "It's faded more than I expected, but at least I have this view. I stopped at a yard sale on my way here and picked up a few things to brighten it up." The blue-and green-patterned ceramic bowl that now sat on the porch's end table and a cheerful quilt hanging on the back of the rocker did little, however, to distract from the sagging front steps, the ragged shingles, and the starburst cracks threatening one of the front windowpanes.

She had chosen this house in the belief that its familiarity would offer some comfort. Instead, its decline only underscored how much had changed. Jim was gone now, a midnight stroke taking him in his sleep, and life felt far too fragile. Instead of support, the house seemed to reflect her grief over the inevitable passage of time. "Come on in. I'll find something for the flowers."

She led the way through the living room. Sara set her bag beside the well-used couch and leaned against the kitchen doorjamb while Kat hunted for a container big enough to hold the bouquet.

"Mom, I'm worried about you." At least Sara didn't waste any time getting to the point. "Your doctor wanted you to start chemo a week ago. Instead, you hide here. It feels like you're giving up." She pushed her shoulders forward as though she were a child again, arguing for an extra cookie or a later curfew.

Kat wanted to hug her, hold her, tell her everything would be okay, but it would be the worst sort of lie. Nothing was okay. She'd retreated here to these mountains to avoid exactly these kinds of discussions.

Three years earlier, during Kat's first round of cancer treatments, Sara had been her staunchest supporter. Jim had manned the front lines, coordinating the countless appointments and taking care of practicalities. But Sara had been there for the toughest moments, driving up to DC each time Kat needed her most.

She'd held Kat's hand when they went in to hear those devastating initial biopsy results. She'd shaved Kat's head when chemo started taking its toll, cranking Gloria Gaynor up to maximum volume, claiming it was impossible to cry while listening to disco. It had been Sara who had gone with her to the plastic surgeon to pick out her new breasts, reassuring her every step of the way, boosting her spirits when Kat faltered.

Their repeated arguments the past few weeks had thrown them into territory Kat was struggling to navigate. This time around, when reassurance was no longer possible, they couldn't seem to find common ground.

"I know this is hard." Kat tried to sound unemotional, but her voice shook and her eyes filled. She kept picturing Sara, alone. She'd spent thirty years trying to keep her daughter safe and protected, and now it felt traitorous to abandon her. "I need time on my own to make a final decision. I've done the surgeries. Taken the drugs. I've fought, and for the last three years I thought I'd won."

It hadn't been a total victory—breast cancer, even when silent, hovered always at the edge of her consciousness, a predator in her peripheral vision, waiting to pounce. She tried not to think about the new lump that lived now in her armpit. The biopsy two weeks ago had merely confirmed the truth she had known in that first heartbeat of discovery.

"Now they're talking about even more chemo and radiation. Enough is enough. I'm done with this battle."

Sara looked away. "Just because it didn't work for Oma doesn't mean it won't work for you. A lot has changed since then—better drugs, fewer side effects. Treatment could mean years."

"What kind of years?"

No answer.

Kat turned away, and her hands closed around the edge of the chipped kitchen sink as she stared out the window above it.

Maybe Sara was scared—Jim gone two years earlier and now her mother threatened as well. Kat well remembered the loss of her own parents and the devastating realization that she no longer had them to lean on. Leaving her daughter was inevitable, but now Kat had to decide what she wanted from the time that remained.

"Sara." She couldn't force herself to look at the lines of worry that twisted her daughter's face, because they wrung her heart and strangled her resolve. "You were so young when Oma died. You don't know what it was like. The vomiting. The weakness. I watched my own mother wither into nothing but bones and teeth and endless pain. I refuse to drag this out and force you into months of caregiving."

Other factors weighed heavily as well. Jim had been at Kat's side through her surgeries, through those first rounds of chemo, a steady reminder that a future existed. They had hopes, they had plans, she had responsibilities. None of that anchored her now.

Since Jim's death, each day had consisted of a series of check boxes: make coffee, pack lunch, drive to work, select the right packet of lecture notes, stand in front of a classroom of high school students who read only CliffsNotes. Say the same things she'd said a hundred times, then return home with stacks of essays to grade. The evening work at least served as a distraction from the silent, echoing house. When she thought about more cancer treatment, the unanswerable question was *what's the point?*

Kat straightened, gave up any attempt to find a vase, and plunked Sara's bouquet into an inch of water in a dented saucepan. The blooms flopped sadly to one side.

This discussion was doing nothing to bridge the gap between them. She turned. Sara looked so sad and alone that Kat's determination to drive home her point seemed irrelevant. She crossed the room, wrapped her arms around her daughter, and hugged her tight. Sara dissolved, hugged back, and buried her face in the hollow of Kat's shoulder.

"*The sense of death is most in apprehension.*" Kat didn't realize she'd spoken the quote aloud until Sara stiffened and pulled away. When Jim had been alive, he had enjoyed hearing her quote Shakespeare whenever it popped into her head, but no one else appreciated it.

"Stop it, Mom. A dead playwright can't solve this. We're talking about cancer. About your life." Sara's jaw was so clenched, it sounded like she spoke through a narrow tube.

"I know you're worried, but I'll only be here for a month." Kat tried to make it sound like no time at all. "I'll think about everything you've said these past weeks. All your arguments for more treatment. I promise. When we meet for lunch, we'll talk it through one more time." A somewhat deceptive promise—Kat didn't think she would change her thinking— but it didn't feel dishonest to offer what comfort she could.

Sara's face pinched in an anxious frown. "I'm worried about you staying up here by yourself. My cell can't even get a signal. What if something goes wrong?"

"Don't be silly. I'll be fine. I'm probably safer here than in the city. I just need some time." Time. The one thing she wanted. The one thing she might not have.

"Okay, okay, okay. I get it." At least Sara now seemed resigned. "I've got one more thing to bring in." She turned and headed out the front door.

Kat sighed and tried to loosen the tension in the back of her neck, but it was there to stay. She glanced at the four large boxes she'd stacked against the far living room wall. Packed to the brim, they held more than thirty years of someday-I'll-organize-all-this memories—photos still in their drugstore packets, programs from DC's Shakespeare Theatre, Sara's school papers, souvenirs, and tennis team certificates. A fitting project for her weeks alone. Perhaps someday in the years ahead, Sara would look through the albums Kat created in these weeks and feel the love invested in them.

Kat's eyes dropped to the canvas bag Sara had carried in with the flowers, and she lifted it onto the couch to see what it held. A book on top—*Coping With Cancer*. Oh good, a little light reading. Her stomach tightened, and she regretted her promise to talk to Sara again about treatment. Under the book, two large, metal, flat-bottomed bowls. A half-dozen fluorescent-green tennis balls. At the bottom, a ten-pound bag of dog kibble.

Shit. Kat took two steps toward the door, but it opened before she got there.

Sara, her expression anything but innocent, held a leash attached to a large yellow Lab who must have been hidden in the back of the SUV. The dog panted, its tongue hanging low and its tail wagging high.

"This is Juni." Sara unclipped the leash and turned the dog loose. "She needs a foster home, and you need company. A perfect match."

"Have you lost your mind?" Kat made no attempt to soften her tone.

Juni came over to sniff Kat's hand, her breath warm and damp. Kat flinched and pulled away. She liked dogs just fine at a distance, but she'd never been around them much. She sometimes wondered whether Sara's passion for animals was simply a pendulum swing away from Kat's refusal to let her have pets as a child. Back then, they had seemed an unnecessary complication to a busy life, and right now, the last thing Kat needed was another complication.

The dog snuffled at Kat's sandaled feet, nosed into the dusty space under the couch, and inspected the crevices between the floorboards. Wisps of pale dog hair drifted behind her.

"You know I've never had a dog," Kat said. "Never wanted one."

"She's perfectly trained. I worked with her years ago. Her owner died after a long illness, and there's no one to take her. She's a total sweetheart, and she needs someone who will spend lots of time with her. I can't do it—I'm already fostering four. You don't want her put down, do you?"

"Come on, Sara, stop with the guilt trip. I don't want a dog."

"You may not want it, but you sure do need it. Up here in the wilds. All by yourself."

"This is a rental. Dogs aren't allowed."

"I stopped at the realtor's on my way up and paid the pet deposit."

"I. Do. Not. Want. A. Dog."

"I. Do. Not. Care." Sara emphasized the words the same way Kat had, but then her face softened, and she launched one of her hard-to-ignore smiles. "Mom, come on. Give it a chance."

Kat tried to think of a snappy response, but the past two weeks had left her with no ammunition. She looked away and silently named all fourteen of Shakespeare's comedies in date order, trying to find a path forward.

If Jim were here, what would he say? Probably something infuriating like *choose your battles* or *look at the intention, not the action.* Perhaps he was right, and this wasn't the fight to cling to. The dog was a present. Misplaced, perhaps, but as genuine in intent as the painted clay ashtray Sara had made in second grade for her nonsmoking mother. An all-too-familiar weight of guilt clamped hard on Kat's chest and forced a decision.

"I'll keep her for one month." The sentence hung in the air, underscoring Kat's foolishness. "No longer."

Sara gave a victorious smile.

Juni disappeared into the front bedroom.

"Don't let her get into my stuff."

Sara turned toward the bedroom door and paused, her head tipping to one side, her gaze focused.

Too late, Kat realized what she was looking at.

She hurried forward to stop her, but Sara crossed the bedroom and lifted the yellow sheet Kat had tacked to the wall. Sara froze, staring at the full-length mirror. The sheet slipped from her fingers and fell back into place. She turned to look at her mother, and her puzzled expression shifted to a gradual understanding.

"You moved the mirror at home out of your bedroom after your surgeries." Sara's voice held nothing but kindness and compassion, and Kat's irritation over the dog dwindled.

"Yes."

Kat's mastectomies and reconstruction had gifted her with nippleless, nerveless, fake Barbie-doll breasts, each with a five-inch scar. The last thing she wanted was a mirror big enough to showcase the damage. The small one in the bathroom was plenty for brushing her hair.

Sara, ever rational, would never hide this way, and Kat braced for a lecture on facing reality. Instead, Sara closed the gap between them, and Kat found herself wrapped in strong, loving arms. Held instead of holding. Cared for. Loved. When Sara let go—far too soon—Kat could still feel the comfort of the embrace.

"Okay, Mom, I get it. Do what you have to do. Maybe this break up here will help." Sara glanced at her watch. "Sorry to head out so soon, but I've got to get back." Her practical side surfaced, and she flipped back to her normal decisive self. "Take Juni for walks every day. Make sure she has food and water. She's well trained, but don't lose her. Call me if you have questions."

"I'll call when I go into town."

"Good. I'll be in Florida for the next week, judging a regional agility competition, but just leave me a message if I don't pick up." Sara gave Juni a pat and her mother a nod. A flicker of sadness on her face didn't fit with her brisk efficiency, but it vanished so fast, Kat couldn't be sure it had actually been there. Sad to be leaving? Sad about the future? Sara provided no clues and simply headed toward the door.

A piercing desire for one more hug, one more bit of connection, sent Kat onto the porch, the dog coming as well but staying obediently at Kat's side. Sara kept going, reaching her car, opening the door.

"Sara." Kat yelled the word, the twenty feet between them suddenly vast. Sara turned and Kat took a deep breath. "I love you." She hoped Sara could hear all the words she couldn't say out loud—sorrow for what the future held, apology for the fact that she couldn't promise to do as Sara wished.

"I love you too, Mom." Sara's face crumpled for a moment. "I wish you weren't so damn stubborn. Be sensible. Call your oncologist. Schedule the chemo. You can hide your mastectomies from your mirror, but you can't hide from the fact that if you do nothing . . ." Her voice broke, and she gulped, her head dropping forward to hide her face. It took a moment before she straightened. "We'll talk in a few weeks. Stay safe up here."

She got into the car, and Kat lifted her hand in farewell. The shouted good-bye left her feeling hollow. She should have followed Sara for a final hug.

Sara turned the SUV around, gave a wave, and headed down the mountain. The last of the dust settled back on the road, the last rumble of the engine faded into silence, and a razor-sharp stab of loneliness overwhelmed Kat. She shook it off. Decisions about her future had to be made on her own, didn't they? That was why she was here.

Juni tipped her head to one side as if she, too, were listening.

"Well," Kat said to the dog. "Looks like it's just you and me." Great. A dog. Something else to deal with.

She glanced toward the overlook and startled. A man and a boy sat on the bench, their backs toward her, staring off across the valley. They must have been there through that whole high-volume back-and-forth with Sara, hidden on the far side of the SUV. Heat rose into Kat's face as she tried to remember exactly what Sara had said. What these people must have heard. Why couldn't Sara have warned Kat of their presence?

Juni looked toward the bench, barked once, and launched herself off the porch, bounding toward the strangers and undermining Sara's claim of impeccable training.

"Juni, no!" Kat raced after the dog, worried she might attack. Who knew what a strange dog would do? By the time she caught up, Juni had reached the front of the bench, but aggression wasn't on her agenda. She stood in front of the seated man, her tail a wagging blur as he scratched her behind the ears. Beside him, the boy had drawn up his legs and tucked himself into a ball to avoid the doggy enthusiasm.

"I'm so sorry, so sorry. My fault. This isn't actually my dog . . . my daughter brought her . . . I don't think she'll hurt you."

"Not a problem." The man sounded more amused than irritated. He was athletically built, in his late forties, maybe early fifties, Kat's age, with long legs and strong hands and graying hair cut close to his head. He wore neat khakis and a buttoned blue short-sleeved shirt. His voice was polite, and he didn't seem to be a threat, but it was odd that he didn't look at Kat when he spoke.

The boy peeked cautiously at the dog, uncurled himself, and held out one hand for Juni to sniff. He used his other hand to retain a firm hold on a small blue day pack that sat beside him on the bench. He wore black shorts that were too big, a long-sleeved dark-blue T-shirt that was too small, and once-red tennis shoes that had seen better days.

Kat stepped closer, her hand extended toward the dog. "I'll take her back into the house. I'm sorry we disturbed you."

"Not an issue. Really."

The boy gained confidence, petting Juni now, and the dog shifted all her attention to him. The man turned toward Kat, giving her a clear view for the first time of the right side of his face, and she gasped. A thick red scar started below his right eye, pulling his eyelid into a slight squint and slicing a jagged path down his cheek and jaw. It continued down his neck and disappeared under his collar. Not a crisp, neat, surgical scar. A raw, vicious slash.

Kat flushed hot and turned away, the fire of her embarrassment catching in her throat and quickening her breath. She hoped the man hadn't noticed her reaction, then realized at once that of course he had. She choked down a lump of shame and forced herself to face him.

He met her gaze calmly with no criticism in his eyes. He must be used to seeing such reactions, but that recognition only made Kat feel worse. If someone reacted to her breasts that way, she'd be mortified.

"I'm Malcolm Lassiter." The man rested his hand on the child's shoulder. The boy, perhaps nine or ten years old, glanced up at him but remained focused on the dog. "And this is Nirav."

"Nice to meet you both. I'm Kat Jamison."

Malcom turned and spoke softly to the child in a language Kat didn't recognize. Nirav nodded and looked shyly at Kat. "Nice to meet." He looked down at his shoes as soon as the words were out.

Kat smiled. She well remembered those days of constantly prompting good manners. "Thank you, Nirav."

The boy slid off the bench and gestured toward Juni. "Papa, I go . . ." His face creased in concentration as he appeared to search for the next word, and then he gave up and finished his question in his own language.

Malcolm nodded and turned to Kat. "May Nirav play with the dog for a few minutes before we head back down?"

Thank goodness she could grant this small favor. Perhaps it would make up for her initial rudeness. "Of course. Her name is Juni."

Nirav apparently understood, because he gave her a devastating smile, grabbed his bag, and tugged at Juni's collar so she would follow him.

Malcolm scooted along the bench, making room. "Have a seat." He gestured to the empty space beside him.

He was a total stranger, and they were in the middle of nowhere, but Kat didn't feel she could refuse. He might think a rebuff was because of his face, and she couldn't let him believe she was that superficial. She sat, glancing first at the dog and the boy, worried they both might disappear into the dense forest. But Nirav had placed his day pack on the porch steps and was playing with Juni in the grass, neither of them giving any indication of wandering.

"Are you and Nirav from around here or just visiting?"

"Only visiting. We just arrived in the U.S. from Pakistan, and we're staying farther down the mountain. The blue house close to the paved road." He glanced behind him at Nirav with a look of pride. "Nirav is my adopted son. I'm a security consultant, and I met him when I was working in Islamabad. The adoption papers were just finalized."

Taking on the responsibility of a child. To all appearances, as a single parent. She might be doubting her own ability to meet the challenges that lay ahead, but here was someone who didn't seem the least bit intimidated.

"You had a long walk up," she said.

"Worth it. The realtor told us we shouldn't miss this view, and she was right." He gazed out at the valley for a moment. "Are you from around here?"

"No. I live in Alexandria. I drove all day yesterday, got here this morning, but we've . . . I've been here before. About ten years ago. This view is as striking as I remember, although it seems like there are a lot more dead trees. More patches of brown among the green."

"I asked about that. Apparently pine beetles and ash borers are the cause. Warmer winters have helped them out, and this drought is killing the weakened trees. We drove in through the national forest, and they had signs up warning of a high fire risk. They've banned campfires and are urging people to be careful. All it takes is one idiot with a lit cigarette."

Kat nodded. She'd noticed the signs but hadn't given them much thought. Drought and fire. Oh good. More things to worry about.

They sat in silence for a few moments, and Kat glanced surreptitiously at the man beside her. His face, which spoke so eloquently of violence, still caused an inward twitch, but his kindness to the boy tempered her normal caution. She wanted to ask about Nirav—the two made an odd pair—but before she could think of the right way to introduce the question, Nirav and Juni rejoined them, the dog dragging a stick, the boy carrying a smooth stone that he proudly showed to Malcolm, who made suitable noises of appreciation.

He got to his feet. "We'd better head back down. Thanks for sharing your view, and for letting Nirav play with your dog."

Kat stood and looked at him head on. "I enjoyed talking with you." Malcom's face considered a smile, although none made an appearance. "Nirav, if you come back, I know Juni would enjoy seeing you again."

Nirav consulted with Malcolm with a glance and apparently found approval there. "Thank you. Yes. Please."

Malcolm took a step down the road, but then he paused. "Listen. We're not far away. If you need anything. If you feel unwell . . ." He stammered to a halt, perhaps seeing in her face that he hadn't chosen his words well. "I mean, if there's anything I can do, would you let me know?"

Kat studied his face. His scarred side was toward her, making it difficult to gauge his expression. Was this a neighborly gesture that he would extend to anyone? Or was this a result of what he'd overheard that morning—a let's-help-the-cancer-victim obligatory outreach?

She hadn't shared details of her current condition with anyone but Sara and a few close friends, but now Malcolm, a total stranger, knew she had cancer, knew she hesitated to treat it, knew her daughter disagreed. If he'd heard every word, he even knew about her surgeries—what else had Sara said?

Pity was not what she needed. That was exactly why she didn't broadcast the news of her illness. She didn't need handouts; she could deal with this on her own.

As soon as she thought it, she knew it wasn't true. Her first round of cancer treatments had slammed hard. Maybe part of her reason for avoiding treatment was because at rock bottom she doubted her own strength.

Malcolm was waiting for an answer. She opened her mouth to respond with her standard no-thanks—*I'm fine, don't think I'll need anything, thanks for offering*—but instead she heard her own voice saying, "Yes, I may need some help. I'll let you know. Thank you."

She looked away, flustered—she'd let her guard down, and she wasn't at all sure that was a good thing. It was odd to accept help from someone she'd just met when she'd avoided seeking it from friends she'd known for years.

Malcolm didn't seem to notice her mixed feelings. "I'll count on it."

He took Nirav's hand and started downhill. Kat grabbed Juni by the collar to make sure she didn't follow. Man and boy disappeared down the road, their heads turned toward one another as if deep in conversation.

That scar on Malcolm's face spoke of violence and rage, of broken bottles in a bar fight or switchblades in a dark alley. Its brutality didn't fit with his polite demeanor and the gentleness he showed toward Nirav, but that scar announced itself, abrupt and startling, wherever he went.

Kat's world was sharply divided between those who knew and those who didn't. She didn't like the fact that Malcolm now fell by chance into the first category, but perhaps there was fairness in it. Her scars were well hidden, while he had to watch people recoil and turn away.

CHAPTER TWO

Quiet settled in at the cottage, the gentle sounds of birdsong and the rustles of the breeze in the stiff leaves of the rhododendron providing little distraction. Kat headed into the kitchen, Juni at her heels, and fixed a turkey sandwich and a glass of iced tea from the supplies she'd brought with her. She filled one of Juni's bowls with water and carried it and the bag of dog supplies to the porch. A scant cup of kibble covered the bottom of the food bowl, and dog duties done, she brought her own food out.

Her conversation with Sara looped endlessly in her head. There had to be a better way to reach her daughter and make her understand. Squabbles and testy arguments were not the sort of memories Kat wanted to bequeath, but at the moment, that seemed all she had to offer. This next month would give them both time to think, and perhaps then they would find a way to move forward.

She sat in the rocking chair and tried to recapture her pleasure at being somewhere new. Her life had been so locked in routine since Jim's death. If nothing else, being here would force some new patterns.

While Kat ate, Juni investigated the band of brown grass between the house and the road, making happy snuffling sounds. She stirred up small clouds of dust everywhere she stepped, which she would no doubt track back inside.

"How does it feel to be dumped onto a new owner?"

Juni lifted her head, pricked her ears, and bounded up the steps. She immediately scarfed her food.

"At least you don't seem inclined to run away." Kat laughed. "And here I am talking out loud to *a dog*. Maybe I really am starting to lose it." If she wasn't careful, she'd end up talking to herself as well.

Juni wagged her tail, trotted to the other end of the porch, and came back carrying one of Kat's sneakers. She dropped it beside Kat's feet and sat, her front paws perfectly aligned, staring with an expectant look. A stare like that communicated far more than words ever could, but Kat wasn't buying it.

"Yeah. I get it. You want something to happen. Yet another reason I don't want a dog." She patted Juni on the head and waved her away.

The dog gave her another long, pointed look; then she went to the canvas bag, stuck her head inside, and got one of the tennis balls. Kat ignored her. Wet tongue lolling, Juni dropped the slobbery ball in Kat's lap.

Kat recoiled and then rolled it off her leg with the tip of one fingernail, but she had to laugh. "Okay, okay. You win." Not just a dog. A dog who gave orders. As persistent as Sara and as difficult to ignore.

She put on her shoes and grabbed her red flowered sun hat and her green shoulder bag with the Arlington High School logo. Juni picked up her ball and headed straight for a tangle of honeysuckle vines at the end of the gravel road. On the other side, a pair of ancient ruts disappeared into the woods, daring them to explore.

Kat didn't follow. Probably nothing in that direction but hungry bobcats and poisonous snakes. The dark, dense forest there unnerved her, with trees of all sizes crowding together in a claustrophobic maze. Particularly forbidding when she was here alone. She reached up and touched the small disk of polished petrified wood she wore beneath her blouse on a silver necklace, and it calmed her as it always did, the talisman that kept her anchored.

She called Juni away. The dog returned at once, so perhaps she was trustworthy. Kat slipped the leash into her bag and started downhill. At least this was an actual road, not just overgrown ruts. Juni trotted a few yards in front, her head held high.

Trees, trees, and more trees. Kat took care to walk in the exact center of the narrow road, as far away as she could get from the little rustling noises on both sides. Patches of dead trees edged the gravel, stripped of greenery like weathered skeletons, yet another harsh symptom of the drought. Malcolm's warnings of the fire risk came to mind, and she shrugged them to one side. Officials tended to be overly cautious, always predicting worst-case scenarios. The odds of a fire were probably low.

Kat had envisioned a mountain retreat as the perfect place for some clear thinking, a reminder of better days with Jim, but she hadn't counted on feeling quite so unsettled. The dog glanced her way occasionally, but Juni's presence wasn't as comforting as she would have hoped. "Fine protector you are." Maybe Sara was right. Maybe it was a mistake to have come.

She set aside her second-guessing and focused on their progress. Steep switchbacks led downhill for fifteen minutes; then they crossed a narrow wooden bridge that spanned a steep-sided gully. Once a stream had run here, but now there were only dust and smooth pebbles to mark where the water had flowed. The bridge's sun-dried planks creaked under Kat's weight, which did nothing to inspire confidence.

She was probably worrying about nothing, but she was relieved to put the bridge behind her. A short while later, she reached a level stretch. Juni stopped, set her ball down for a moment to bark, picked it up, and raced ahead.

Kat hurried to catch up. They'd reached the other two cottages that shared her road. On the left, a nondescript blue cottage had a snazzy-looking silver two-door BMW parked in front. That must be where Malcolm and Nirav were staying. Opposite stood a pretty yellow cottage with a front border of bright red and purple tulips. A shaded porch held a white porch swing. It all looked homey and happy, nothing like her own bland rental, and Kat shrugged off a wave of envy. She drew closer and only then realized the tulips were molded plastic.

Juni lunged forward. Kat tried to grab her, regretting that she hadn't learned her lesson the first time, but the idiot dog evaded her grasp and jumped onto the porch, tail wagging.

"Hey, where'd you come from?" A young girl moved out of the shadows and into the sun where Kat could see her. Thin, tan, and graceful, with short, dyed-orange hair and clashing pink lipstick. Twelve, maybe thirteen. She offered a quick, uncomplicated smile.

Kat smiled back. "Hi. Sorry. I should have had her on her leash."

The girl knelt in front of Juni, a book in her hand, and the dog dropped her ball and licked the girl's face. She laughed and wiped her cheek. "That's okay. I like dogs."

She wore a pair of faded jeans that looked just right for the woods and a pale-green sleeveless top with crocheted trim that looked drastically out of place. Silver glitter on her fingernails sparkled as she stroked the dog.

"I'm Mrs. er . . ." Kat caught herself. This was not one of her English lit students. "I'm Kat. I'm staying in the house at the end. This is Juni."

"I'm Lily." The girl handed the ball back to the Lab and stood. "I've never met a dog who carried her own toys." She sounded impressed.

"She's been taught well, that's for sure." So far, Sara hadn't been totally wrong about that. "Not by me."

Lily scuffed the toe of one tennis shoe along the porch floorboards. "I don't have a dog. Mom says they're dirty."

Kat started to say she'd never had a dog before, either, but the door behind Lily swung open, and a man stepped into the doorway.

"Lily, you shouldn't play with strange dogs." His hand on her shoulder drew her away from Juni.

Lily set her jaw, but she let herself be shifted.

The man stepped forward, off the porch. He stopped at the right distance—close enough to be understood, but too far away to be intimidating. Kat noticed details like that more often with Jim gone. He looked about thirty, Sara's age, and he wore faded jeans with holes in the knees and a Georgia Tech T-shirt. Dark wavy hair hid his ears, and wire-rimmed glasses magnified his thin face, making him look boyish and nerdy. His dark-brown eyes and the shape of his chin were an exact match for Lily's.

Juni wagged her tail and offered him her ball, either a stamp of approval or further evidence that she was no guard dog.

"I'm Scott Bradford." He inspected Kat with an up-and-down look that appeared to file every detail. "And this is my daughter, Lily."

"Kat Jamison." She stepped forward for a quick, neutral handshake. "I'm your new neighbor. Up the road. The cottage called Mountain Ease."

"You've got the cottage with the great view. Lily and I walked up there yesterday."

That overlook must be far more popular than Kat had realized. She hadn't planned on manning a tourist stop. "It's beautiful up here. I'm looking forward to a quiet month." She meant it as a hint, but he didn't look like the sort to tune in.

Now that no one was showering her with attention, Juni returned to the road and stood poised to move on. She watched Kat, waiting for a signal. The perfect excuse to leave.

"Nice meeting you both." Kat started to follow the dog. "Juni and I are out exploring."

Lily took a half step forward. She stayed silent, but her eyes were on Kat, and it was easy to guess she'd like to come along.

Kat paused. She had not come to these mountains to hang out with a kid no doubt bored in the boonies, but some company in these woods would be nice.

Lily waited.

Kat caved. "Want to come with us?"

Lily's dazzling grin made her look half her age. "Can I, Dad?" She took a few steps toward Juni. Scott started to shake his head *no*, and Lily cut him off. "Come on, Dad. Please? You have to do your computer stuff. And you keep bugging me about that backpacking trip. Think of this as training."

Kat smothered a smile, and Scott gave her an if-you-only-knew-what-I-put-up-with look that emphasized how young he was.

Lily's plea had the melting effect she'd obviously hoped for. "I guess you can go," Scott said. "How long a walk? Where are you going?"

"We'll stay on the road." Not that Kat would ever consider leaving it. "An hour or so? I won't let Lily out of my sight."

Scott gave Kat another careful once-over, and whatever doubts he harbored seemed alleviated. "Thanks. Lily will enjoy it, and I can get some work done."

"Thanks, Dad." Lily took Juni's ball, tossed it down the road for her to fetch, and raced after her.

Kat followed. Perhaps entertaining random children was an unexpected by-product of having a dog. First Nirav. Now this girl. Sara had always been surrounded by a whirlwind of girlfriends, but they were simply passing faces whose names Kat could never quite keep straight. It had been a very long time since she'd spent time with a child outside a classroom.

Lily waited and fell into step beside Kat, and as they walked, she tossed Juni's ball ahead of them for her to retrieve. The heavy scent of evergreens hung in the air, and with company along, Kat relaxed enough to notice.

"It smells like Christmas here," she said.

They had always decorated a real Christmas tree when Sara was little, complete with construction-paper chains, popcorn strands, and glitter-laden preschool art. Kat had filled tin after tin with fudge and iced sugar cookies, and on Christmas morning she and Jim would set the alarm for 5 AM to watch the look on Sara's face when she first saw the presents.

Kat had done her best to keep all their family traditions alive—a new candle added to the table at each December dinner until the whole dining room glowed on Christmas Eve, flour spread on the back porch so reindeer hoof prints could magically appear Christmas morning. Then the year came when, flattened by chemo, Kat had found it all more trouble than she could manage. The decorations now lived only in their boxes, gathering dust in the attic.

Perhaps, if she were well enough, she could take them out this next Christmas. Perhaps she and Sara could decorate together. Then again, perhaps not. Who knew what kind of shape she'd be in by December?

Lily said nothing. The silence grew awkward.

Be checked for silence, but never taxed for speech. This time, Kat took care not to speak the line aloud.

Maybe a direct question would work. "You're staying here with your father? That must be nice."

Lily shrugged. "Yeah, I guess so."

Kat didn't believe her, and Lily obviously didn't expect her to. Probably best to ignore it, but too many years as parent and teacher made her ask, "What's wrong?"

Lily blew out a long breath. "This summer bites. I only get to stay with Dad for a month every summer. He takes me somewhere different each year, and I try to guess where." Her words tumbled out in a rush. "My best friend Myra and I figured this summer would be New York City. You know, Statue of Liberty like X-men. Empire State Building like *Elf.* Instead, he's planned all kinds of hiking and backpacking crap, and it all sucks."

Kat resisted a sigh. The smiling child she'd invited had transformed into a whining teenager.

"I called Myra last night—can you believe the phone in that house Dad rented has *a cord*?—and she says she's going to the mall this afternoon with Caroline Wagner. *Caroline*

Wagner. They'll end up best friends and they'll spend all their time together and I won't have anybody at all."

By the time she reached this pitiful ending, her face was pinched and she was sniffling.

Kat fumbled in her pocket and found a wrinkled tissue. Lily blew her nose.

"Maybe you'll like the hikes with your dad."

Lily snorted, gave a major eye roll, and launched into a soliloquy on all the other things Myra said, did, and planned.

Kat's attention wandered. Her students fell into two distinct categories by the time they hit high school—those who twisted with every peer-pressure breeze and those who ignored the wind. Lily appeared to already be accomplished at pretzeling herself into whatever shape her friends demanded. Sara's stubbornness might be frustrating, but at least she knew her own mind.

Lily ran out of complaints at last, and this time, Kat enjoyed the silence.

Her thoughts turned to Malcolm and Nirav, wondering what their story was, wondering whether she'd see them again. Sara, Juni, Malcolm, Nirav, Scott, Lily. Her mental picture of a month of unbroken solitude was already in need of some serious revision. She couldn't decide whether she resented the invasion or enjoyed the unexpected neighbors. Maybe a little of both. She needed space on her own to make up her mind, but perhaps she didn't need to be lonely.

When the gravel ended, Kat and Lily turned downhill on the paved road, lined on both sides by brown overgrown fields, their withered plants another reminder of the drought's relentless progression. Half-rotten fence posts leaned at crazy angles amid head-high saplings, and weeds grew thick and tangled. Juni tired of playing fetch, and she ranged a little ahead, nosing the undergrowth. She startled a pair of mourning doves, who took flight with whistling wings, and Kat added them to her lengthening bird list.

They'd walked farther than she'd planned, time to turn back, when Juni stopped and stared to one side. She dropped her ball on the pavement and stalked into the scrubby weeds, her head down, her tail stiff, a low growl rumbling deep in her throat.

"Juni, no." Kat looked, but she couldn't tell what had prompted such a sudden change.

Lily moved to the edge of the road and leaned forward, as if a few added inches would clarify the situation. "I can't see anything. What's wrong with her?"

Kat shook her head, apprehensive. She called again.

Juni ignored her and continued to walk stiff-legged into the weeds, the hair on her back standing up like bristles on a scrub brush. Twigs and thorny vines snagged her coat, pulling at her skin, but the dog ignored them, too. When she reached the old fence line, she stopped growling, lifted her head, and gave a hesitant wag of her tail. She whined, her full attention focused on something ahead of her. Something Kat couldn't see.

"Juni, come here." Kat tried to sound suitably stern and commanding. Juni glanced in her direction, but she didn't come.

"Shit," Kat said under her breath. If Lily hadn't been there, she would have said something stronger. She shouldn't have trusted this dog. She called one more time, but Juni stood rock solid and barked, giving no indication she had any intention of obeying.

The mass of vegetation between Kat and the dog was the perfect hiding place for ticks and chiggers. Maybe even snakes. The skin on Kat's arms prickled at the thought, but she couldn't abandon the dog. She gulped and plunged in. Vines grabbed her ankles and brambles attacked her bare legs, scoring her skin in long red scratches. She would have a few choice words for Sara the next time they talked, that was for sure.

"Damn dog." She paused to detach a tall thistle plant from her shorts. "Honestly, Juni, couldn't you find a nice open lawn to disobey on?"

She finally reached the dog, who barked again and nosed Kat's leg. Kat took a firm grasp of her collar, ready to drag her back to the road, but a whimper came from the bush ahead. Kat flinched, but she let go of Juni and bent low, careful not to move closer, unsure whether the noise came from something needing help or something dangerous.

Another dog lay hidden. A young dog. Not tiny, but his oversized paws meant he was not yet full-grown. Brown and black, some sort of mixed-up combination of hound or shepherd or who knew what, with a broad forehead and floppy hang-down-low ears. He crouched, trembling, beneath a snarl of rusted barbed wire that hung from one of the old fence posts. Not something overtly dangerous, and Kat inched forward as close as she could. Brambles studded the dog's short coat. He was caked with dirt and skeleton-thin.

Juni started forward, but the web of vines and wire blocked her.

"Stay."

Juni sat and panted.

Kat cautiously extended a hand, unsure whether that was the right move, but she stopped before she touched the dog. *What if he's rabid? What if he bites?* "Hi there."

The puppy ducked his head and flattened himself still further. He tried to back away, his paws scrabbling against the churned-up dirt around him. A length of taut, once-white wire-core clothesline stretched from his neck to disappear into the jumble of weeds and decrepit fence, preventing him from moving.

The suspense must have been too much for Lily, and she thrashed her way through the undergrowth and came up behind Kat. She stopped, looking at the pup. "What's wrong? Is he hurt?"

"He's caught. Hang on. Let me see if I can get him loose." Just what she needed. Another dog. Another worry. But leaving the poor thing like this was too cruel to even contemplate.

Kat wished her heart would slow. "Easy now. Easy. No one's going to hurt you." She tried to keep her voice calm, tried to imagine what someone who actually knew what they were doing would do, but the puppy whined and pulled at his tether, his eyes wide and frightened, searching in all directions for escape.

Kat stretched, grabbed the clothesline, and traced it back. It snaked in and out of the jagged branches of a long stick, which had in turn lodged in the old fence. The dog must have dragged the rope behind him, picking up debris as he went. Who knew where he had come from. How far he had traveled. How long he had been stuck here.

It took an endless few minutes to untangle the snarls, but Sara would never let her hear the end of it if she gave up. When the rope fell free at last, Kat turned again to the dog. "It's okay. Come here, little one." The pup didn't budge.

If only she understood more about dogs. Sara should be the one here in this situation—she'd know what to do. Kat kept the tension constant on the clothesline and moved cautiously forward. The pup whimpered, flattened his head, and tucked his tail even farther under his belly. He was shaking so hard, the sun-scorched grasses around him rustled.

Kat leaned forward, reaching, close enough now to breathe in the cloud of stink rising from the dog's coat. The smells of urine and feces and indefinable muck slowed her hand, but it was the sweet metallic smell of fresh blood that made her gasp and pull back. She closed her eyes, and the memories rushed in, the bloody drains after her surgeries, her mother's years of illness, the constant doctor visits and blood draws. Her stomach churned and a swell of nausea caught in the back of her throat.

"Kat, are you okay?"

The urgency in Lily's voice jerked Kat back to the present.

"Give me a minute. I'm fine." A blatant lie. Kat licked dry lips and wiped damp palms on her shorts. She could do this.

She reached up and touched her necklace, and her scrambled insides detangled themselves.

The dog watched her with wary eyes. Kat leaned forward again, apprehensive of what came next, breathing through her mouth this time to avoid the smell. She held out her hand for the dog to sniff, and he looked up at her. No growl or snarl. She patted him on the back, slipped her hand underneath his body, and picked him up. He was about one-fourth Juni's size, but he felt hollow, as light as papier-mâché.

"You got him. Is he all right?" Lily tried to come closer, but Juni blocked her way.

"Hard to tell yet."

Dirt tumbled off the dog's coat, and Kat tried to avoid the worst of it. Despite the filth, she nestled him securely in her arms, worried he would scramble away if she didn't keep a firm hold.

What a mess. The pup's left front leg had a long ragged cut that dripped blood onto Kat's new tennis shoes, and tendons glistened white below the elbow, exposed by the peeled-back skin. Kat shook with the effort to hang on instead of flinging the animal away, and her breath came fast. Grape-sized brownish-purple lumps distorted the dog's shoulders and back, and Kat's stomach gave another lurch. Engorged ticks.

Dried blood crusted the loop of clothesline that encircled the dog's neck. Sara would probably try to get it off right away. Kat shifted her hold, pinning the pup against her chest with one arm so she could use her free hand to investigate. She ran her fingers along the rope collar and tried to loosen it, but she couldn't get a firm grip, her fingertips sliding seamlessly from rope to skin.

Then she understood. She fought against a mighty wave of nausea and swallowed hard against the bile that scalded her throat.

The rope was embedded.

The clothesline must have been tied in place when the dog was smaller and then ignored. As the pup grew, the collar dug in, and the skin split as it tried to grow around it. She held the dog more tightly against her, dirt, blood, ticks, and all.

"Kat, what's wrong?" Lily stretched forward, trying to see.

Kat's entire body shook, a formidable tremor of pure anger. No, she corrected herself, *anger* didn't begin to describe it. Rage. Rage at such ignorance. Rage at the overwhelming neglect that had left a helpless animal in such slow relentless agony.

"Let's get back to the cottage. This dog needs a vet."

She waded through the brush to the road. The pup continued to tremble in her arms, and he tucked his head between her elbow and her side as if trying to make himself invisible. Otherwise, he made no effort to move, no attempt to escape. Juni stuck close, her head stretched high to sniff at the new arrival, but the pup acted oblivious.

Kat forced aside a feeling of panic and another flood of disastrous memories—other overwhelming situations where she had been only a powerless spectator. Jim's sudden death. The cancer. Its spread. If only someone else would materialize to take care of this mess.

"What are you going to call him?" Lily asked.

"Nothing. I'm not naming him. I'm not keeping him."

What in the world had she gotten herself into? Kat didn't want complications. She didn't want to be involved. She didn't want one dog, much less two. Yet here she was, trudging uphill, her legs crisscrossed with bramble scratches, her clothing plastered with dirt, clutching an injured half-starved pup who probably needed endless care. But when she shifted her hand, it rested below the dog's chest, and she could feel his heart beating steadily against her palm.

CHAPTER THREE

Malcolm and Nirav arrived back at their rental cottage and headed for the kitchen. "Hungry? Want some lunch?"

"Yes, please." The orphanage had drilled the kids on manners, and Nirav had been an avid learner—*you must act polite, children, or you'll not be chosen.* The message didn't settle well with Malcolm. As if a child without manners deserved less.

Nirav sat in one of the kitchen chairs—always close by, always watching, as if fearing his new father would disappear if given half a chance.

Malcolm's business partners in the security firm had been incredulous when he told them he'd filed papers for adoption. Fifteen-countries-in-ten-years Malcolm? Everything-he-owned-in-one-duffel-bag Malcolm? Raise a kid? On his own? He'd heard the chatter. Seen the headshakes and the dubious frowns.

Now, here he was, back in the States, arriving in Atlanta with his new son and detouring to the mountains for some

37

quiet time together while he negotiated a mortgage in DC for a house seen only on video. Worrying about kid's clothes and kid's shoes and school registration. It all felt a bit overwhelming, but whenever he doubted his sanity, all it took was a hug from Nirav to remind him what was important.

He pulled some leftover dal from the fridge and plopped it into a skillet to warm.

"Papa," Nirav said after a while, "in our new house, is there room for a dog like Juni?"

Papa. The new name still sounded strange, but every time Malcolm heard it, he was infused with a pride no other title or rank had ever given him. "A dog, huh? Well, the backyard is fenced. We can think about it. A dog has to be cared for. It's a big responsibility."

Nirav beamed, apparently confident that *thinking about it* meant *yes.* "I can do that. I can take care of him. When can we get him?" When they were around other people, Malcolm tried to stick to English, but when it was just the two of them, they both slipped into Hindi. In his own language, Nirav always had plenty to say.

"Hold on, hold on. We'll see." A son. A house. Now a dog?

"What do you want to do this afternoon?" They hadn't checked out the lake yet, and they needed to get groceries from town.

"Can we read one more chapter?"

Malcolm laughed. That woman at the bookstore had been right—all kids loved wizards and flying broomsticks. "Not a whole chapter. How about four pages?"

It was slow going, reading aloud in English, then pausing after each paragraph to translate any bits Nirav didn't understand. He was catching on fast, so it was worth the effort, even if Nirav's English vocabulary now included some pretty strange words.

Malcolm stirred the dal. Pulled plates from the cupboard and dished it up.

Nirav held a small bowl in his lap and ran his hand over its smooth rim, deep in thought. Not one of the kitchenware bowls—this one had a pretty pattern on it. Probably a piece of bric-a-brac from the cluttered shelf in the living room.

"Everything all right?" Malcolm asked.

Nirav looked up. "Papa, the things in the book are all pretend, right? There are no real Quidditch matches, or delivery owls, or magic sorting hats."

"That's right. It's only a story. Like the stories you've told me about Ekalavya." Maybe this magical stuff was too strange or too scary. Maybe they should be reading something more mundane.

"But is there a mirror like the one Harry found? Where you can look and see what you most want?"

Malcolm carried the plates to the table. Filled glasses at the tap. But delaying the disappointment wouldn't make anything easier.

"I'm sorry, Nirav. I'm afraid that mirror is pretend, too."

Nirav's face barely flickered, but Malcolm knew what that composure cost him. Should he leave it at that or dig deeper? What if he said something that made things worse?

Nothing was the same with Nirav in his life, not even answering a simple question. In the past, when he'd been with Special Forces, and now, heading up his own security firm, the risks had always been well defined. Regardless of whether he was working with an individual or a company, the steps were the same: evaluate threats, identify weaknesses, put an effective protection plan in place. And although he was ultimately responsible, he had an experienced team backing him up every step of the way.

But now he'd been entrusted with the care and safety of a child, and he was on his own. These risks were strange territory, and Malcolm felt constantly on the verge of screwing up. Perhaps someday he would discover a map and compass for parenthood, but for now he was making it up on the fly.

Nirav poked at his food without eating.

"If you had a mirror like that, would you like to see your parents the way Harry did?" Malcolm froze for a moment, not even breathing, hoping this was the right path.

Nirav nodded. Kept his focus on the bowl in his lap.

The kid didn't even have a photograph. Malcolm scrambled for a solution. "Try this. Close your eyes. Picture yourself stepping in front of that magic mirror, like in the book. Can you see your parents standing beside you?"

Nirav closed his eyes, and after a moment the tension in his mouth and jaw relaxed, and he almost smiled. Malcolm gave silent thanks. Nirav didn't say anything more, but when he opened his eyes, he dug into his lunch, and Malcolm chalked it up as a success.

This was all new for both of them. Nirav had remained in the orphanage while Malcolm spent a year fighting through endless legal paperwork, and their visits had been limited to an occasional meal or afternoon trip to the park. Now they were together full-time, and every day was a new journey, often along narrow, unpredictable paths.

In his job, Malcolm had no choice but to remain detached from the pain of those around him, and he'd gotten very good at it. Trouble with the wife or girlfriend? Worried about Mom back home? Well, we all have challenges; deal with it on your own time. Malcolm was happy to offer an encouraging word or listen to details over a beer, but he wasn't invested in the outcome unless it impacted the task at hand.

With Nirav, that sense of distance had evaporated. Every moment of the boy's worry or pain tore into him like shrapnel. Every moment of joy or contentment was a victory. It was a roller coaster that left him off balance, and it had been years, perhaps decades, since he'd tackled anything for which he felt so untrained.

After lunch and four pages of Harry Potter that somehow turned into six, Malcolm and Nirav pulled together water bottles and a snack to go check out the lake. They locked up the cottage and were halfway to the car when a call stopped them. "Hi there, neighbor!"

It was the guy from the cottage across from them, coming down his front steps. Pale. Slouched. Ten pounds out of shape. He held a half-empty Corona in his hand.

"Hi, I'm Scott," he said. "Scott Bradford. Wanted to introduce myself. My daughter Lily and I are staying right across from you. Came over to say hello." He came closer, and Malcolm watched with amusement his initial startled flinch as he noticed the scar. Scott certainly had no ability to hide his thoughts.

"Hi. I'm Malcolm Lassiter." Malcolm shook Scott's hand, cold and damp from the beer bottle. "And this is my son, Nirav."

Scott looked closely at the boy, and Malcolm tensed. He had grown used to being an outsider in his years in Asia and the Middle East, but here in the States, it was Nirav who looked out of place. Strangers gawked at the two of them together, or else they frowned and turned away. They'd been delayed at Immigration for more than an hour, Nirav's new U.S. passport inspected in detail, a manager called in for consultation.

Every suspicious glance at the bewildered boy left Malcolm seething. Even the cashier at the grocery store outside Atlanta had treated Nirav's halting English as a sign of imbecility. Scott looked like he was checking off categories—*dark skin, foreign name, someone appropriate to ignore.*

Malcolm fought down a strong desire to say something pointed. He gave Nirav's shoulder a reassuring squeeze instead.

Scott didn't seem to pick up on the cooling atmosphere. "Quiet out here, isn't it? Makes sense to be neighborly. I've been trying to get some programming work done, get my boss off my back so I can actually start on vacation. Lily and I plan to do some backpacking—never done it before, but I bought all the gear on the REI checklist, so we should be all set. How hard can it be? Just load up and walk."

Malcolm had a hard time keeping his face neutral. *Just load up and walk?* It was easy to picture Scott sinking to his knees under the weight of a forty-pound pack, but he let it go. Few fathers would arrange a backpacking vacation with their daughters, so Scott earned some points there. "Sounds like you've got it all planned out."

"Yep. The Appalachian Trail is just up the way. We can—" He broke off and turned. Kat and a young girl with fiery orange hair were approaching, walking uphill with Juni trotting beside them.

Kat's arms sagged with the weight of whatever she was carrying, and her steps were uneven.

"How was the walk?" Scott called.

Neither answered, and it wasn't until they got closer that Malcolm saw the worried look on Kat's face and the lump of dirty fur in her arms.

"Dad, look!" Lily raced up to them. "We found a puppy, and he's hurt." Her face held equal parts concern and excitement. Juni ran forward to greet Nirav, who knelt to pet her.

Kat stopped when she reached them. "I'm afraid he's in pretty bad shape. He's cut, and he's got a horrid rope around his neck."

The puppy was buried in her arms as if trying to hide from the world. It was little more than a skeleton, and blood oozed steadily from one of its legs. A strong stench rolled off the dog in almost visible waves. Scott wrinkled his nose and took a step back.

"Kat's going to take the dog to the vet," Lily said. "Can I go, too, Dad?"

Kat looked startled, as if this was the first she'd heard of the idea, but she nodded agreement. "If you don't mind letting Lily come, it would help if she could hold the dog in the car."

"Are you sure you want to go, Lily?" Scott's doubt came through loud and clear. "You can if you want to, but the vet is probably just going to put him down. Probably best, the way he looks."

"Dad!" Lily looked shocked and indignant, and Nirav stood up, looking concerned. How many foolish things could one guy say in five minutes?

"It may not be quite that bad," Malcolm said. He came closer, and Kat shifted the dog in her arms so he could see. He glanced at the bloody leg and then reached out to feel around the dog's neck. The rope had done a wicked job. "The leg will be okay. The neck . . ." He shook his head. "I've never seen anything like it. You're right, you need a vet."

"There should be one in town," Kat said. She turned to Scott. "Hopefully this won't take long. I'll bring Lily right back." She shifted the dog awkwardly in her arms.

Scott glanced at his Camry and then looked down at his feet. Once again, his thoughts were clearly telegraphed. Offer a ride to two stinky dogs? No way.

Malcolm gestured toward his BMW. "Nirav and I were heading down to the lake, but if you need a ride into town . . ."

"Oh no," Kat said. "There's no need. I've got my car, and with Lily's help, I should be fine. I need to get my wallet from the house anyway. But thanks. I appreciate it."

"At least let us give you a lift back to your cottage. You don't want to carry that dog uphill the whole way."

Kat looked indecisive. "Your car . . . we're a mess . . . are you sure?"

Malcolm answered by pulling his keys from his pocket. "Come on. It will save you a long hot walk and get you on your way faster." He'd have little chance to help Kat with her more serious problems, but this, at least, he could manage.

CHAPTER FOUR

An hour later, Kat and Lily were in a glistening exam room at Laurel Grove Animal Hospital. Kat had expected a rural vet clinic straight out of James Herriot, but the antiseptic smell, the bright lights, and the long counter lined with medical devices mimicked Kat's visits to her own doctor. One of the advantages of avoiding new cancer treatment had been cutting down on the countless medical appointments, but now here she was anyway.

Lily sat on an upholstered bench with Juni at her feet, and Kat stood beside the steel examining table. The puppy cowered on the table while the vet checked him out.

Dr. Lawrence was young, blonde, and thin, almost frail, with skin so pale it bordered on translucent. Kat thought *Ophelia* and wondered if she was too fragile to cope with this mess, but the vet didn't balk at the filth, and she examined the dog from nose to tail with efficiency.

"He's not mine," Kat said, even though no one had asked. "We found him like this. Juni's not mine either; she's my

46

daughter's. I can't take on another one." Her call to Sara once they'd reached town had gone to voice mail. She was probably already on the road to Florida. Kat dug her fingernails into the palms of her hands. "That rope. His leg. Those ticks. I had to bring him in."

The vet finished her exam and stood back.

"I'm glad you did." Her voice resonated with a deep-South drawl, and Kat had to concentrate to pick the words out of the accent. "The good news is he's about five months old, and all his problems appear treatable. The not-so-good news is he's got quite a few problems. The embedded collar is the worst of it. I'll need to remove it under anesthesia, see how things go. I know the leg looks bad, but the cut is recent, and closing that wound will be pretty straightforward."

The thought of anesthesia and surgery on such a helpless creature made Kat cringe.

"He'll need bandage changes for a few weeks," the vet went on. "He's malnourished, and he's dehydrated. His gums are white, likely anemic from the ticks, and he's probably loaded with intestinal worms."

Dr. Lawrence stopped and waited. Her face remained expressionless, but her hands twisted the tubing of her stethoscope into a rubbery tangle.

It took Kat a moment to realize she was supposed to say something. "I'm glad you can help him, but he's not my dog. What happens after he gets better; does he go to a shelter or something?"

The vet looked at Kat and shook her head in a definite *no*. "We'll talk to the county shelter, but when they learn it's a surgical case with no tags and no microchip, not to mention a history of neglect, they'll ask me to put him down."

Kat's stomach clenched.

"Oh no." Lily's voice was shocked, and Kat cursed herself for bringing the girl along to hear this.

"There's a local rescue group, but they're swamped, and they usually don't have funds for something this complicated." Dr. Lawrence's voice was even. She wasn't pushing, she wasn't trying to create a guilt trip, she was just laying it out. But her face had lost its last hint of color.

Brutally unfair not to give the pup a chance at some sort of future. Death instead of treatment would be giving up.

Kat pulled up short. Was this what Sara felt when she thought about Kat's decision? She hadn't thought of it in quite those terms before, and the wave of empathy she felt for her daughter's perspective caught her off guard and left her unsettled.

The pup took that moment to scramble across the examining table and bury his head under Kat's arm, exactly as he had when she carried him up the hill. He brought with him a new wave of his revolting smell, and Kat tensed for a moment before she gave him a tentative pat. Dogs-at-a-distance might have been her history, but today she was getting a crash course in up-close-and-personal.

Another dog? The last thing she needed.

Euthanize this little guy? Not an option.

"I can pay for his treatment." She had completely lost her mind. "And then maybe you or my daughter can find him a home."

The vet's body relaxed, and she smiled, showing deep dimples. Kat realized Dr. Lawrence had braced herself to hear Kat say she wanted none of it, to hear she'd have to put the dog down.

The vet nodded toward the puppy, who had now welded his body to Kat's. "I think he's already found a home."

Kat's lips tightened around the resolute *no* that fought to escape. A dog was a long-term commitment, and *long-term* was no longer part of her vocabulary. "Not me." Her voice squeaked. "I don't know anything about puppies. Juni came to me fully trained."

Juni sat up straight and pricked her ears when she heard her name.

Dr. Lawrence waved one hand as if sweeping away something completely irrelevant. "People who say they don't know anything make the best owners, because they make sure they learn. It's the idiots who think they know everything who let their dogs get in this sort of shape."

She picked up a pen and clipboard and made notes on some sort of form.

"We'll need to keep him here overnight, get him rehydrated, do the surgery, and take care of all these parasites. He'll need vaccinations and heartworm preventive." She slid a pen across the table along with the paper—an estimate form with a space at the bottom for Kat to sign her acknowledgment. "This total should cover it. We'll need a deposit."

Kat's lips tightened at the long column of numbers. So much for a low-budget mountain vacation. The pen felt heavy and awkward, but she signed.

"We don't have a name for the dog entered here," the vet said as she finished her paperwork. "Any thoughts?"

Lily and Juni sat expectantly, two pairs of watching eyes. Kat frowned at the grungy, tick-laden puppy. Paying for treatment was one thing. Naming was another. A name was a commitment. One she didn't want.

Dr. Lawrence stood with her pen poised, and Kat stood outnumbered. She sifted through a handful of boring dog names—Spot, Rover, Chief, maybe Lily had ideas—and then remembered the river she'd seen on her Virginia map on the drive here.

"Call him Tye. T-Y-E."

The vet grinned as she wrote it down, and Kat could tell she chalked it up as a victory. The simple act of naming, of no longer thinking *that dog*, was added insurance Tye might now have a home.

"Give us a call in the morning, and I can tell you how the surgery went. You should be able to take him home tomorrow afternoon."

Kat led Lily and Juni back to the car, her arms unexpectedly empty and useless without the pup.

"That wasn't so bad. Now what?" Lily asked.

What indeed. Heat shimmered on the asphalt parking lot, and Juni jumped into the back seat of the car and hung her head out the open window, panting. Peace and quiet sounded tempting, but Lily had been a genuine help. Kat cast about for some sort of reward. "How about some ice cream?"

Lily whipped out her cell phone and tapped at it. "There's a fudge and ice cream shop four blocks to the left?" She made it a question, but her voice was hopeful.

"A nice change from blood and ticks." Kat put the car in gear, and they arrived in minutes. "I can't go in like this." Kat's clothes looked like she'd stumbled off a battlefield. She fumbled for cash and handed it to Lily. "You're in charge. Anything is fine."

The grin Lily gave her made Kat wonder what bizarre flavors they'd end up with, but the choices proved sensible. They carried the ice cream cones to an outdoor picnic table—mint chocolate chip for Kat, double peanut butter for Lily, and plain vanilla for Juni.

Half of the vanilla ended up dripping onto Kat's leg as she held it for the dog, but after everything else that had dripped on her that afternoon, it ranked as only a minor inconvenience. She tried to remember the last time she'd sat outdoors eating ice cream. It had been years, maybe decades, and the simple pleasure felt surprisingly good.

When she and Jim had been in these mountains ten years earlier, they'd sat outside like this. Coffee back then, not ice cream. They had driven north to Asheville so she could see *As You Like It* performed by the Montford Park Players at Shakespeare in the Park. It was a perfect night and a great outdoor performance—a casual, bring-your-own-chair, pass-the-hat-for-donations event—but Kat's sharpest memory was of a peaceful hour before dinner when they stopped at a small café.

She and Jim had talked of nothing serious—Sara's news from college, carpet they'd ordered for the townhouse, Kat's plans for the next school year. What highlighted the memory wasn't the place or the conversation; it was the pleasure of being with someone she could share it with.

The same pleasure existed now. It wasn't the mountain location or the drippy ice cream that held this moment still for her; it was the fact that she was spending it with Lily and Juni. They'd shared an adventure, and it felt as if she'd known them both for far longer than a day. Such a shame she had so little time left for more moments like this with Sara.

When they were done, Kat drove them all back up the mountain. Malcolm's car was still gone, but Scott came out to meet them when she pulled up. She rolled down her window, and Lily gave Juni a final pat and climbed out of the car.

"Thanks for letting Lily come with me. She was a big help. And they didn't have to put the dog to sleep."

"Glad she could help." Scott gave Lily a smile. "I got a lot done. A win-win. I should finish this project in the next day or two, and then Lily and I can start a real backpacking vacation."

Lily wrinkled her nose at the word *backpacking*. "Kat, can I come see Tye tomorrow after you pick him up?"

"Of course, if it's okay with your dad. Juni would enjoy that, too."

Scott frowned and tried to push his glasses back into place, even though they already looked right to Kat. "I thought we'd go for a hike tomorrow morning," he said to Lily.

"Later in the afternoon? Please?" Lily gave her father a begging look, and his face softened. He laughed.

"Yeah, okay. That should work."

"Thanks, Dad. See you tomorrow, Kat!" Lily turned and raced into the cottage.

Scott looked after her and sighed. "Thanks again for taking her with you. She seems to have enjoyed herself, which is a better track record than I've had. She used to love the out-doors when she was little, but it's like a different person stepped off the plane this year. She just hangs around the cottage and whines about missing her friends."

He sounded clueless, but then again, it couldn't be easy to jump in and out of a daughter's life with once-a-year visits. "Lily and I talked a little on our walk." Kat paused and tried to choose the right words. "Maybe if you scaled back your plans. Let her make some decisions."

Scott tensed, and Kat regretted offering the unsolicited advice. "Thanks," he said, sounding like he didn't mean it. "My ex keeps telling me I don't understand a thing about twelve-year-old girls, but she's my daughter. She can't have changed that much. She'll come around."

His words were neutral, but his tone was dismissive. Kat suspected nothing would change.

Enough. She had earned some solitude. She said a firm good-bye and started the car. She didn't want to think about Lily or Tye, Malcolm or his scars, or even her own problems. She didn't want to think about anything at all. Maybe a good book and a cold drink would do the trick.

She drove back to the cottage with Juni, dumped her stained clothes and blood-splattered tennis shoes in the deep kitchen sink to soak, and relaxed into a long hot shower, climbing out only when the water pressure dropped, and she remembered the drought. She slid into jeans and a fresh blouse and tried to forget the day's problems and the smell of filthy dog.

But when she sank into the porch rocking chair and reached to set her glass of iced tea on the table, she froze. She had placed her little multicolored bowl on that table when she unpacked that morning. Had it been there at lunch? She couldn't recall. Now it was gone.

She looked around as if it could have moved on its own, but it was nowhere in sight. Gone. Some person had done this.

The hair on Kat's arms stood up straight, the day suddenly colder. Sara and Lily hadn't touched it. Malcolm hadn't gone near the porch. Nirav had been running around, but it was an unlikely thing for a nine-year-old boy to take. She glanced at Juni, but that was even more absurd.

The woods had lost some of their menace as the day moved on, but now the trees closed in around her, once again dark and forbidding. The remote location. A man with a scar. An injured dog. Her retreat was proving anything but restful.

That night Kat slept with her windows closed and locked, banning the breeze and muffling the sounds of the tree frogs, the cicadas, and the *who-cooks-for-you* call of the local barred owl. In the middle of the night, she reached out for Jim, the memory of his comforting warmth intensely real. She woke, startled, when all she found beside her was empty space.

Empty space. In the end, it was all she would leave behind her as well.

CHAPTER FIVE

Malcolm sat in front of his cottage with his coffee the next morning, surveying the parched landscape and the cloudless sky. Still no sign of rain. He was delaying breakfast until Nirav woke, and frankly, the chance to be on his own for a bit was too good to pass up. Such a change, this business of being tethered to another person. He and Nirav had been together full-time for only a couple of weeks. It was going to take time to adjust.

His cell phone showed only one flickering bar. He'd need to go farther down the mountain to get enough signal to check email and see if a date for the house closing had been confirmed. This stay in the mountains was great as a transition into so much that was new, but it would be nice to get Nirav settled in a real home. They needed to start their new life.

The sound of a car engine grew closer, and Malcolm looked uphill. That had to be Kat, since hers was the only cottage higher up the mountain. He'd thought of her often since he'd overheard that awkward conversation the previous day. Kat was facing serious decisions. Covering her mirror? He understood plenty about that temptation. It had taken him more than two years to get to the point that he no longer startled himself as he faced his mirror to shave each morning.

Her car slowed and then stopped in front of him. Kat waited a few seconds for the dust to settle and then rolled down her window.

"Good morning," she called.

Malcolm closed the distance between them. "Good morning. How's that poor dog doing?"

"The vet seemed to think she could patch him up. I'm heading into town now to run some errands, and I'll give them a call. In theory, I should be able to bring him home later today."

"Good. I'm glad they think he'll be okay, and I know Nirav will be, too."

The slam of a screen door caused them both to turn toward Scott's cottage, and sure enough, here he came.

Scott waved and walked across the road to join the conversation, jabbering long before he even arrived. "Morning! How's everyone doing? Looks like another beautiful day. No rain to deal with. Lily and I are going for a hike, but she's still sound asleep. I swear, she's up until the wee hours and then hibernates for half the day. I promised to make her animal pancakes for breakfast. She won't have that luxury on the trail."

Kat smiled, apparently more patient with all this than Malcolm was. "I used to do that for Sara—bear shapes and fish shapes were her favorite."

Scott nodded. Malcolm didn't think eating animal-shaped food would appeal to a vegetarian, but perhaps Nirav would like plain round ones. He'd have to remember to pick up pancake mix next time he was at the grocery. Something else to think about—American breakfast food.

"Please thank Lily again for all her help yesterday," Kat said.

"She had a great time. Talked about nothing else last night." Scott didn't sound overly happy about it.

Malcolm took a step toward his cottage, conscious that they were delaying Kat from her errands, but she held up her hand to stop him. "I'm glad you're both here. Something odd happened yesterday—someone must have been up at my cottage while I was away. A thief. Nothing of consequence taken, but keep your eyes open."

"That's not good news," Malcolm said. They were isolated up here—both a protection and a risk. "I'll definitely pay attention to anyone heading up the road."

"Thanks," Kat said.

She started to say something more, but Scott jumped in first. "Did they break into the house? What did they take? Did they do any damage?"

"The only thing missing is a ceramic bowl I had left out on the porch. It's not worth anything, but I liked it. It's creepy to know it was there and now it's gone."

Scott snorted. "A bowl? No thief is going to drive all the way to the top of this mountain and only steal a bowl. You must be mistaken. It's probably there. You probably put it somewhere else and forgot." He waved his hand to dismiss any alternative and gave Malcolm a pointed can-you-even-believe-such-foolishness look.

Kat's jaw tightened, and Malcolm's irritation spiked. Scott was right, it was weird, but that was no reason to doubt Kat. "If Kat says someone took it, then someone took it. We'll need to be careful."

Scott's eyes narrowed, but Kat gave Malcolm a grateful look. "Thanks. Well, I guess I'll head into town. You both have a good day. I'll look forward to seeing Lily later." She waved a farewell and put the car back in gear.

Malcolm once again started toward his cottage, but then he stopped. A bowl. Missing yesterday. "Kat!" he called. She braked and looked back at him. "What did your bowl look like?"

"It had a blue-and-green pattern on a white background. A dark-blue rim."

Malcolm's throat tightened. The bowl Nirav had been holding at lunch the day before looked like that. He had taken it into his bedroom when he went to bed, placing it on his nightstand, touching it as if it provided some hidden comfort.

Malcolm couldn't accuse Nirav out of hand. He needed to talk to him. "Okay. Thanks."

Kat looked puzzled, but the car started forward again and soon disappeared down the hill.

"Guess I'll go wake Lily," Scott mumbled, obviously still annoyed that Malcolm hadn't backed him up. "Get her moving."

Malcolm didn't reply, his thoughts churning. Surely Nirav couldn't have stolen that bowl. He would never have done such a thing.

He went into the house and quietly opened the door to Nirav's room. There it was on the stand—a small decorative bowl, nothing all that special about it. Nirav slept on undisturbed, but the covers were twisted around him as though he had spent the night tossing and turning. The director at the orphanage had told him Nirav sometimes woke with nightmares, but Malcolm hadn't heard him in the night.

He leaned against the doorjamb and watched the boy breathe. Nirav's face was smooth and calm, whatever memories that haunted him well hidden, at least for the moment. Malcolm's chest tightened. Nirav was the most precious gift he'd ever received, and he wasn't looking forward to the conversation he now had to have with him.

The day Malcolm first met Nirav, he had gone to the outskirts of Islamabad, toward Taxila, to get a sense of the neighborhood. One of his security firm's most important clients planned to hold a series of meetings there, and Malcolm wanted to scout it out. On paper, low risk, but an on-site look would fill in the gaps far better than a remote assessment. In person, he could evaluate traffic patterns. Local hangouts. Possible threats.

He spent an hour exploring the area on foot, getting oriented, and then he settled at an outdoor table at the café across from the meeting site, ordering coffee and mutton stew with chapati. From this location, he could watch and learn. It would be far easier to detect the abnormal on meeting days if he was thoroughly grounded in what was usual for the neighborhood.

He felt the weight of eyes on him. This sixth sense he possessed, hidden in his skin or buried deep in the reptile part of his brain, had served him well, and he never ignored its warning. He got stared at a lot—first, because he was a tall white foreigner, second, because of his face. He could never assume such an intense look was simple curiosity, so he turned in his chair to find the source of his disquiet.

No threat apparent—it was only a small boy. Empty-handed. Shaggy-haired. Very thin. He stood in the dirt that edged the café patio, barefoot, his left arm held tight to his side. His clothing was faded, well worn, and too large for his slight frame.

Usually when Malcolm met the eyes of someone at random, one of two things happened—either they stepped forward with a greeting or request, or, more often, they turned away, embarrassed by their nosiness. This boy did neither. He studied Malcolm's face so intently, Malcolm could feel the boy trace every twist of his scar. He waited for him to hold out his hand in the universal beggar's appeal—he sure as hell looked hungry enough—but the kid just stood there, his hands at his side, watching.

"Would you like this?" Malcolm gestured toward the untouched chapati in the basket beside his plate. The boy's eyes jerked to see what he pointed to, and he looked startled, as if he hadn't yet noticed the food. His tongue moistened his lower lip, and he nodded.

Malcolm waved him closer, and the boy looked around the patio, most likely searching for the waiter, who would undoubtedly chase him off. Coast clear, the boy stepped to the table, and Malcolm placed the bread in his hand. The boy tore into it with small white teeth, seizing huge hungry bites, the food disappearing with astonishing speed. His eyes never left Malcolm's face.

There was no more food. Malcolm expected the child to leave. Instead, he gave a nod of thanks and returned to his post a few steps off the patio, feet planted, body still, simply watching. Malcolm resumed his walking tour of the district, but this time the boy followed, five paces behind every step of the way. Completely silent. For an hour, the two walked, past storefronts and houses, past the neighborhood mosque and a small school. Malcolm and his shadow.

At last, Malcolm sought out a bench, found one in the shade, and sat. "Come here," he said in Urdu.

The boy hesitated, but he came.

"Sit down." Malcolm gestured to the space beside him.

The boy sat at the far end of the bench. Wary. Poised to run if he glimpsed danger.

"What's your name?"

"Nirav." The boy spoke quietly.

A name more common in India than in Pakistan. "Does your family live around here?"

Nirav looked uncertain. Chose his words. "I have no family."

No family. It explained a few things, but not everything. "Why are you following me?"

Nirav hesitated, as if there was more than one answer, but then he seemed to make up his mind. "My family is from Mirpur Khas." Malcolm had read about the area—far to the southwest. "My father came here to Islamabad for business. My mother and I came with him to see the city. There was a train wreck. An explosion. They are both dead. I am here."

Orphaned and stuck in a strange city. Malcolm felt a surge of pity building, and he pulled himself back from feeling sorry. This was just one little tragedy in a country that had seen many.

"So, why were you following me?"

Nirav hesitated, and then he came to stand in front of Malcolm. He reached out with his right hand and traced the scar on Malcolm's face with an extended finger, not touching, but his hand so close Malcolm could feel the air shift across his skin.

Then, Nirav lifted his left arm, which until then he'd held pressed to his side, and Malcolm saw the burn scar. It covered the back of his hand and his entire lower arm, healed but still red and raw, with a broad band of damaged skin that extended farther up toward his shoulder, disappearing into the sleeve of his shirt. "We are the same."

The words hit home like a punch beneath the diaphragm, and Malcolm had to remind himself to breathe. Nirav sat down again on the bench, but close this time, their legs touching. He reached out with confidence and took Malcolm's left hand in his good right one, his fingers closing fiercely. Malcolm hesitated for only a second, then turned his hand so he could hold on tight in return. *We are the same.* By any standard measurement, the world would judge the statement a lie, but the two of them knew its truth.

The memory of that first meeting returned to Malcolm often. It had been the day that transformed his future, a day when a chance encounter had seismic impact.

Nirav stirred in his sleep, then opened his eyes. He saw Malcolm standing there, and his face eased into a smile that sprang directly into Malcolm's heart.

"Good morning." Malcolm's voice was quiet, but it didn't mask his determination to face whatever his son had done. "Let's get you some breakfast. Then you and I need to talk."

CHAPTER SIX

Kat dreaded seeing Tye again, but she needn't have worried. The cute wiggly dog the technician carried into the exam room at the vet clinic that afternoon bore little resemblance to the quivering tangle of dirt she had dropped off only the day before. His right front leg had been shaved along most of its length, and a thick line of purple plasticky stuff—skin adhesive, according to the tech—replaced what had been a bloody wound. They had removed the horrific rope collar, and a bright blue bandage swathed Tye's neck. No ticks remained, and the pup had been bathed and smelled faintly of orange groves. Kat relished the improvement—a spirit-lifting break from the hovering apprehension that had pervaded her cottage.

The pup sniffed at Kat's hands with curiosity.

"Things look pretty good, considering," Dr. Lawrence said.

She demonstrated how to change the bandage while Kat stayed at a safe distance, but the process turned out to be far less disgusting than she'd feared. The wound encircling Tye's neck where the clothesline had dug in looked raw and wet, but at least it wasn't bleeding.

The vet put the last wrap of the bandage in place. She made it seem easy. "Change this daily, but also if it gets wet or seems loose. And don't use a collar—use a harness if you need him on a leash. Definitely now. Probably forever."

Kat fumbled in her shoulder bag for her pet-store purchases. "Do you think this is the right size?"

She held out a bright-red harness and matching leash, as recommended by Sara on the phone that morning. Her daughter had been astonished to hear that Kat had acquired yet another dog, and she hadn't held back on advice.

The vet dimpled. "See, I told you people who claim they don't know what they're doing put the most thought into owning a pet."

She showed Kat how to put the harness on, and when it fit perfectly, Kat felt like she'd received an A+ on a difficult exam.

"Bring him back in a week, and we'll see how he's doing." Dr. Lawrence gave Tye a farewell scratch behind his ears, and he gave a quick wag of his tail in response.

Kat left the clinic somewhat dazed, the dog in one arm, a bag bulging with bandage material and dog-training brochures in the other. She put Tye down on the front passenger seat and started the car, but the dog scooted over and climbed into her lap, wedging himself underneath the steering wheel.

As a toddler, Sara had hit phases where she wouldn't let Kat move more than a foot away without throwing a fit, and the clinginess had made Kat feel hemmed in. This puppy was claiming her in the same way, but this time it felt good. Maybe the difference was that this time, Kat was the one who needed something to cling to. Perhaps this was why Sara liked being around animals so much.

"Okay, okay," Kat laughed. "Hold still. Don't make me wreck." Oh good. Talking out loud now to two dogs instead of one.

Once back at the house, Kat let Juni out and sat in the rocker on the porch while she leafed through the puppy brochures. The dogs played in the clearing. Juni occasionally looked at Kat as if asking what she'd done to deserve such a boisterous companion, but she treated Tye gently, only nudging him away when he tried to chew on her ears.

It was after four when Scott and Lily walked up. Scott stopped in sight of the cottage, gave a wave, and turned back. Kat had to give him credit for escorting his daughter, but she wasn't disappointed to see him go. He had been rude and dismissive of her concerns about the stolen bowl, and his skepticism still rankled.

Lily ignored her father's departure and rushed forward to pet Tye. "Wow. He looks great."

She started rolling tennis balls to the pup and tossing them to Juni, all three of them appearing delighted with the simple activity. Kat kept a watchful eye, and eventually Tye burned off much of his puppy-energy. He flopped to the ground at the foot of the steps, the wrap around his neck loose and sagging from all the roughhousing.

Kat sighed, went inside, and got the bandage materials. She had hoped to avoid that awful wound a bit longer.

"I wish I had a dog." Lily's voice bordered on a whine.

She had said it about thirty times. Maybe forty. The cards hadn't been dealt right—Lily wanted dogs and Kat didn't.

"Okay, dog lover, come over here and give me a hand."

They sat on the wooden steps with Tye in Lily's lap, the ointment, pads, gauze, scissors, and blue vet wrap lined up in a neat row. Juni stretched out at their feet and watched the preparations with interest.

Lily scratched Tye behind his ears, and he gazed at her with the doggy version of pure bliss. "He's better now that he's not gross and bloody and covered in ticks. And he's pretty smart."

Lily had been trying to teach him to sit. Tye wagged his tail and pricked his ears at each command, but Kat hadn't noticed any evidence of overwhelming brilliance. She unwrapped the layers of the old bandage and exposed the raw neck wound, which hadn't improved any in the few hours since she'd seen it last.

"Yuck." Lily scrunched up her face and leaned as far backward as possible.

Yuck, indeed. The wrappings smelled like medicine, not blood, but the scent still set Kat's heart racing. She reached up and touched her pendant. She could do this. She set the used bandage down on the step behind her. "Hang on to his head, and I'll try to spread this ointment."

The two of them focused intently on Tye, but they hadn't made much progress when Juni got to her feet, barked once, and trotted across the yard, her tail wagging. Kat looked up. Malcolm and Nirav had walked up the road.

"Good afternoon." Malcolm bent to pat Juni on the head and then came over to the porch. "We've come to apologize."

"Apologize?" Kat set down the bandage she was holding. "Whatever for?" She had been trying to figure out how best to thank Malcom for his kindness in giving them a ride the day before. An apology from him was nowhere on her radar.

Lily looked interested. Tye sat, content, on Lily's lap, his neck still unbandaged.

Malcolm spoke a few words to Nirav, and after a moment, the boy stepped forward, his head hanging, his eyes fixed on his shoes, the smiles and laughter Kat had seen the previous day nowhere in sight.

In Nirav's right hand, held with great care, as if it might shatter at any moment, was the missing bowl.

Kat struggled to understand. "You found it?"

Malcolm shook his head. "We didn't find it, exactly."

Again he spoke to the boy, his tone impressively gentle.

Nirav answered with a few words in the same language, and then he came closer, his eyes still cast down.

"I am saying very sorry. I not good to take. Not mine." He spoke the words with great concentration, as if he had practiced them. He held the bowl out to Kat, and only then looked directly at her. His mouth was drawn tight with effort. "Mama had like this."

Kat inhaled sharply, and her chest clamped down hard. A small boy, not a burglar or a lurking maniac.

She belatedly reached out to take the offered bowl, and only then saw that red, puckered skin covered the boy's left hand and arm, visible today because he wore short sleeves.

The skin looked fragile, more like opaque plastic wrap than actual skin. The muscle of the arm was withered. It must have been a horrible burn.

Kat turned the bowl in her hands, the surface cool and smooth. She looked back up at Malcolm.

"He really is sorry." Malcolm met her gaze head on. "He saw the bowl when he was playing with Juni yesterday, and he slipped it into his day pack because it reminded him of one his mother had." He glanced at the bowl. "When I saw him with it, I thought it belonged to our cottage. It wasn't until you told me yours was missing that I started asking questions."

Throughout this explanation, Nirav's eyes never left the bowl in Kat's hands, but he listened carefully. He appeared to understand what Malcolm said, nodding agreement at all the right moments.

"Nirav lived pretty much on his own for a long time in Islamabad, and he was used to taking anything that had been abandoned or thrown away. This is his first week in the States. He's still learning the rules." Nirav glanced up at his father, and Malcolm gave the boy's shoulder a reassuring pat.

Kat pictured this fragile-looking boy, alone on the streets of a strange city, and the image shifted to become Sara at that age, equally lost and alone. Unbearable. The world treated the defenseless with cruel indifference. She gave the boy what she hoped was a reassuring smile. "Nirav, thank you very much."

Lily had been staring at Nirav's burn. "What happened to his arm?"

Kat bit back her instinct to admonish her. At least Lily hadn't asked Malcolm about his face.

Malcolm looked from the bowl to Nirav and seemed to decide some sort of answer was necessary. "Nirav was traveling with his family from western Pakistan into the capital when their train derailed. There was a fire, and his parents were killed."

He reached up and touched his own scar without seeming to realize he was doing so.

She had thought these two were an unusual pair, but they had this in common—both were survivors. That's what she had been called these past three years—a cancer survivor—but the term never seemed to fit. You survived a storm or a battle, events that had a distinct ending, but when the fight kept going, you were simply a combatant.

Kat turned the bowl in her hands. Too much trouble over such a small thing. "Thank you for explaining." She wasn't sure what to do. She would be happy to give the bowl back to Nirav if he valued it so much, but she didn't want to undermine Malcolm's efforts.

Nirav was looking around now with a little more confidence, and he caught sight of Tye, who still sat in Lily's lap, waiting for his new bandage. He had seen the dog wrapped in Kat's arms the day before, but the extent of his neck injury had been much less obvious then. Nirav looked now at the dog's wound, and his face tightened, his brow furrowed. He tugged on Malcolm's hand. "Papa, dog has hurt. Dog . . ." He paused, struggled for the next word, and then gave a frustrated snort and rushed on in his own language. He pointed to the dog and gestured to his own throat, obviously upset.

"It's better now," Kat said. "The rope collar did the damage, but now that it's off, his neck should heal."

Nirav looked puzzled, and Malcolm translated.

The boy came forward to pat Tye on the head. He spoke to the dog, and then to Kat, then turned to Malcolm and waited for him to translate.

Malcolm let out a breath that traveled from deep down. "I have so much to learn. He told the dog that the person who did this has brought very bad karma upon himself, and he assured the dog he is now cared for. And he's telling you that your *bhuta daya*—I think it means compassion toward an animal—marks your divine quality." He ruffled Nirav's hair and gave him an approving nod—one of those tough-guy equivalents of a hug. Nirav beamed.

Kat had to swallow twice before she could speak. "Thank you." Those two words didn't convey the breadth of what she wanted to say, the sense of honor his words granted her, but Nirav responded with a brilliant smile and turned back to the dog. Juni, apparently feeling neglected, chose that moment to drop a tennis ball at Nirav's feet, and he picked it up with a surprised look.

Lily promptly handed Tye to Kat and stood up. "Come on, Nirav." She waved toward the Lab. "This is Juni. *Juni*. And that's a ball. *Ball*."

"Juni." Nirav had already met the dog, but he appeared eager to practice. "Ball." He held up the tennis ball.

"You got it."

Nirav looked at Malcolm and waited for his nod, then followed Lily into the yard. The two started throwing the ball for

Juni, and Lily chattered on with their game, naming things in English at a bewildering pace.

Malcolm gestured toward the lineup of bandage materials. "You've lost your extra pair of hands. I'm no medic, but would you like some help? Nirav was excited to meet Lily yesterday. If you don't mind, I know he'd enjoy a few minutes to play."

"Thanks, I'd love some help." Kat settled Tye more firmly in her lap. "I'm in over my head with this puppy."

Malcolm knelt, gave Tye a pat, and spoke to him in the same quiet tone he'd used with Nirav. He tackled the bandage job with an air of confidence. The raw gash on the dog's neck didn't seem to bother him in the least.

Not a medic, but someone who knew a lot about wounds and bandages. Kat resisted the urge to glance up at his scar. "So Nirav had no family after losing his parents?"

Malcolm nodded as he finished a neat layer of gauze and picked up the vet wrap.

"As a Hindu in a Muslim country, and with his arm as it is, he didn't have much chance of adoption. The Hindus in western Pakistan, where Nirav's from, got cut off from India when British India was partitioned, trapped by a line on the map. There's still a lot of persecution." He shook his head. "Anyway, when I worked near the orphanage on assignment, Nirav saw my scar and came and took my hand. He wouldn't let go."

Malcolm looked toward his son, and his composed expression slipped for an instant to reveal a complicated mix of compassion, pain, and contentment. The flash of naked emotion vanished, veiled once again, before Kat could fully sort it out. "That was a year and a half ago. I've been fighting paperwork and court approvals ever since, but it's official now. Nirav is my son."

Each time he said those words, *my son*, Kat was struck by the proud delight in his voice. If she said *Sara is my daughter*, she hoped the same joy would be obvious.

Kat sat quietly for a moment, thinking through it all. "A new son. You mentioned challenges yesterday. That's a big challenge for anyone."

"It's the little things I'm finding difficult. When we were in Islamabad, there was no issue finding vegetarian food, but now we're back here, and I'm learning to cook all over again. I have to figure out schools and clothes and a thousand other details. Need to think about all sorts of things differently."

Malcolm had spoken carefully, as if his sentences were new and rarely shared. A restful person. Not like Scott, with his casual disdain of anything she said. More like Jim, thoughtful and kind. A Benvolio, not a Brutus. Kat wasn't looking for anything romantic, that was for sure, but she couldn't deny it was nice to feel a connection to someone new.

"Looks to me like you're doing fine," Kat said. "I always knew my daughter would change my life, but no one ever warned me she would change who I was. Children have a way of cutting to the heart of things." And sometimes slicing into it as well.

Malcolm finished the bandage—as neat a job as the vet's version—and Kat leaned forward to set Tye on the ground. Her necklace tumbled from inside her blouse and swung forward. Tye bounded off to join Juni and the children, and Kat straightened. She grasped the chain of the necklace to slip the pendant back against her skin, and the smooth polished surface caught the sunlight.

"That's unusual," Malcolm said. "What is it?"

Kat usually answered that question in only a few words, but Malcolm seemed genuinely interested. It felt right, somehow, to share this story, to reach out. There was so little time left to do so. She slipped the long chain over her head and handed it to him. "It's petrified wood—stone now, not wood, but if you look closely, you can still make out the annular rings."

"I've never seen anything like it. Where did it come from?"

Kat grimaced at the memory. "When I was fourteen, my parents took me to visit the Petrified Forest National Park out in Arizona. I couldn't wait to get there. I held the map. I counted down every mile. I had built up this fantastic expectation of a forest turned to stone, a forest exactly like a living one. Trees with trunks, branches, leaves, all of it, standing like a grove. Magic, like a frozen scene from a fairy tale." Malcolm handed the necklace back, and Kat ran her thumb over its cool surface. "We got to the park, and I was devastated. There's no standing forest there, just a bunch of broken logs on the ground. Random chunks of wood mineralized into stone. My mother felt so bad, she bought me the necklace."

"Those kinds of disappointments hit hard. A nice reminder of family, anyway."

"Something like that."

Kat put the necklace back on. Her mother hadn't actually felt bad, but it was an easier explanation than the full truth.

Stay tough, like this stone, her mother had said when she gave it to her. Her face had been tense and flushed with embarrassment, mortified that her daughter had let herself sob in public. *Stay tough.* At first, Kat wore it simply to remind herself. Over time, it had become a talisman, a source of comfort and strength when life got hard. She'd promised herself she'd be a better mother than that to her own daughter, and she'd succeeded.

The necklace had a second meaning. *Don't believe in fairy tales.* A much harder lesson to learn, but she'd accepted its truth. Her doctors had been straight with her. Once breast cancer spread like hers, there was no cure, only an ongoing battle. Her doctors supplied the ammunition, but she was the soldier, and her body was the battleground. The goal was remission, a furlough marked by constant vigilance, the enemy always poised and present, waiting.

Happily-ever-after was the fairy tale Sara believed in. Kat knew better. She wished there was some way she could make it easier for her daughter.

She motioned for Malcolm to join her on the porch steps. *Sit by my side and let the world slip.* She would have to get a second chair for the porch if she kept having so many visitors.

Malcolm sat, and his eyes found Nirav. "I never expected to have a family." His original formal manner had evaporated, and he spoke more to himself than to Kat. "A son. All this sudden responsibility. I resisted at first, but I finally decided to embrace what life handed me, even though it wasn't what I was seeking."

Kat debated whether to leave it there. But Malcolm was a true survivor. "What do you do when life forces something into your hands that you don't want?"

Malcolm looked at her, his face grave. "You embrace that, too. As well as you can." He looked away, as if his thoughts were elsewhere. His hand moved up to his scar again. "If it weren't for this scar, Nirav never would have sought me out. Think what I would have missed. That alone is reason enough to accept it."

Acceptance. That's what Malcolm had that she didn't. Kat had fought her cancer, fought hard. But she'd also fought the support of friends by walling them out. Fought her own peace, not just with mirror tricks, but with pretend-it's-not-real mind games. For the first time, Kat wondered what she might have missed by hiding as she had.

She had talked to only a handful of people over the years about her cancer. Conversations with Sara were how-are-you-feeling updates, with plenty of emphasis on medical details—neutral, unemotional, safe. Much easier than admitting the turbulence that rocked them both.

When he was alive, conversations with Jim had been pep talks, encouragement offered against the challenging back-drop of the significant changes to Kat's body, her nonexistent sex drive—the curse of her estrogen-blocking drug—and the shifts in their relationship to accommodate both.

Even conversations with a few close friends skirted around uncomfortable issues with a fixed determination to pretend nothing was wrong. It had been easier that way, less likely to cut to the bone.

All these people meant well, but none had faced anything similar. Her doctor had recommended a cancer support group, but she'd avoided that, thinking *don't dwell on it, move on*. Perhaps that, too, had been a mistake. Kat longed to talk with someone who wasn't invested but understood.

Malcolm sat leaning back, his elbows propped on the step behind him and his long legs outstretched. On the surface, he looked as relaxed as a house cat soaking up the sun, but his body hummed with compressed energy, like a spring coiled under pressure and barely restrained, ready to explode at any instant. A panther, not a house cat, but sympathetic and kind.

She cleared her throat. "You heard what my daughter and I said yesterday. When you and Nirav were sitting at the overlook." She made it a flat statement, not a question.

The corners of Malcolm's eyes crinkled for a moment, as if a smile waited somewhere. "Sort of hard to miss. Yes, I heard."

"Yeah. Sorry about that—we didn't know you were there." She took a deep breath. "So . . . I have breast cancer. Bilateral. Two different tumor types. I did the whole nine yards of treatment three years ago—mastectomies, chemo, hormones. The outlook wasn't too bad. But now . . ." Her voice cracked, and she stumbled to a halt, astonished that she had confessed so much to someone she'd just met.

Malcolm didn't flinch. He held her gaze and nodded. "It sounds like you have some tough choices to make. Your daughter sounded upset about your decision."

Kat swallowed and resurrected her voice. "I haven't made a final choice. Sara has this blind faith that if you follow directions, everything will be fine. I know better."

"That's the voice of experience."

The way he said it, Kat knew his own experiences had taught him the same.

"I remember having that sort of faith at her age," he continued. "After a while, you figure out that life gives you no guarantees. There are always risks." He looked toward Lily and Nirav, sprawled now on the grass with the dogs beside them. "The hardest choices to make are the ones that have big risks regardless of what you do."

Big risks regardless. That defined it exactly—the risk of dying sooner without treatment balanced against the risk of struggling through the treatment itself only to end up prolonging the horror. "When you don't want either option, how do you decide?" This was a question with no answer, but she asked it anyway.

Malcolm shook his head. "I'm the last person you should come to for advice. I've made plenty of bad choices."

"So, you think deciding against treatment would be a bad choice?"

"Not at all. I think it's your choice to make. Listen to yourself. If you reach a decision and feel settled with it, fair enough. But if you find yourself questioning, that's when you want to step back and reconsider."

Nirav called to his father, eager to show him how high Juni could jump to catch the ball. Kat and Malcolm joined the children, and their conversation turned away from serious topics. When dinnertime approached, Malcolm gathered Nirav up to head back to their cottage.

"Thanks again for bringing me the bowl," Kat said to Nirav. "And Malcolm, thanks for helping with the bandage."

"No problem at all." He waved and headed down the road with Nirav beside him.

Kat wished she could find the words to thank him for what he'd really given her. Not help with the puppy, but the sense that someone out there understood.

CHAPTER SEVEN

Kat took the dogs out before breakfast the next morning, and the brittle grass crunched louder than usual underfoot. If these mountains didn't get rain soon, even more trees would die. She sat in the rocker and sipped her coffee as the sunlight brightened the colors of distant trees. A red-tailed hawk soared effortlessly in the warming updrafts, its shadow rising and falling as it sped over the rolling contours of the land.

Calm. Peace. That's what this view provided, but the serenity offered only a fragile defense against the sadness that swamped her every time Kat thought of her cancer, its tendrils silently invading her otherwise healthy body. She had no belief in an afterlife, and death itself didn't frighten. It was the absence of life that saddened her.

She had always planned for *someday*. Someday, she and Jim would travel the world. Someday, she would know with certainty that her teaching had made a difference. Someday, she would reach the point where she didn't second-guess herself. But now the days she had left flew past, torn from the calendar and tossed casually aside, with no way to know how many remained. She could picture her future narrowing, tapering ahead of her until it shrank into nothingness.

Not what she wanted. Not what she'd planned.

Kat shook herself back to the present. *Stop it.* She had a beautiful day in front of her. She carried out the first of her scrapbook boxes and began filtering through its contents, the dogs dozing at her feet. By chance, this one contained a mixed-up jumble of items from the last thirty years. The tassel from her college graduation, faded and frayed. The offer letter for her first teaching job, the salary ridiculously low. The fuzzy snapshot of a pregnancy ultrasound, the technology of the time making Sara appear as only an indistinct blob in one corner of the image. She sat for a long time holding a pre-school plaster cast of Sara's handprints. So tiny. Her hand used to disappear in Kat's when they crossed the street.

A thick sheaf of stapled pages caught Kat's eye, and she pulled it out. Leaf rubbings. Brightly colored crayoned pages from an ill-fated weekend. Sara must have been eight or nine, assigned to collect as many kinds of leaves as possible. Jim had seized the opportunity for a family camping trip, and against her better judgment, Kat had agreed to go along.

Sara loved every minute of it—pitching the tent, starting the campfire, eating frying-pan toast off the Coleman stove for breakfast. She led the way on every hike and collected leaves with the fervor of a young Linnaeus. She and Jim consulted field guides, searched for animal tracks, and waxed poetic over every butterfly and turtle.

Kat hated it. Too hot. Too muggy. Too many mosquitos. The strange night-noises and rocky ground made sleep impossible. When she stumbled into the bathhouse the next morning, she was horrified to see that the entire floor undulated with newly hatched black caterpillars, squirming in all directions. They were so close together, it was impossible to even walk to the sink without squishing them.

"What's wrong, dear?" Jim asked when she returned to the campsite.

"There are . . . bugs . . . in there. Everywhere. Some sort of caterpillar. I couldn't even brush my teeth." Kat could hardly force the words through her dismay.

Jim gave her a sympathetic pat on the arm. And Sara? Sara leaped to her feet, said, "Wow, sounds cool," and ran to go see. She even brought one of the tiny caterpillars back to show her father, the fuzzy black squiggle crawling up the length of her arm. Even at that age, any sort of creature drew Sara in like iron to a magnet.

Kat turned the pages of the leaf book, each rubbing labeled in childish block-print. White oak. Tulip poplar. Red maple. Back then, leaves and bugs. Now, a life filled with animals. Such a far cry from Kat's bookish world.

Every item, every photograph she touched brought memories. Stories she had almost forgotten. Stories she had never told Sara. Bringing all this here had been the right impulse. If she got it all neatened up and organized, she and Sara could go through it together.

Her spirits lifted as she worked, and the morning flew past.

Lily had asked to come visit again, but Kat was a bit surprised when she arrived after lunch in Scott's car instead of on foot. She was even more surprised when Scott got out and walked toward her, looking—could this be right?—sheepish.

Lily hung back and called out a subdued, "Hi, Kat."

Today she wore khaki shorts and a simple green T-shirt, and she'd abandoned her experiments with makeup. A single charm bracelet hung on her wrist. She walked over to greet the dogs but stayed close enough to Kat and her father to listen.

Scott nodded a good morning. "I have a huge favor to ask."

Kat suppressed a sigh. "Ask away."

Scott glanced at his daughter, and his face softened. "I've been working toward a deadline on my current project and was all set to make it. But the bastar—sorry—my boss called last night to say he wants something different."

He launched into a long description of technical details, but the only thing that snagged in Kat's brain were catchphrases—*strategic . . . critical . . . twenty-four hours . . . deadline.* How could anyone generate this level of urgency about a computer program? She swallowed her irritation.

Scott rambled on. "I've told them for weeks we were on the wrong path, but they wouldn't listen. Now I'm going to have to work the rest of the day and pull an all-nighter to make the changes." His tight frown thrust his jaw forward, reminding her of a petulant five-year-old forced to clean his room.

Kat made no attempt to stifle her sigh this time, but other than that, she stayed silent and waited for him to get around to it.

"Is there any way Lily could stay with you tonight? I've brought her things. And two quick-bake pizzas. She's promised she won't be any trouble, and she'll do the dishes and anything else you ask. This is it. Honest. After this project is done, I'm on vacation and we'll be off hiking. You won't see us again."

Out of the corner of her eye, Kat could see Lily studying the ground, looking tense and likely feeling more than a little embarrassed to find herself handed off by her father like an unwanted parcel. Kat wasn't wild about a houseguest. She barely knew these people, and the implication that a woman alone must exist only for childcare annoyed her. But if she said no, it would catch Lily in the middle. She was a nice enough girl, there was plenty of room, and it was only one night.

"All right. She's welcome to stay."

Scott did not appear to notice the lack of enthusiasm in Kat's voice. Lily straightened, and her hunched shoulders relaxed. She raced off to play with the dogs, puppy-energy in human form.

"Thanks. I really appreciate it." Scott paused and glanced down the empty road. "Oh, by the way, we passed Malcolm and his kid walking this way when we drove up."

Kat gave him a sharp look, which Scott didn't notice. It sounded like he hadn't even offered them a lift.

"That Malcolm guy." Scott said the three words with an air of imparting critical information. "You have to be careful when you're dealing with someone you know nothing about."

Kat glared. There was no way she could let a crack like that slide. "I know he's taking care of his son. That's plenty to start with. After all, you don't know anything about me, either, and that doesn't stop you from leaving your daughter here overnight."

"Yeah, but that's different." Scott paused for a moment, apparently considering the merits of saying nothing more, but unfortunately, he plunged on. "I grew up in Norfolk around military guys like him. Always bossing people around. Acting like they know everything. Dragging that poor kid back to this country where he doesn't belong . . . I mean, their cottage smells like one of those weird foreign restaurants with menus nobody can understand. Walk by at lunchtime and you'll see what I mean."

Scott acted like he'd presented an irrefutable argument, but Kat could only stare at him, appalled and speechless. Poor Lily, having to put up with this.

After an awkward moment, he appeared to tune in to the idea that he hadn't made any headway. He gave a dismissive snort. "I'll get Lily's stuff out of the car."

He fetched Lily's day pack and the food, and Malcolm and Nirav arrived on cue. Nirav and Lily immediately went into a huddle involving numerous hand gestures. Scott and Malcolm gave each other stiff and formal hellos, but before Kat said much more than good-morning to Malcolm, Nirav raced up to his father and tugged on his pants leg for attention.

A long conversation ensued, with Nirav speaking long paragraphs in Hindi as he pointed to Lily and the dogs, and Malcolm repeatedly shaking his head *no*. Malcolm finally held up his hands and let them fall in defeat. He turned to Kat.

"Nirav and Lily have some idea they're staying here tonight?"

Kat hesitated, fully prepared to say no this time—this was ridiculous, she wasn't a B and B—but Scott, who was standing slightly behind Malcolm, shook his head vigorously and mouthed the words *no, don't do it*. Kat's neck and back stiffened along with her resolve.

"Lily is staying. Nirav is surely welcome if he'd like to stay as well."

Malcolm looked startled, and Scott looked furious, both of which gave Kat immense satisfaction.

Malcolm recovered first. "Thanks. He seems excited about the idea. Says Lily and the dogs are his first three friends here."

He turned for a long conversation with Nirav, which Kat suspected consisted of mind-your-manners instructions, and then the boy ran off happily to play with Lily.

"I'm a little hesitant about this, but Nirav says he'll be fine overnight. I'm glad he feels this adventurous. I'll bring his things up, and I can bring some food. This is very kind of you." He smiled somewhat ruefully. "I admit it's also nice not to be the only source of entertainment for a while."

"No problem at all. Lily is great with Nirav. She makes everything a game. If pizza is okay, Scott brought plenty."

Scott stood sternly silent. He walked over to say good-bye to Lily, pulled the car around in a three-point turn, and headed downhill in a rattle of gravel.

* * *

The afternoon passed quickly. Two children plus two dogs equaled perpetual motion, impervious to the heat, and Kat sorted through more of her scrapbook items while keeping an eye on them all. Lily gave up trying to train Tye to understand *sit* or *stay*, but she had success in teaching Juni to switch between her and Nirav when they played ball. Lily's stern voice saying, "Take it to Nirav" alternated with Nirav's softly accented, "Take it to Lily," while Juni ran happily between them.

Both children helped with Tye's bandage change. The wound didn't look quite so raw this time, and Kat's stomach didn't lurch quite so much, but she had to admit her version of a new bandage used twice as much vet wrap as Malcolm's and had way too many lumps.

For dinner, she picked off all the pepperoni from Scott's greasy-looking pizzas, not wanting Nirav to feel different, and fortunately, Lily declared a love for cheese-only pizza. Nirav peered at it with suspicion, but after a few careful bites, he dove in. The little patterned bowl—Kat thought of it now as Nirav's bowl—sat in the center of the table with several apples in it, and twice Nirav reached out to touch it with a tentative finger.

"How'd that hike with your father go?" Kat asked Lily.

"Okay, I guess."

She didn't roll her eyes, and she sounded sincere, so perhaps things had indeed gone a little better than she'd feared.

"We hiked a really steep trail to a pond—Dad said beavers used to live there, and we found some stumps where we could see their teeth marks. There was an overlook nearby where we could see all the way down to the lake."

She used her hands while she talked. Nirav's brow crinkled as he listened, but he hung on every word.

"I got to read the map myself—Dad showed me how to look at the elevation lines to know whether you'll go up or down, and I could tell where we were and how much farther we had to go. Dad said I had a great sense of direction."

After dinner, Lily showed Nirav how to build houses out of playing cards, and Nirav taught her to count to ten in Hindi, but once it started getting dark, they both began yawning. Kat suggested an early bedtime. She got them both settled in the back bedroom, then stepped outside with the dogs.

The sun had slipped over the horizon, and ominous dark clouds massed low overhead. The warm air rested thick and heavy against Kat's skin, and it smelled densely wet, a seashore wetness without the salt. About time. A storm might cool things down a bit.

As if reading her thoughts, the wind picked up, swirling puffs of road dust toward the cottage. A flash of lightning lit the sky to the east, and Kat counted quietly to herself—*one one-thousand, two one-thousand.* She had reached only ten when the corresponding thunder arrived. Juni whined and shifted uneasily, trembling at each deep-throated rumble, and Kat pulled Tye onto her lap.

Jagged lightning leaped from one cloud to the next. The mountains loomed dark around her, heavy clouds masked the last few stars, and small twigs skittered along the gravel road. Tye snuggled against Kat's belly, and Juni sat as close to the chair as she could get and rested her head on Kat's knee.

Despite the din, no rain materialized. No help for the drought and nothing to cut the fire risk. A half hour of celestial fireworks provided entertainment, but then a particularly forceful gust of wind pelted Kat with dead leaves. "Okay. Time to go in." Juni leaped to her feet and nudged the screen door.

Kat stepped inside and moved silently across the darkened living room to check on the children, Tye still content in her arms. Lily was sprawled on top of her covers, lost in the deep sleep only fast-growing children could achieve. Nirav's bed was empty.

"Nirav." Kat whispered the name. "Nirav, where are you?" He had to be here—he couldn't have opened the front door without her noticing.

She fumbled for the living room light switch and blinked in the sudden glare of the overhead bulb. Something thumped gently against the wooden kitchen table, and she spotted Nirav, backed against the inner wall of the kitchen as if seeking its protection. He shifted from one foot to the other and didn't meet Kat's eyes. The bowl of apples sat off center on the table, directly in front of him. That bowl, placed quickly on the table, would have made just such a thump as Kat had heard.

She set Tye on the floor, went over, and knelt in front of the trembling boy. "Nirav, are you alright?" He nodded, but he kept staring at the floor. "When my daughter was little, she used to hate thunderstorms. She couldn't stand to be by herself."

At this, Nirav looked up, his body rigid. He nodded again. "Sky too loud."

Kat opened her arms, and the boy launched himself from his retreat at the wall and pressed his thin body into Kat's embrace. She held him tight and some of his tension ebbed, but the next thunderclap exploded close enough to rattle the windowpanes, and he shuddered.

Idiotic, sitting out to watch the storm without even thinking about the children. She was out of practice with motherhood. No wonder the thunder frightened the boy—a strange country, a new father, a sleepover, and now a full-fledged storm. Nirav shifted in her arms and pulled back slightly, calmer now.

"The storm won't hurt us here."

Nirav nodded against her, but he made no effort to leave the safety of her arms. Tye trotted over and flopped at his feet, and Kat simply hung on. Two long comforting hugs in the same week—this one and Sara's. She hadn't realized how starved she'd become for human touch. One small part of her brain kept counting down—how many hugs did she have left? How many thunderstorms?

"Nirav, if it's okay with your father, I'd like to give you the bowl you like so much."

That worked. Nirav's eyebrows lifted high, and the faint trace of a smile appeared. "You are giving? To Nirav?"

Kat gave him an added hug. "Yes. To keep. We'll ask your father tomorrow."

The partial smile blossomed into a full-fledged grin. "I am giving you thanks. Yes."

Whew. Maybe not so out of practice after all. "Your mother had a bowl like this one?"

The smile dropped to half wattage, and Kat regretted the question.

"She had one like." He stared at his feet again, and there was such a long pause, she thought he wasn't going to say anything else. Then he looked up at her. "I am running in house." He whispered the words, and Kat strained to hear above the noise of the storm. "Bowl drop at many pieces. Mama very sad."

The sharp pain in his voice stabbed deep. He pulled away, but Kat held his hand. "Your mother loved you, Nirav, even if you broke a hundred bowls."

He frowned.

"Your Papa—Malcolm—loves you even though you took this bowl."

Nirav's face cleared. "He says. Yes."

"Your mother, the same."

Nirav slowly nodded.

Kat gave him a quick hug. "We probably need to get some sleep." Nirav didn't look very happy about the idea. She glanced at Tye, who was contentedly chewing on the floppy toe of one of Nirav's socks. Nirav patted the puppy, and the stiff line of his shoulders relaxed.

"Would you like to keep Tye with you?" Kat asked. "Because of the storm."

Nirav's expression smoothed. "Thank you."

This probably broke every dog-training rule in the book, but when Kat lifted Tye onto the bed beside the boy, the pup snuggled in close, and Nirav slipped an arm around him. The right thing, at last.

Kat took a final look at Lily, who hadn't budged, and she and Juni went into her bedroom. She was tired and ready for bed, but as she started to undress, she stopped, staring at the sheet she had used to cover the mirror.

She stood for several long moments. Streaks of distant lightning lit the room like random camera flashes, and deep rumbles of thunder shook the house.

Malcolm and his scarred face.

Nirav playing ball one-handed.

She went to the wall and pried out the three thumbtacks she had used to fasten the sheet. She put the tacks on the dresser, folded the sheet with the edges precisely aligned, and placed it on the bed.

Kat faced the mirror directly. She unbuttoned each button of her blouse, fumbling the last few. Then quickly, before she could change her mind, she took her blouse off and let it fall to the floor.

She wore no bra, the sole advantage of a reconstructed chest. The overhead light hid nothing. Symmetrical, factory-perfect breasts, cool to the touch compared to the rest of her skin, and, even after three years, distinctly alien. Twin long, broad scars from the mastectomies, spanning the space where her nipples used to be. Two thin curved scars from the lymph node removals. Four tiny puckered stars marking the exit wounds from surgical drains. The fresh red welt of the recent biopsy.

Such radical changes, and yet the cancer still lurked inside her.

The scars will fade over time, her surgeons had assured her, but Kat had a scar on her knee she'd gotten when she was five, and it still looked as fresh as the day it happened. These newer scars weren't fading either, arcing red across the whiteness of her skin as vividly as the lightning arced across the darkness of the sky.

She forced herself to look. It had taken only days to accustom herself to Malcolm's face, but she doubted she would ever achieve the same level of acceptance when looking at herself.

CHAPTER EIGHT

The storm quieted sometime after midnight, its energy spent, and Malcolm slept deeply, no longer on alert for Nirav's nightmares. Vague dreams of campfires and burned toast were easy to ignore, but he woke at 0603 to the smell of actual smoke.

He was fully awake, out of bed, and moving fast before his brain framed a single coherent thought. He checked the kitchen—no fire. The rest of the house—nothing. But smoke drifted in through the open windows.

Nirav up at Kat's.

Shit.

He should never have let his son out of his sight.

Clothing, shoes, wallet, phone, keys. Out the door, sky dirty gray, wind from the east, seven or eight miles per hour, no fire visible but smoke sweeping up over the treetops. The fire must be lower down the mountain, but the wind would push it this way.

No movement in the cottage across the way. Malcolm crossed the road in three strides and pounded on the front door. "Scott! Scott! Wake up! Fire! We have to get the children."

Nothing.

He pounded again, the glass in the top half of the door rattling with every blow. "Scott! Wake up! Come on!" At last he heard a sleepy voice, a mumbled *what the hell* from inside. The door opened. Scott. Tousle-haired. Barefoot. Fumbling his glasses into place.

"Come on. We have to go get the children. Move. Now."

Scott shook his head as if he was still half asleep, and he backed up a step as if determined to do the opposite of whatever Malcolm told him.

"The mountain's on fire. Probably from that storm last night. Kat hasn't brought the children down—they may not even know yet. Come on." Malcolm jiggled his car keys. Two more seconds and he was leaving on his own.

Scott's gaze shifted to the smoke-tinged sky, finally tuning in. He gulped visibly. "Oh my god. Why didn't you wake me sooner?" He scuffed his feet into a pair of tennis shoes by the door and grabbed his car keys and cell phone off the hall table. "I'll drive. Your car's too small."

The idea of letting someone else drive in such an emergency made Malcolm want to pull rank, but Scott was right, and they'd already wasted too much time. He said nothing, just raced to Scott's car and slid into the passenger seat.

Scott picked up on the full urgency at last, and he wasted no time getting the engine started. He stomped on the accelerator, and the car lunged up the gravel road, its engine howling.

Malcolm rolled down his window. Popping and crackling sounds were disturbingly close. "Does your cell work up here?"

"No." Scott's voice shook. His face had no color, the whiteness of severe shock. "Doesn't matter. We can't warn them. Nothing works at Kat's place either—Lily didn't even take her phone with her."

Malcolm leaned forward, wishing sheer willpower would make them move faster. "I should have gone up during the storm and brought Nirav home. I'm sure he was frightened. By the time I made up my mind to do it, the storm had moved on, and I didn't want to wake anyone." He had seen the drought, the deadwood, the lightning. He should have assessed the risk and kept his son safe, not abandoned him to a stranger. His absolute failure tasted harshly bitter.

Scott seemed to be having similar thoughts. "Lily has to be okay. She has to be. That sleepover was my idea."

No point in assigning blame. "The smoke woke me. Fire can race in this wind."

Scott nodded, doing a better job than Malcolm would have expected on the steep, treacherous switchbacks. They weren't high enough on the mountainside to see any details yet, but a shroud of smoke hovered over the treetops and sent thin wisps of haze floating across the road.

"I don't want to get cut off." Scott spoke through tight teeth. "When we get there, we grab the kids and go." Both hands clenched the steering wheel, and he fought to stay on the road as they blasted through the rough potholes that pockmarked the surface.

"And Kat. All three." Malcolm's tension made his voice even harsher than usual.

The smoke thickened as they drove, and both men started to cough.

Small explosions echoed up the mountainside, sounding like small-caliber fire. Or firecrackers. Like the Fourth of July. Malcolm had planned on taking Nirav to a Fourth of July parade. Marching bands. Festive floats. *Welcome to your new country.* His throat tightened.

They crested the edge of the gully, ready to head down to the bridge, and Scott hit the brakes. The car skidded across the gravel in a sickening curve and finally lurched to a stop.

The wooden bridge was on fire, and flames had already enveloped both sides of the steep creek bed. Smoke streamed into the car through Malcolm's open window, the smell sharp and acrid. Two downed trees and a tangle of burning debris blocked the road on the far side. *No way up; no way down.* The phrase had a sickening finality.

"No bridge! What do we do now?" Scott banged his palm against the steering wheel.

Malcolm scanned the flames. *Not good, not good.* This road was the only way in. "This gully is funneling the wind. A faster path for the fire."

They bolted out of the car. Smoke swirled from all directions, and the intense heat seared Malcolm's face and scalded his throat with every breath. He knew more than he wanted to about gunfire, mortar fire, bombing raids, IEDs. About pain and fear and lurking death. *Please. Let Nirav be safe.*

"Lily! Lily!" Scott shouted over and over, but it was pointless, Kat's cottage still more than a half mile away. Even if Lily had been standing right there on the other side of the roadblock, she probably couldn't have heard him. The fire's roar drowned everything else.

Perhaps there was still a way to circle around the worst of it. Malcolm leaped over a patch of burning grass and forced his way a few feet into the trees on the uphill side of the road. Hopeless. He turned back. "It's catching like tinder." He slapped at a few blackened spots on his pant legs. Thin curls of smoke rose from the fabric.

"We have to get them," Scott said. "There has to be a way." His voice shook, his hands shook, and he looked increasingly panicked. A gust of wind tossed a burning twig onto the hood of the car, and he flinched as it tumbled to the ground.

They were surrounded by smoldering trees and at risk of being hit by far more than a twig. They needed to get moving. "We'll get them." Malcolm snapped the words, hoping they would shake some sense into Scott. "But not this way. We have to go back before the fire loops behind us and traps us, too."

Behind them, smoke poured in from all directions, thicker than it had been only a few moments earlier.

"Leave? Hell, no. Lily's up there!" Scott looked fearfully at the flames, but then he turned to Malcolm with a snarl. "If you were a real parent, you'd understand."

"Don't be a fucking idiot."

Scott bristled at the word *idiot*, but Malcolm didn't give him a chance to snap back.

"I'm heading back to let people know the three of them are trapped." Malcolm took two strides away from the car— he had no time to cater to a fool. He could sprint back, grab his car, and head down to where he could pick up a cell signal. If Scott wanted to stay here and burn to death, that was his call. "Am I running, or are you driving?" The surging flames were getting closer every instant.

Scott pounded a fist against his thigh, staring up the road as if his glare would open a path. He wiped his face with his shirt sleeve. "Okay. You win. Driving. Driving in the wrong direction."

He lunged into the car, threw it into reverse, and before Malcolm even had his door shut, backed helter-skelter down the road in a frantic search for a space wide enough to turn around.

CHAPTER NINE

The *click-click-click* of Juni's toenails on the bare wooden floor woke Kat from an all-too-brief, unsettled sleep. The sound was a ticking clock, counting down. As soon as she rolled over, Juni whined and poked Kat's arm with a cold nose.

"Go away. It's too early." Kat pushed the dog away and burrowed back under the covers.

But Juni kept whining and nudging, whining and nudging. The children would wake soon. Kat rolled out of bed and pulled on a shirt and shorts. Something was different this morning, something was off. Too quiet. That was it. Almost silent. She could usually hear the early-morning chatter of birds. This morning, nothing.

She opened the front door to let Juni out, and the smell of woodsmoke hit her at first breath. An illicit campfire. Or some farmer burning trash. But a gray haze tinted the air, too dark and dense to be fog, and Juni stuck close, underfoot instead of snuffling through the grass, even clingier than during the thunderstorm. Kat slipped on her flip-flop sandals and walked across the road for a better view of the valley.

At first all she could see were shifting shreds of smoke that hovered low over the mountainside, but a sudden change in the breeze cleared a window in the gray, and scattered patches of bright orange and yellow came into view. Flames. Fire. A forest fire. A forest fire, in the midst of all this drought. Kat's throat closed on a hard lump of fear that threatened to choke her. She froze, staring, unable or unwilling to take it all in. Nothing improved, and at last she shook herself into motion.

She needed to take the children to their fathers. Now. Scott had a landline at his place—Lily had laughed about a phone with a cord—he could call the fire department. If they said she should evacuate, she could come back and pack.

She hurried into the cottage, opened the children's bedroom door, and found Nirav sitting up in bed as if he had just wakened. Tye sprawled in his lap. Lily still slept soundly.

"Lily, wake up." Kat's tension strangled the words, and she tried again. "Wake up, Lily. We need to go use your father's phone."

Lily opened one eye and made a disgusted face. "What time is it?"

"Time to move. Come on, get up and get dressed." Kat picked up Nirav's shirt and shorts from the chair in the corner and handed them to him. "Get dressed, please."

He took the clothing with some obvious nervousness, watching her closely, but he climbed out of bed and started across the room. Lily snuggled back into her pillow and closed her eyes.

"Lily, come on. I don't want to scare you, but there's a small fire down below. It's far away, but we need to call the fire department. Your father's phone is closest."

Lily sat bolt upright and swung her feet out of bed, wide-eyed and fully awake. "A fire? A forest fire?"

Nirav might not have understood the words, but he obviously picked up on Lily's frightened tone. He froze in the doorway, looking from Lily to Kat and back again.

"Get dressed. Now."

Nirav hurried toward the bathroom, Kat headed for the living room, and Lily closed the bedroom door to change. Kat gathered her cell phone, car keys, and green canvas shoulder bag from the living room, and she stuffed in Tye's harness and the leashes for both dogs. Lily and Nirav joined her, each with their day packs of overnight things.

"Got everything?" she asked. They both nodded. "Okay, come on."

Juni stayed fused to her side. Kat opened the door. The smoke had thickened in the minutes they'd squandered and was darker and more threatening now. Not horrible, at least not yet, but very present. Kat took a deep breath to calm herself, but that only triggered a cough. Tye whimpered and backed up a step.

Nirav's eyes widened with full understanding. "No fire. No." He tucked his injured arm more tightly against his body.

He had far more experience with the consequences of fire than the rest of them. Kat reached around his shoulders and gave him a quick hug. "It's okay." She prayed that was true. "We're going."

Lily took Nirav by the hand, and they started down the steps, but Nirav stopped as soon as he saw Tye no longer followed. He dropped Lily's hand, set down his day pack, and scooped up the puppy with his good arm under Tye's chest and his bad arm bracing his hindquarters. He hurried to the car. Lily grabbed his pack, and she, Nirav, and both dogs wedged themselves into the back seat. Kat tossed her shoulder bag in front, fumbled the key into the ignition, and sped downhill as fast as she dared.

"I'm sure . . ." Her voice cracked, and she cleared her throat and began again. "I'm sure we'll meet your fathers as they're coming up." There, that sounded better. That sounded almost confident. Even she believed it. Almost. There was dead silence from the back seat.

They made it through the first switchback, then the second, and with each drop in elevation, the smoke got thicker and visibility got worse. Small flecks of ash dotted the windshield like discolored snowflakes, tiny gray specks of alarm. Kat tried to clear it with the windshield wipers, but that only left gray streaks, making it even harder to see. She hit the brakes to avoid a raccoon who trundled uphill in the center of the road.

"Where's Dad?" Lily whispered, as if talking out loud could make things worse. "Shouldn't we see him by now?"

"Any minute." Surely he and Malcolm had noticed the smoke. They would come. Kat would meet them. She braked again to let two deer pass. They weren't in any rush, they acted like they were out for a morning stroll, and Kat found their nonchalance reassuring. But they, too, were moving uphill, while she and the children were moving down.

She slowed the car to a crawl as she approached the next switchback, which led steeply down to the small bridge over the gully. Once they crossed the bridge, it would take only a few minutes to reach the other two cottages.

She eased around the curve, then slammed on the brakes so abruptly she was thrown against her shoulder belt. The children yelped, and she could hear them scramble back in place. The road ahead was gone, replaced by a wall of flame. Kat's insides twisted into barbed wire. *No. Please no.*

The dry stream bed burned along its full length, as if the fire had known it would be an easy pathway up the mountainside and had pursued it first. Grasses and ground cover crackled as they burned, yellow-orange and vaporizing fast. Dead limbs and fallen tree trunks flamed. Two of the dead trees Kat had seen on her earlier walks had toppled, and they lay tangled, blocking the road. They had knocked down adjacent saplings as they fell, and the resulting mess was a snarl of burning branches and debris.

"How are we going to get to Dad?"

Lily's voice choked, and Kat turned to the back seat. Lily, her eyes huge and panicked, sniffled with each breath. Nirav stared out the car window at the flames, and he clung to Tye with both hands. Juni sat between the two children, panting. She whined when Kat looked at her.

"We're going to be fine." Kat fought to keep her rising panic out of her voice. *Shit. Shit. Shit.* If only she'd wakened sooner. Moved faster. Gotten here in time. "Wait here. Let me see if there's some way around."

"Don't leave us." Lily's scream ripped into Kat's jangling nerves.

"I'm not leaving you. Watch. You'll see me every minute."

Kat climbed out of the car, coughing as she took in a lungful of smoke. Her eyes watered, and she blinked hard to see. Intense heat pulsed toward her, as if the fire were exhaling to warn her away. She stood at least ten yards back, but the heat seared her face and the fronts of her arms and legs. She broke into an instant sweat.

Glowing cinders blew forward from the flames, two landing on her shorts. She brushed them off fast, but they left flecks of black on the fabric. Ashes clung to her hair, her face, her clothing. She took a few tentative steps toward the tangle blocking their way, but the fire advanced, jumping toward her along the dry grass that lined the verge of the road.

Bizarrely, birds—red-winged blackbirds, sparrows, even a few bluebirds—swooped low to the ground at the very edge of the advancing flames. Kat watched in confusion until a grasshopper leaped high in panic, only to be plucked from the air in midjump by a barn swallow.

Kat wanted to run, wanted to scream, but her legs froze and her voice locked. She stood hypnotized, staring at the flames, transfixed like a mouse immobilized by the sight of a cat. The fire spoke in tongues: pops and crackles as pockets of sap exploded, whispers as the dry grasses caught, shuddering crashes as branches and whole trees fell in the distance.

She had imagined a nicely behaved fire, something managed by a friendly red fire engine with a stream of water sufficient to quell a nuisance. Such suburban approaches would be hopeless here. This fire wasn't domesticated. It was a predator.

Kat trembled, tentacles of fear tightening down on every muscle, her body crackling with tension. She'd convinced herself she could meet death head on, but she hadn't expected it so soon. She was going to die on this mountain, not home in her bed. She had minutes, not months, and she couldn't even tell Sara good-bye.

Grief flooded every cell and swamped her thinking. She shook herself, forcing herself back into action. *Move, damn it. Do something.* She couldn't afford to waste time. She glanced into the trees and underbrush on the right, thinking perhaps they could scramble around the burning roadblock on foot, but the thick undergrowth already smoldered. Even if she'd been alone, she didn't think she could outflank the flames.

Kat coughed and wiped her eyes against her sleeve, her head pounding, then hurried back to the car and got in. She twisted in her seat and gave the children what she hoped was a reassuring look, but based on the horrified expressions on their faces, they must have recognized the truth.

"We'll be fine." Perhaps if she kept saying it, she'd believe it. The words didn't stop her heart from pummeling her ribs with a force that shook her whole body. She glanced at her cell phone. No bars. No signal. No surprise.

"We'll be fine. Honest." She threw the car into reverse. "We'll just move on to plan B."

Her voice shook only a little, sounding almost confident, an actress playing her part. Inside, pure terror was winning.

They weren't going to drive down this mountain to safety. They weren't going to reach Scott and Malcolm. They weren't going to call anyone for rescue.

Plan B didn't exist.

CHAPTER TEN

Malcolm debated their options in silence as the car rocketed down the mountain road. If the advancing fire was only now reaching the bridge they'd just left behind, then they might have time before it reached Kat's cottage higher on the mountain. Time, but not much. They needed a helicopter, and Malcolm had no clue how fast the Forest Service would move in mobilizing equipment. They had to act on their own.

Scott slammed on the brakes when they reached his cottage.

"What the hell are you doing?" No reason to stop.

"Landline." Scott was already climbing out of the car. "I'll call. Let the authorities know people are trapped."

Fair enough. Get people moving. Malcolm tried his cell phone again, but it was hopeless. They needed to get farther down the mountain. The smoke smelled even more caustic now, his throat burning with each inhalation.

Scott must have gotten through—he was taking long enough. Too long. More minutes wasted. Malcolm had his door half open, ready to switch over to his car and leave on his own, but here came Scott at last, loaded down with a laptop, a suitcase, and a computer bag. He tossed them into the back seat, climbed behind the wheel, and placed a handful of jangly girl's bracelets on the console between the front seats. Malcolm settled back. He could get his car later. Or not at all. It made no difference.

Scott threw the car back in gear, wrenched it back onto the road, and sped off.

"What did they say?" Malcolm hoped Scott had emphasized the essentials. He wasn't used to working with such an inexperienced person.

"No luck. Phone line down."

"You spent all that time in there *packing*?" Unbelievable.

Scott shrugged and said nothing.

Malcolm checked the mountainside below them as Scott drove. No fire visible, but smoke cloaked the trees and ash wafted past like scraps of gray confetti. He tried the phone again. And again. At last, they hit pavement and the phone sprang to life. He hit the auto-dial code for his DC office and relaxed infinitesimally when it was answered on the first ring.

"Lassiter and Associates, how may I direct your call?"

Thank goodness. Stephanie on phone duty. She wouldn't waste a precious second. "Steph. Me. I need a helicopter. Now. This minute. We need a winch and harnesses for rescue. About twenty miles southwest of Franklin, North Carolina."

"Roger that." The steady click of computer keys came through clearly. Steph was already searching through the company's database of contacts. The agency didn't often have a need for wilderness rescue, but it routinely used helicopters for secure transport.

Scott stared at him, his jaw hanging open, his attention returning to the road only because they approached a sharp turn.

"I've got a possible." Stephanie's voice held no hint of tension, but Malcolm knew she understood the urgency. He could picture her—alert, focused, efficient. "Hold while I call."

The phone went silent. "Working on it," he told Scott.

"What the hell? You're whistling up a *helicopter*?" Scott's voice was incredulous, a little kid awed by a magic trick.

His reaction did nothing to improve Malcolm's assessment of him. How did this guy think rescue operations were run, anyway? By mystical incantations?

"Okay, got it." Steph was back. "Pilot happened to already be at the airport; copilot is twenty minutes away. They're hustling."

"How long?" He glanced at his watch. 0652. They'd wasted almost an hour going up the mountain and coming back.

"They promise to pick you up by 0810."

Too slow. "Tell them it's an extra K for every minute they cut off the estimate. Don't worry, this is my dime, not the company's. Have them call me when they're in the air. I'll scout a landing site, give them specifics on where to pick me up."

"Got it. Call back if you think of anything else you need."

"Roger that." At least things were moving. If he could get that chopper here, they had a chance of beating the fire to Kat's cottage. "And Steph. Thanks. It's Nirav . . . out there in a forest fire, trapped with two others." His voice shook on that last sentence, giving away more than he intended.

"Oh my god." Her tone reflected both shock and concern. "That's horrible. Let us know what else we can do at this end. And keep us posted."

"Will do." It felt good to know there were others out there rooting for their success. He disconnected the call and turned to find Scott glaring.

"Where to pick *me* up? You're telling them to pick up only you? What about me? I'm coming with you."

"Not necessary," Malcolm snapped the words. "I can—"

A black pickup rounded the curve ahead, headed straight for them.

"Watch out!"

Scott hit the brakes too late, his reflexes bad, but fortunately the other driver was paying attention. The truck stopped inches from their front bumper. They had almost reached the main state road, and smoke drifted only in vague ribbons here, the worst of it blowing up the mountainside behind them.

Scott and Malcolm scrambled out of the car. The other driver lumbered from his seat, a middle-aged guy with sagging cheeks, sagging chins, and a sagging belly. His denim shirt had *Jake* embroidered over the breast pocket, like a mechanic or a clerk at Home Depot. Local. Not a professional, but he might be some help. They could afford the time while they waited for the chopper to arrive.

"Fire Department. You two okay?" the guy called.

"We're fine." Malcolm gave the answer in an intentionally calming tone before Scott even had his mouth open. "We've got three people trapped up the mountain."

"One is my daughter." Scott's voice held all the urgency Malcolm had banished from his.

Jake reached without haste into the cab of his truck, pulled out a large folded paper, and flattened it on top of the pickup's hood.

It was a high-resolution map of the area, printed in black and white with topographic lines. Roads and trails spider-webbed across its surface, and small squares, hand-drawn in ink, were labeled with names and numbers. Each represented a building. The corner of the map read *West Valley Volunteer Fire Department*. Malcolm scanned it carefully, looking for another possible route to Kat's. Nothing.

He might have been only a volunteer, but Jake stuck to the point. "Three cottages up this road. What's the situation?"

Scott opened his mouth, probably to give some long-winded account of his summer vacation plans, so Malcolm jumped in again.

"These two cottages are empty now." He pointed to two squares. "The road's blocked here." He tapped the spot where the bridge had been. "No cell service. We couldn't get through, and it's probably worse now." Malcolm pointed to the third square. Kat's cottage. "Three people here. One woman, early fifties; one girl, about twelve?"—he glanced at Scott and paused for a split second to wait for his nod of agreement—"one boy, nine. The boy speaks limited English."

Nirav. He must be terrified—but alive and terrified was better than dead. Malcolm quelled his roiling insides and ordered himself to wall off such distracting thoughts. No emotion, no sentiment, just facts.

"Not good." Jake scratched his chin and shook his head. "The fire's headed straight at them. Does the woman know these mountains?" He unclipped a walkie-talkie from his belt.

"I don't think so." She'd been here before, but she'd acted nervous up there alone. Not the outdoorsy type, that was for sure.

"Look, the girl is my daughter." Scott hit the hood of the truck with his fist, his face creasing with pain at the impact. "You have to do something." He acted like Jake had options.

Jake nodded and depressed the call button on his walkie-talkie. Scott shifted from one foot to the other, his panic radiating outward in waves, but Jake reported only the bare facts—two houses clear, three people trapped.

"We've notified the Forest Service firefighters, but it will take time for them to mobilize." Jake's voice was apologetic, but Scott took a step toward him and brought his hands up as if he planned to grab Jake by his shirt and shake some sort of action out of him.

Malcolm grabbed Scott's arm and pulled him back. "Stop it. That won't help."

Scott subsided, grumbling, and Jake gave Malcolm a nod of thanks.

"I've never seen a fire get so big so fast," Jake said. "This whole area is long overdue for a burn—way too much deadwood—and this wind isn't helping. It's nothing like those freight-train speeds they get out west, but it sure as hell is spreading." He hesitated. "I'm sorry, but there's no easy way to get to that last cottage if the road's blocked."

"I've called in a helicopter," Malcolm said. "My company uses them often, and I had one of my staff members get things moving."

Jake straightened, almost standing at attention. "A helicopter?" He nodded his approval. "That'll help. We can send people in on foot from the other side cross-country, but that will take time."

Malcolm pointed again to the map. "I thought this field by the road here would be the best place to land the chopper. I saw it when my son . . ." His voice cracked, and he cleared his throat. "When my son and I went down to the lake. Is it far enough from the fire to be safe?"

Jake nodded. "Should work." He tossed the map back into his truck. "I need to go check a few more houses on the old forest road south of here. I'll radio the chief again and tell him you two are on your way. He's down there with a crew now, trying to keep the main road clear."

Scott and Malcolm returned to the car and waited while Jake inched his truck in a slow semicircle to head back downhill.

Scott wiped his palms on his shirtfront. He didn't look at Malcolm. "Won't the Forest Service have their own equipment and rescue teams?"

"The fire crews will bring their own choppers in, but this one may get here faster. It's our best chance of rescue." It was their only chance. Malcolm checked his watch again. 0720. Time had slowed.

Scott picked up the tangle of bracelets he had rescued from his cottage and held them for a long moment. He started to say something. Stopped. Malcolm expected some sort of complaint, but when he looked more closely, Scott seemed calmer, the touch of the bracelets perhaps a reminder of how much was at stake. "I keep picturing Lily. Frightened. Trapped without me." He was shaking, but this time he looked Malcolm in the eye. "A helicopter. Thank you. I wouldn't have known how."

CHAPTER ELEVEN

Kat backed her car uphill on the narrow road away from the wall of flame and at last found a space wide enough to turn around. She sped on as fast as she dared, wary of the steep drop-offs beside her, showering gravel at each precipitous switchback. In minutes, Kat, Lily, and Nirav were back at her cottage. Exactly where they'd started, but now worse off than before.

"Wait in the car." Kat glanced back at the children, who huddled together with Juni sandwiched between them and Tye still crouched on Nirav's lap. Now that the fire didn't loom directly in front of them, Nirav no longer looked rigid with horror, but his eyes darted anxiously, and his breath came in audible gasps.

Lily clung to her armrest with whitened fingers. "Where are you going?" Her fear was reined in by a very thin strand.

"I need to check the fire. See which way it's moving."

Kat hurried to the edge of the drop-off, her eyes stinging and her stomach churning. Perhaps the situation had improved.

But no. In the time she had wasted waking the children and driving down and back, the fire had eaten through acres of dry forest on the lowest stretch of the mountain, its appetite insatiable. She couldn't hear it from this distance, but smoke laced her every breath, and a dark oppressive cloud hovered over the valley. A hot breeze hit her in the face, crisping her cheeks.

She glanced at the cottage. Its weathered clapboards would be no protection. She was tempted to believe the rocky span below her would do some good, perhaps even divert the flames, but she tossed the thought aside as soon as it occurred to her. Too narrow. She'd already seen how the flames could jump.

Nothing lay between her and the fire. A switchblade of panic slashed through her thin veneer of calm.

"Kat, come on. Where are we going to *go*?" Lily's last word screeched her terror.

Go. Escape.

But go where?

Kat's head throbbed and she couldn't concentrate. She needed Jim. Sara. Someone. She dug her fingernails hard into her palm, hoping the pain would help her focus. She couldn't do this. Couldn't make such choices. What would Jim do if he were here? He would probably pull out some sort of back-woods magic trick. No help there.

Her shoulders slumped. Her feet were encased in concrete. If she made the wrong decisions, the children would die and it would be her fault, *her fault, her fault*. But there was no one else.

Kat reminded herself to breathe, her throat the width of a pencil. She forced herself to turn slowly. Ahead of her, the rocky drop-off, the advancing fire. To the right, the road, already hopeless. Behind her, the cottage, backed by a steep uphill tangle of rhododendron and mountain laurel, impenetrable on foot. To her left, the end of the gravel road, the mass of honeysuckle, the endless forest.

We're trapped.

Kat's gaze rested for a moment on the delicate white honeysuckle flowers, trembling in the breeze, and the sudden image of each blossom vaporizing into flames added yet another layer of horror to her waking nightmare. Then she froze.

A gap.

She'd noticed it before. A gap in the trees where two abandoned but still-visible ruts ran on the other side of the honeysuckle. An old logging road, a forgotten homestead road, perhaps a road to nowhere, but it had once been in use, and it led forward along the ridgeline. It wouldn't take them directly away from the fire, but it led north, along the side of the mountains that overlooked the burning valley to the east. With luck, it could take them out of the fire's direct path.

Kat raced to the end of the gravel, trying to see. Overgrown. More like a pair of unused footpaths than a road. It was a chance. Maybe their only chance.

She rushed back to the car and called to Lily and Nirav as she passed the open car door.

"Stay here. There's a way out. I'm going to get things from the house." Kat recognized the lie as she spoke it—*a way out* was far too optimistic a description.

She threw open the cottage door with a bang that rattled the windows and scanned for anything useful.

Camera. No. Laptop. No. Bird book. No. Clothing. No.

She ran into the kitchen, turned on the tap full force, and filled an empty wine bottle with water. She glanced in the cupboards, but the poorly equipped kitchen had no pitchers or large pots she could use. She grabbed the half-full Mason jar of iced tea from the fridge and searched the near-empty shelves—eggs, butter, lettuce, no help—but she seized a block of cheese. She tucked a bag of granola under her elbow, grabbed the bowl of apples from the table.

She skidded to a halt in the living room. The scrapbooks. Four huge boxes crammed with her history. Sara's history. Her legacy to her daughter.

It would take four slow trips to lug them to the car, and even then, they wouldn't fit in the trunk—she'd crammed them into the back seat on her way here.

The children. The dogs.

Compared to the importance of saving the children, these lifeless boxes of paper were meaningless.

She locked her mind tight and turned her back on the past. She left the cottage door standing open behind her and tried not to picture the house and its dreary furnishings going up in flames.

Kat jerked open the back door of the car, ready to thrust her handful of supplies inside, but she stopped. The children's faces were pale and shocked. Tears scoured Lily's cheeks, her eyes swollen and her nose running. Nirav sat tight beside her, trembling, his body drawn inward to occupy the least space possible. He patted Tye over and over again as if the motion could stave off terror. Juni had scrambled into the front seat. Kat had to protect them all, the weight of that truth overwhelming.

"I want my dad." Lily snuffled between each word.

"Dad. Yes, I am wanting Papa." Nirav's voice shook.

Kat squatted so she could look directly into the children's frightened eyes. "Your fathers are out there working to find us."

She thrust aside the horrifying possibility that they, too, had been cut off from safety. Or burned alive in their cottages. They had to be out there. Somewhere. Fighting for their children. They were the only ones who would realize she and the children were trapped.

"We can't stay here. The fire is moving this way. I'm going to try and force the car down that old road." She gestured ahead of them. The futility of what she proposed washed over her, threatening her resolve.

Lily leaned forward to see, and she grunted an inarticulate sound of denial. "That's not a road. We need to stay here. Dad can't find us if we leave." It was a very Sara-like protest, and Kat closed her eyes for a split second, grateful Sara was safe but missing her terribly.

Lily's body vibrated with tension. Nirav looked back and forth between Kat and Lily, uncertain, and Tye watched his every move. Juni rested her head on the back of the front passenger seat, her eyes anxious.

The overwhelming need to *move move move* made Kat want to scream, but she couldn't let herself freak out.

"Lily. Stop. We need to help each other."

The words had no impact. Kat's jaw creaked as she ground her teeth together. There was no way she could tackle this without at least minimal cooperation. She tried again.

"Lily, I need you to help Nirav."

That got through. Lily looked at the boy beside her and nodded.

"Make sure your seat belts are tight." Kat waited for Lily to check them both, then handed the wine bottle of water to Lily and the bowl of apples to Nirav.

"Okay. We're going now."

"We go. Yes. No fire." Nirav clutched his bowl with both hands.

Nirav had a knack for summing up the essentials.

Kat hurried to the driver's seat, stuffed the jar of tea and the other food into her shoulder bag, strapped herself in, and backed the car twenty yards down the road to give herself room to accelerate. From here, the bank of honeysuckle looked like a solid wall, and the gap in the trees where the old road lay was invisible. Kat's hands tightened on the steering wheel, and she closed her eyes.

If there were rescuers out there, they would search here at the cottage, not farther along the mountain. Ahead, she and the children faced only wilderness and heaven-knew-what.

This wasn't going to work. She didn't want to die by fire, but death chased her regardless. It might be best to simply wait here. Wait here and accept. The temptation was overwhelming. Kat reached for her pendant, and her panic escalated when she couldn't find it resting against her chest. In her haste that morning, she hadn't slipped the necklace over her head. Too late to get it now. Like her boxes of mementos, she had to leave it to fate.

Focus. On. Priorities.

Juni whined and nosed her arm.

Children. Dogs. No choice.

"Juni, down." Kat pointed to the floorboard in front of the passenger seat. Juni gave her a look that seemed to question Kat's sanity, but she wedged herself into the foot space.

Boldness be my friend. "Hang on," she called to the children.

She didn't look back at them, afraid their fear would undermine her resolve. In a single swift motion, she pushed the pedal to the floor, the engine screamed, and the car surged forward, accelerating faster and faster as it raced across the short stretch of remaining gravel.

They hit the end of the road at forty miles an hour with a jolt that threw them against their seat belts. A horrific crunching sound echoed as the front bumper collided with something solid hidden in the honeysuckle, and both children cried out. A mass of green vegetation obscured the windshield, and metal shrieked as tangled vines scraped along the sides of the car. Kat kept her right leg locked. In only seconds, they were through.

They were on the old roadbed. The instant Kat recognized that fact, their left front wheel caught on a massive rock, and her head slammed into the driver's side window as the car rocked violently to the right. The children screamed. Kat braked to a halt, dazed by the blow.

She shook her head, trying to clear it. Twisted around. "You two all right?"

Nirav nodded. His good hand clutched his precious bowl, the apples scattered across the floorboards. Tye, wedged now between Nirav's hip and Lily's, panted hard.

"Okay," Nirav said.

A little color returned to Lily's face, an improvement over the white of complete terror. She brushed at her shirt, which looked darkly wet. The wine bottle she held was now half empty, much of their water lost.

"I'm okay." She leaned forward to peer at Kat. "You're bleeding."

Kat explored the rapidly swelling bump on her head, and her fingers came back bloody. The sight threw her off-balance as it always did, and she fought to stay rational. A small cut on a wicked bruise. In the total scheme of things, nothing to panic about. It just needed an ice pack.

She stifled an out-of-place laugh. She dabbed at the wound with a tissue from her shoulder bag, then tossed it aside. Juni climbed off the floor and back onto the passenger seat.

No turning back now. She'd signed up for a fight. They'd tackled the first step and made it, so perhaps that was a good sign.

"Hold on to something solid. This is going to be bumpy." Assuming the car could still even move forward.

She took a quick look back. The children grabbed on to armrests and the front edges of their seat. Behind the car, thin tendrils of dark smoke slithered stealthily toward them with the patience of a serpent seeking its prey.

CHAPTER TWELVE

At the main road, Malcolm told Scott to turn left, toward the lake and toward the field where he planned to rendezvous with the helicopter. Three fire engines were clustered along the road near the lake, one of them an enormous tanker truck. Small figures in heavy yellow coats lumbered along the roadside, lugging fire hoses and wielding shovels. The forest burned with intensity here, and flaming trees towered high over the firefighters, dwarfing their efforts. Trying to quell this fire with water from individual hoses was as effective as spitting into an inferno.

"This is all they have?" Scott kept looking around as if other equipment was hidden somewhere. "Where's all the high-tech?"

"It takes time to mobilize," Malcolm said. "This looks like a local force, and the Forest Service will call in reserves. It looks like they're trying to keep the fire from moving south, and the lake is a natural firebreak to the east. The wind is

124

pushing the flames west and north, up the mountainside, up toward the ridge and the Appalachian Trail."

"Up toward Lily and Kat and your boy." Raw words when spoken out loud.

Malcolm tensed. *Nirav.* How could he have let Nirav out of his sight? Maybe Scott was right. He wasn't a real parent. A real father would never have let this happen. Nothing he'd done in his years in the field, nothing he'd done in his current role of security consultant, had prepared him for parenthood, but it had given him the skills and discipline he needed to function in an emergency. That's what he needed to access now.

He pulled himself back under strict control. "We'd better check in with Jake's boss. Too soon for the helicopter."

Scott pulled the car as far off the road as he could, and the two men started along the last fifty yards on foot. The road rose to a small hill here, and the full scope of the danger became apparent. Low on the mountain, flames and smoke extended to the north and south as far as Malcolm could see. Higher up, the fire moved forward in narrow bands, following the easiest pathways first, like the gully that had blocked their efforts to reach the children. Malcolm searched the hazy horizon, but he couldn't identify the stretch of mountain where Kat's cottage was located.

The wind hit their backs as they walked, pushing the smoke out of their way, but the closer they got to the fire, the more intense the heat became. Malcolm's face blazed, and sweat dripped off his chin.

Scott wiped his forehead with the back of his hand. "No wonder those firefighters wear all that stuff."

A dozen people were working here to dig a broad trench to block the fire, using two enormous hoses to wet the exposed earth and douse stray sparks that jumped the firebreak. Textbook strategies, consistent with everything he'd learned in Special Forces training, but it didn't look like it was going to be enough.

Malcolm's cell phone chimed, and he answered. "Yes."

"This is Wolfpack two-seven-foxtrot, in the air and heading south. Need landing location. Advise. Over."

The voice crackled over a spotty connection, but it was definitely female. Good. They needed careful and meticulous support on this flight, and that's what Malcolm had learned to expect from the women pilots he'd flown with. "Roger that. Landing site is a level pasture near Quarter Moon Road." He gave specifics. "Over."

"Ten minutes. Out," the voice replied.

Malcolm disconnected. "Ten minutes," he told Scott. He glanced at his watch. 0750. Not bad. The chopper should easily beat the 0810 estimate.

He walked faster, leading the way toward the person who was obviously in charge—a tall, lean, middle-aged man who alternated between terse commands to his crew and static-filled conversations on a walkie-talkie. Every aspect of his posture radiated authority.

The chief gave Scott and Malcolm a two-second glance. "Clear out. Civilians aren't permitted here."

Scott made a choking sound and seemed ready to argue, but Malcolm responded in a neutral tone. "Jake called about us."

The chief gave them a longer look, then nodded curtly. "The guy with the chopper? Jake said you had some sort of corporate connection. Must be nice." He gestured toward the mountaintop, using his walkie-talkie antenna as a pointer. "We've got a problem along the AT. Four hikers. Saw the smoke and flames, cut off the trail to get away. One of them fell, broke a leg. They have a SPOT satellite messenger, so we know their position, but your chopper will likely beat ours here. You can go pick them up."

Scott again started to protest, but this time a glance from Malcolm silenced him.

Chase off after strangers? They'd do no such thing, not when they needed to get to Kat's cottage fast to beat the fire. Time to pull rank. Malcolm drew himself to his full height, broadened his shoulders, and turned his head so his vivid scar faced toward the chief. "Happy to help. Right after we get our children out."

The fire chief tensed. "There's already a Temporary Flight Restriction in place, and a fire's updrafts are nothing for an amateur pilot to mess with. I can block you from flying, and I can commandeer your chopper anytime I want."

"I'm well aware of that." In an emergency like this, individual rights flew out the window. Malcolm gave the fire chief a scathing look, and out of the corner of his eye, he saw Scott flinch, obviously glad it wasn't directed at him. "I'm equally sure you want to prioritize your rescue operations to target those at highest risk first."

The chief glared right back, neither of them backing down.

An edgy fifteen seconds of immobility ticked away, and then the fire chief slowly nodded acceptance. "Agreed. You go get your children. We'll stay in touch with the hikers. But let me make myself clear." He pointed the walkie-talkie antenna at Malcolm, its tip almost touching the other man's chest. Malcolm forced himself not to move. "If I call and tell you those hikers can't wait for our helicopter, you break off immediately. We know precisely where those hikers are, and they're staying put. But if your kids aren't waiting where you think they are, you could end up searching the whole mountainside."

Malcolm closed his eyes and took a deep breath, hating the implication that Nirav could be anywhere but safe at Kat's cottage, waiting for help. This helicopter was *his*, and he was going to use it to rescue his son. Period. But he had to have a pilot, and the pilot had to obey regulations. If he didn't play his cards right, he'd lose the chopper completely.

The chief had his priorities straight—Malcolm would be saying the same thing if he were in charge and didn't have a vested interest. His hands unclenched and his shoulders relaxed. He opened his eyes. "Okay. I'll play it your way."

Scott gave a derisive snort but kept quiet. The chief stepped over to a nearby pickup truck and rummaged through an orange box of equipment. He pulled out a chunky phone with a short thick antenna and tossed it to Malcolm.

"Sat phone. Press one and you get me. Keep me posted."

"Any drones in your equipment?"

The fire chief had already turned back toward his team. "Coming on our chopper." He tossed the sentence over his shoulder. "Their thermal imaging is good for tracking the fire, but not too good for finding people unless they're far enough away from the heat of the flames. Yet another reason we don't want your chopper out there cluttering up the airspace."

He started shouting orders, once again immersed in the immediate crisis.

Malcolm gave the chief a final nod and crossed the road, hurrying back toward the landing field. He scanned the sky, but nothing yet.

Scott scowled. "What the hell do you mean, 'I'll play it your way'? Some jackass hiker breaks his leg, and it's suddenly our problem?"

Malcolm whirled, all patience lost. He let his tight anger show on his face, and it had the impact of a blow. Scott stepped back. "Shut the fuck up. If I hadn't agreed to help, we'd have nothing. That fire chief had every right to keep me off my helicopter."

"Keep *us* off *our* helicopter. I'm coming with you."

Malcolm snorted. "You'd just be in the way." Scott was a worried father; he got that. But trap himself in the helicopter with someone this clueless? No upside. Not an option.

Scott flushed brilliant red, but he straightened and faced Malcolm head on. "It's my daughter out there. I'm coming."

Malcolm took another one of his deep breaths and swallowed his frustration at working with amateurs. He had to set aside his fears for Nirav and stay practical. Another pair of eyes wouldn't hurt, and once they had Kat and the children on board, Scott could take care of Lily. That might help. Twelve-year-old daughters were probably even harder to understand than nine-year-old sons. "Fair enough. You can come. Hopefully it will be a quick trip."

Kat and the children should either be at the cottage or on the road below. If they tried to come down and found the road blocked, they would probably return to the cottage. That open patch of gravel out front was big enough to land. They just needed to get there before the fire did.

Scott looked at his phone. "I thought you said ten minutes."

Malcolm tipped his head to one side. "Listen."

The sound came closer. The roar of an approaching engine. The chopper skimmed toward them, barely above the tree-tops, flying in fast from the north. It hovered over the field, pivoted slowly through a full circle, then settled to the ground.

Malcolm ran forward. The chopper looked like one of the old Bell 427s, with pilot and copilot in front and cabin space behind that could hold either passenger seats or cargo. Exactly what they needed. As he got closer, dents and scratches became obvious, but it had made it this far, so he had no grounds for complaint.

The backwash from the rotors kicked up huge clouds of dust and grit. Malcolm ducked under the still-spinning rotor, and Scott panted at his heels. A young guy in cutoff jeans, a USC Wrestlers T-shirt, and a three-day beard waved them closer. Not exactly the sort of uniform Malcolm expected, but the crew of this chopper could dress in tie-dye and beads for all he cared, as long as they knew what they were doing.

The two scrambled on board. There were no seats other than the pilots' chairs. A large piece of canvas-covered equipment hulked in the center of the cargo space—the winch he'd asked for—leaving only narrow aisles around the edges for passengers.

"I'm Pete," the young guy yelled over the engine noise. "And this is Lou, our pilot."

He gestured toward the woman sitting in the right-hand cockpit seat. A gloved hand lifted in acknowledgment.

Pete gave Malcolm's damaged face a slow double take, but not with any more reaction than anyone else did, and then he banged the door shut behind them. He clambered into the copilot seat on the left, threw some switches, and tapped his wristwatch. "Beat the estimate by ten minutes." He had to yell to be heard over the engine's roar. "Does that really mean a ten-K bonus?"

Damn right. Ten minutes might make all the difference. Malcolm nodded and yelled back. "Double if you can rescue my son and two others from this fire. Get this thing back in the air."

CHAPTER THIRTEEN

Kat clung to the vibrating steering wheel of her lurching car and prayed its frame would hold together. They were moving forward, away from the fire, but they were making miserable, inch-by-inch progress. The car canted first one way and then the other as they bounced over rocks and dropped into washed-out potholes. Branches screeched along the roof and sides of the car, and it shuddered horribly each time they hit a sapling or a shrub. Kat kept her foot on the gas pedal and her fear locked away. Hopefully nothing essential would get punctured.

"Where are we?" Lily asked.

"Not sure exactly, but we're moving in the right direction."

The question reminded Kat of car trips when Sara was little. Trips on smooth four-lane highways, with Triple-A TripTiks highlighted in colored magic marker to show the route. Trips Jim conceived, planned, and led, while Kat just had to keep Sara entertained. If only someone else would take

132

charge now, someone who would take care of her and these children. Keep them all safe.

Instead, she was on her own and driving on faith. The smoke faded as they progressed, revealing a corridor of green vegetation free of flames and floating ash, a tiny glimpse of hope.

She glanced in the rearview mirror. The children hung on grimly as the car's jolts tossed them back and forth. All of them would have bruises, and Kat's head still throbbed from her collision with the window. Her waist and chest ached from being thrown so often against her seat belt, and she wondered if her implants would hold up to the beating. It was a stupid, inconsequential thought, but far better to think of stupid things than to meditate on reality.

Their right front tire hit a particularly large rock, and the steering wheel jerked out of Kat's hands. She fought to regain control and slowed even further. The road—assuming anyone in their right mind would call it a road—appeared to be curving steadily to the right. Kat tried to picture the contours of this part of the ridge as she had seen it from the cottage, but she couldn't remember the details well enough to envision their route.

"How will Dad find us?" Lily asked. She had calmed enough that a whine was easily detectable.

Kat picked up her cell phone for the thousandth time and checked its screen. Still no signal. "Your father will find us. Or we'll get word out. Find a spot where my phone will work."

She hoped the words faked a calm confidence. How the hell would anyone find them now? She risked another glance at Nirav, who sat silent. Far more silent than normal, even for him. "Nirav, are you okay?"

He nodded his head *yes*. A foolish question. He wasn't okay—none of them were. Lily reached over and squeezed his hand, and Kat returned to the bone-jarring task of clutching the wheel.

They forced their way forward almost a mile, assuming the odometer could be trusted on such uneven terrain, and then they reached a barricade. A huge tree had toppled long ago, and its rotting trunk blocked the ruts ahead as effectively as the fire had blocked their path off the mountain. Kat slowed to a stop and turned off the engine. She rested her forehead against the steering wheel for a moment. Helpless. Frustrated. Trapped.

She wanted to sit in the silence. Perhaps take a nap. Instead, she pulled herself out of the car. The children and dogs got out as well. She walked up to the downed tree and nudged it with her foot. Chunks of bark broke free, but the bulk of the trunk remained immovable. A job for chainsaws and a backhoe.

She checked her cell phone, walking back and forth to see if she could get any glimmer of a signal. Nothing but more disappointment.

Dense undergrowth edged in on all sides. No easy path around the roadblock. No more driving. If they wanted to keep moving forward, their only option was to keep going along the old roadbed on foot.

She walked back to the children. Lily leaned against the scratched and dented back door of the car, her forehead deeply creased as she glared at the downed tree. Nirav stood to one side, watching Juni and Tye sniff their way through the underbrush. He still clutched his bowl, which he'd refilled with the apples.

They were out of immediate danger, and they all needed a moment's break.

"Okay." Kat tried to make her voice cheerful, but the fear that wrapped itself around every nerve ending made it difficult. "Let's rest for five minutes and eat something."

"I am hungry," Nirav said.

Kat managed a half smile. "Yeah, me, too."

Nirav set his bowl on a tuft of grass and handed out apples. Kat retrieved the bag of granola and block of cheese from her bag. No knife—damn, she should have thought of that—but she broke off small chunks of cheese and handed them around. Nirav gave half of his to Tye, and the puppy nuzzled him for more. Kat didn't have the heart to make him stop.

"So, how do we get the car around the tree?" Lily asked.

Kat gave her a sharp look. Lily knew better. It was obvious they couldn't move the car any farther. "We don't. From here, we walk." Kat used a no-big-deal tone of voice and hoped Lily would buy it.

Lily's eyes widened. "Walk? We can't—"

Kat cut her off. "Just until we get a cell signal. Hopefully not far."

"Why can't we stay here in the car?" Lily wasn't quite whining this time, but she wasn't far off.

A tantalizing prospect—sitting still in upholstered comfort instead of tromping across a wooded mountainside with two children and two dogs in tow. They could even have air conditioning until they ran out of gas. The fire might be headed in a different direction by now. They might be safe here. They could rest and wait for rescue. Maybe they didn't need to reach a cell signal; maybe all they needed was patience.

Undecided, Kat took a deep breath. And smelled smoke. Not strong, not piercing, a vague smell like friendly smoke drifting from a distant fireplace chimney. But definitely more than she'd noticed a few minutes earlier.

"We need to keep going." Maybe she'd made the wrong call in leaving the cottage. Maybe they would have already been rescued if they'd stayed. Instead, she'd brought them here. They'd made it this far. They couldn't just sit and wait.

She peered ahead into the overgrown forest. The old road served as only a feeble indicator of where the mountain might be passable, a tenuous path through an intimidating wilderness. The shifting shadows below the trees took on menacing shapes, and at that moment, fear owned her.

The best safety lies in fear. Shakespeare certainly had a line for every occasion. Kat steadied herself, and she gave the children a lying smile. Cue the actors. *In this scene, you pretend you know what you're doing.* Action.

"We need to keep going," she repeated. Her voice hardly shook.

She picked up her shoulder bag, stuffed her cell phone into her back pocket, and clapped her floppy red hat on her head. She didn't trust Tye to stay with them the way she trusted Juni, so she put on his harness and attached his leash. "Nirav, can you take care of Tye?"

"I am taking Tye." He took the end of the leash and gripped it tightly. The food seemed to have restored both his energy and his spirits.

"Lily, you help Nirav. And keep an eye on Juni."

Lily frowned, but she took a step closer to the boy.

"Is there anything you need to take with us?"

Lily opened her day pack and pulled out clothing, a toothbrush, toothpaste, and a hairbrush. Kat checked Nirav's and found the same.

"Leave it all here."

"Leave our stuff?" Lily's voice rose high, thin and anguished, the trivial loss more immediate than the larger danger.

"We can come back for it after we're rescued."

Another lie. Kat doubted she'd ever see this car again, and the thought ate at her like acid. She and Jim had bought it together, test-driving dozens and choosing this one only after Jim read every *Consumer Reports* car review for the previous ten years. She was leaving behind more than an automobile. She stuffed the last apple and their dwindling supply of cheese and granola into her shoulder bag along with the Mason jar of tea, and then she passed the open wine bottle of water to the children.

"Drink up."

Nirav and Lily gulped thirstily, and Kat drank the last swallow. She dropped the empty bottle beside the car and suppressed a feeling of guilt as she looked at the panting dogs.

"All set?" she asked.

"I guess." It would have been hard for Lily to show any less enthusiasm.

Nirav said nothing, but his eyes fell at once to his bowl, which still sat by his feet. The bowl Kat had chosen. The bowl so like the one treasured by Nirav's mother.

Kat sighed. Nirav couldn't carry it and also deal with Tye. "Would you like me to take it?" she asked.

Nirav's face lit up at once. "Yes. Please. Thank you."

"What!" Lily's hands were on her hips, again reminding Kat of Sara and reigniting her need for her daughter. "You mean he gets to take what he wants, and I have to leave everything behind?"

You're not the only one who's left things behind. Kat resisted the temptation to say it out loud, and her glare silenced Lily. She wedged the bowl into her bulging shoulder bag.

"Okay." She returned to the downed tree. "Nirav, you first." She hoisted him up so he could scramble over the top, and then she lifted Tye onto the trunk so he could jump down the other side. Juni bounded up and over with no problem.

Lily waved aside Kat's offered hand and swung one leg over the broad trunk. "Ew, gross." She clambered to the other side and looked down at her legs with a horrified expression. Slick, black, half-rotted tree crud coated her skin and transferred itself to her hands when she tried to rub it off. She glanced down at the tree and took a step back—white larvae squirmed in the area where she had knocked a chunk of bark out of place. She gave a small whimper. "We so need a car."

Kat picked a different spot to climb over but ended up equally filthy. The least of their worries. "It's just dirt. Come on, Lily, you can do this."

Kat paused to take a final look at the car. Torn leaves and broken twigs hung from the side mirrors, the door handles, the windshield wipers. Deep cracks split the front bumper, a sapling-shaped dent deformed the hood, and huge gouges scarred both sides where branches had grabbed hold. It was trashed, but Kat's feet didn't want to move on. Leaving it meant they were abandoning their last tie to civilization.

*   *   *

They trudged along the old roadbed, three humans and two dogs, making slow progress. Brambles scratched every inch of exposed skin. Rocks lurked to stub toes and twist ankles. Th children at least wore tennis shoes, but Kat regretted h flimsy sandals with every step on the rough, uneven grour

They walked in single file, Kat and Juni in the lead. stuck close, and she nosed Kat's leg repeatedly, askir reassurance. A vague smokiness clung here, but they co see or hear any actual fire, and the rush of adrenaline been riding on ratcheted down a half notch, leaving and full of doubts. What if she'd made the wrong running? An endless tunnel of trees and rhoc imprisoned them, leaving no way to see where they or where they had been.

Where were Scott and Malcolm? They had t out by now, worried about the children. If trapped, they must have called in the fire. Let rescue was needed. They were probably in so in town, pacing, worried, waiting for news. wasn't the anxious, pacing type. He would

the surface. His anguish would be hidden underneath. easy trick, as she was learning now, trying to hide her from the children.

Would Sara see the fire on the news? Would she worry? Forest fires usually got only a ten-second clip—a shot of busy firefighters, then a return to the latest political scandal. She probably didn't even know what was happening.

Kat forced a powerful wave of sadness aside and forged onward.

Lily's pace slowed, but Nirav plodded on, his eyes never still as he examined everything around him. A tough kid. No tears, no complaints. He reached down to untangle Tye's leash from a dead branch, and Kat wondered where his thoughts took him. He'd already lived through enough horror, and now he'd have plenty of fodder for new nightmares.

If he lived long enough to have nightmares.

Lily asked for the third time for something to drink, and Kat reluctantly passed around the jar of tea. The children drank sparingly, and Kat gulped the last two swallows. No more tea, no more water. She returned the empty jar to her bag, hoping there was some chance they would find water ahead. A thin dusting of cinders settled on her arm, and she brushed it off, angry at yet another reminder of their danger. Other than the whispery talk of the breeze in the branches, an eerie silence pervaded the forest. No birds. A bad sign.

"How much farther?" Lily asked.

Kat checked her phone. No signal yet, but they'd only been walking for half an hour. "I don't know. We need to get to an open area to see where we are."

"We need a map." The criticism in Lily's voice implied that Kat had intentionally launched them on a poorly equipped expedition.

Kat repressed a sharp reply. Lily was twelve and scared, and Kat had indeed launched them on a hopeless trek. She rubbed her thumb along a particularly bad scratch on her thigh and concentrated on putting one foot in front of the other.

They needed more than a map. They needed a phone that actually worked. Water. A fairy godmother.

She should have wakened earlier. She should have known the dry lightning of the night before meant danger in a drought. She should have grabbed the children bodily and hauled them to the car in pajamas instead of wasting precious minutes while they dressed. She should have left a note at the cottage. Or in the car.

Stupid. Stupid. Stupid.

Too many mistakes. Someone different might have known what to do. She might be making matters worse now by insisting they keep moving instead of sitting still and waiting for help. This was far worse than making decisions about her cancer. With cancer, the only life at risk was her own.

Less than five minutes later, they approached a break in the trees, a patch ahead where Kat could see an expanse of sky. She walked faster, hopeful. Perhaps a road. A real road, not an overgrown trail, a road that would lead them to safety.

But when she reached the edge of the gap, she stopped, dismayed. A rockslide. The mountain dropped steeply here at almost a forty-five-degree angle. At some time in the distant past, the slope above had broken loose and cascaded downward, obliterating the ruts they followed and clearing a swath about a hundred feet wide through the vegetation. Waist-high boulders. Stones of all sizes. Loose dirt and gravel. The whole area looked haphazardly tossed together, as if it could destabilize and plummet farther down the mountainside at any moment.

The old roadbed continued on the other side of the rocky jumble, but to get there, they would need to pick their way across the slide. Uphill, to the left, the rockslide looked equally difficult to cross. Downhill, to the right, the drop-off steepened even more, becoming almost vertical. The slightest slip and they would tumble into free fall. Trying it with two children would be nothing short of idiotic.

The tears Kat had held in check all morning threatened to spill, and she turned away from the others and wiped her eyes hard with the back of her hand. She hadn't asked for this. A quiet month in the mountains, that's all she'd sought. Not smoke and fire. Not this frightening hike. Not the overwhelming responsibility of these children.

She dug deep, struggling to find the strength to hang on. She'd survived her surgeries and those long weeks of chemotherapy. She'd survived Jim's sudden death. She had to keep it together now.

She composed her face and turned to tell Lily and Nirav they would wait here and hope for rescue. They couldn't go farther. Lily stood beside Juni, her body sagging. Nirav squatted, petting Tye. All four sets of eyes turned toward Kat.

Waiting.

Trusting her.

Behind the children, in the area of sky visible in the space cleared by the rockslide, a dark roiling cloud of smoke loomed over the valley like an omen of evil. They hadn't outrun it. The fire must still be approaching.

Kat tried to tap into some reserve she hadn't yet exhausted. If they stayed here, action on their part was done, and all they could do was sit and hope. If they stayed here, they'd be giving up.

She forced the words out. "We need to cross these rocks."

Lily looked from Kat to the landslide, and then she peered to the right at the drop-off. "No way."

"Straight across." Kat pointed to the ruts on the other side. Close enough that she could see individual grasses, but impossibly far.

"Do we have to?" Lily's voice cracked.

Kat checked her phone. Nothing. She replaced it in her back pocket.

"Yes. We have to."

Nirav followed the conversation closely, and he now looked downhill, his face apprehensive.

"We'll be fine." Kat stepped over and gave him a quick hug.

She hoped they believed her. All of them were tired, and even Tye now walked sedately on his leash instead of zigzagging all over the place, all his puppy-energy spent. This wasn't at all a sensible attempt, but another glance at the smoke cloud fortified her resolve.

Kat settled her shoulder bag more firmly in place, and she gripped a child's hand in each of her own. She sandwiched the loop handle of Tye's leash between her palm and Nirav's.

"We'll go single file. Lily, you lead us. Head straight across."

"I'll fall." Lily's face had lost all its color, and her voice shook.

"You won't. Be careful and hold my hand." She turned to Nirav. "You okay?"

He nodded, but he never took his eyes from the steep drop.

Kat squeezed his hand. "I've got you."

She tried to quell her own doubts. No choice, she reminded herself. No choice.

They started out. Lily, then Kat, then Tye, then Nirav, linked together and moving sideways as they faced downhill. Juni followed. Rocks and pebbles rolled out from under their shoes with each step, and for each few feet of headway, they slid downhill a foot, eliciting gasps. Nothing gave solid purchase. Lily angled uphill in an effort to keep them from slipping too far down the slope, but they still lost ground.

Kat's sandals had no traction, and her feet slipped within the straps. Pebbles sliced into the soles of her feet. She gritted her teeth, but she didn't stop. Little by little, they inched forward. Tye walked between Kat and Nirav, his slight body barely disturbing the loose gravel. Juni scrambled a bit, but she had an easier time than the heavier humans, with four legs to balance instead of two.

They made it a third of the way across. Two-thirds. Maybe Kat had worried over nothing.

Then Lily slipped.

She cried out, an incoherent animal cry that shook the hillside, as she fell forward. She flailed her free arm, tried to regain her footing, and jerked at Kat's restraining arm. In a chain reaction, Kat lurched and pulled Nirav off-balance, his slick palm slipping from her grasping fingers. Lily teetered and pulled herself upright at the last possible moment, frighteningly close to sliding out of control. Kat sat down hard on the edge of a boulder, the cell phone in her back pocket making a sickening crunching sound. Nirav stumbled, tripped over Tye, landed on his side in a heap of fine gravel and at once began to slide downhill, shouting in Hindi as he went.

"Nirav!" Kat's panicked voice echoed down the valley, and her heart sledgehammered so high in her throat it threatened to choke her.

Nirav skittered down the slope in a cascade of stones, the fingers of his good hand grabbing uselessly for purchase. At last he managed to slow himself, and he finally came to a stop on his belly, more than thirty feet below Kat and Lily and well out of reach. His feet and lower legs hung over the edge of the precipitous drop, and his arms stretched spread-eagled as if trying to cling to the loose slope. He lay there, frozen, his face scratched and bloody, looking frantically at Kat for help.

CHAPTER FOURTEEN

The helicopter sped up the mountainside, leaving the fire-fighters behind. Pete, in the copilot seat, rummaged in a compartment beside him and handed back two wireless headsets. Malcolm crouched behind and between the pilot's chairs to look through the glass canopy and slipped his headset in place. Scott held his up, turning it back and forth, trying to figure out how to put it on.

"Head south-southwest to the cottage located here." Malcolm pointed to a map on a clipboard wedged onto the console between the pilot seats.

Scott moved forward and grabbed a handhold strap mounted on the cabin wall directly behind the pilot's chair. The engine noise clattered through the body of the chopper at a deafening volume, and the walls, the floor, and the ceiling all vibrated steadily. The engine showed its age by an occasional missing beat, and the whole helicopter shivered. Scott flinched every time.

"Follow this road," Malcolm went on, "in case they tried to come down the mountain and got stuck partway."

Malcolm's finger traced a line along the map, and Pete nodded.

"Will do," Lou said. "Hang tight."

The helicopter accelerated, retracing the path they had just taken down the mountainside. Visibility sucked because of the smoke, but Malcolm could make out the road below them. It took only a few minutes to reach the two lower cottages, still unscathed.

As they curved into the next hollow, they reached the point where they'd been forced to turn back, and Lou hovered in place. Malcolm sucked in a tense breath, and his empty stomach knotted. When they had left the area earlier, fires had started on both sides of the road, but now the entire length of the gully blazed. The wooden bridge had collapsed at one end, and its planks were hidden by tall orange flames. Fire ate the grasses, shrubs, and trees on both sides of the gravel road, racing uphill as if bent on destroying everything it touched.

He'd counted on reaching Kat's cottage well before the fire, but for the first time, cold logic argued against it. *What if we're too late?* He pushed the thought aside. If he dwelled in that space, he'd never be able to function.

Lou moved the helicopter to a higher altitude to avoid the thick column of smoke, and they lurched suddenly sideways.

"Updrafts." Lou compensated instantly, and her voice was dead calm, but Scott paled and took an even tighter grip on his handhold.

"Head up the mountain," Malcolm said. They started forward again, following the burning road. All of them peered ahead.

"Almost there," Scott said. "They should hear us by now. They should be standing out front."

Malcolm wished it were so. They had reached the top of the ridge. Directly below them was the broad patch of gravel at road's end, the stone bench, the overlook. Everything that surrounded it was in flames, shrouded in smoke. No one standing anywhere. "Stop. This is it." His voice belonged to a stranger. A wave of nausea rocked him, and his eyes burned even though they could barely smell the smoke in the enclosed cabin.

Nirav. He would have been safer left to beg on the streets of Islamabad. All of Malcolm's hopes for a new life, all his good intentions, gone. Nothing left but fire and smoke.

Lou circled the area at slow speed. Pete glanced her way and shook his head.

"Why are you stopping?" Scott's voice was shrill and panicked. "Kat's cottage is higher up. Above the fire. We need to keep going."

No one answered. Malcolm couldn't form the words to tell Scott he was wrong.

Fire was consuming everything below them—trees burning, shrubs burning, bright yellow flames mixed with the red glow of hot coals. An endless expanse of fire had surged directly up the steep mountainside, and it had already swallowed this whole stretch of land.

A shift in the breeze cleared the smoke for a moment. The cottage, what was left of it, sat directly below them, its roof and all four walls blazing. Scorched dirt, littered with burning branches and debris, replaced the yard the children and dogs had played in.

"Oh my god." Scott's face turned sickly white, and his whole body shook. He glared at Malcolm. "You said we would rescue them. You said we would beat the fire. What if they're trapped? We have to go down. We have to get them out." His voice screeched as it reverberated into the headphones.

Malcolm rested a hand on Scott's shoulder. He had lost a son, and Scott had lost a daughter, but their feelings changed nothing. He shook his head. "We can't go down. It's an inferno."

"You bastard, we can't abandon them. What if they're down there?"

Pete twisted in his chair to look at Scott. "No one's alive down there." His face showed his sympathy, but his flat voice emphasized his seriousness.

Malcolm had known that truth the instant they arrived, but hearing the words spoken out loud made it difficult to breathe. Then again . . . "No one would sit still for this fire." His voice grew stronger. A faint glimmer of hope. "Kat must have taken the children. Left the cottage. We should search uphill—they would head directly away from the flames."

"I hope not," Pete said.

"What do you mean?" Malcolm asked. If only he knew more than the basics about forest fires.

"The mountain is steepest here," Lou answered. "That's why the fire got here so fast."

She glanced back at both Scott and Malcolm, brown eyes in a worried face, and she must have seen their confusion.

"Picture the way a match burns when you hold it flat." She held her left hand flat, palm down. "Then picture what happens when you tip it with the flame at the bottom." She tilted her hand.

Malcolm could indeed picture it. Uphill would be a deathtrap, even if Kat and the children could have forced their way through. That tangled undergrowth needed a machete, and they had no skills to tackle something like that.

"A fire's speed doubles with each ten-degree increase in slope." Lou seemed to think they needed more detail.

Malcolm closed his eyes for an instant, the sharp reality slicing deep. Kat's cottage had been the one with the view, the one with the steepest slope at its doorstep.

"TMI, Lou," Pete said quietly. "TMI."

Lou looked away, the back of her neck bright red. "Sorry." She stopped talking.

Scott jostled Malcolm's arm, leaning forward, searching the scene below as the helicopter continued to hover. Everything on fire. Nothing untouched. Soon there would be nothing left. Nothing at all.

"Wait." Scott clutched Malcolm's arm with frantic fingers. "Where's Kat's car? It's not here. Steel wouldn't burn. It's gone!"

CHAPTER FIFTEEN

Nirav clung to the loose gravel of the rockslide, balanced at the very edge of the sheer drop. The sky glowed an eerie orange behind him, and its gray haze of smoke moved in their direction, making it even more difficult to see clearly.

"Nirav, don't move." Kat yelled so loud, her voice bounced back from all sides.

Nirav nodded, and then, apparently not understanding, he tried to pull one knee up under his body, sending a cascade of small stones over the drop-off.

"Stay, Nirav." Lily yelled. "Stay."

This time the boy froze.

Kat wanted nothing more than to plunge down the mountainside, grab Nirav's hand, and yank him to safety. But she couldn't race down such a steep slope. She glanced along the adjacent forest edge, looking for a less risky way down, for a long stick that could help her reach Nirav, for anything at all she could use. Nothing. She ran through the list of things she had with her.

"Lily, come here. Be careful." They had to act fast, but she couldn't risk losing Lily, too.

Lily, pale and shaking, sidestepped across the slope, and Kat gestured to the boulder she had fallen against.

"Sit here and don't move."

She picked Tye up and plunked him onto Lily's lap, then rummaged in her shoulder bag and pulled out Juni's leash. She disconnected Tye's leash from his harness and clipped the two leashes together. Twelve feet. Not nearly long enough—she needed another twenty feet—but perhaps she could inch partway down and get close enough to toss one end to Nirav.

"Keep Juni with you," she told Lily.

Kat sat down on a boulder-free patch of gravel and started scooting downhill on her butt. She moved as slowly as possible, a few inches at a time, but the stones she dislodged bounced down the slope and hit Nirav. He buried his head in his shoulder, trying to protect his face.

"Kat, stop! You'll hurt him."

Kat stopped. *Screwing up again.* She inched sideways three or four feet and tried again to edge downhill. She inched her way along for a third of the distance to Nirav, but then she began to slide, the drop-off frighteningly close. She grabbed at the loose gravel with her fingers. She dug in her heels, her sandals skewing sideways off her feet, her ankles twisting, sliding faster, out of control. She slid another two or three harrowing feet and then finally stopped. She couldn't risk moving any farther.

Nirav lay motionless, still too far away for the leashes to reach. There had to be another way. Kat looked behind her, where Lily leaned forward, her face pinched, her eyes darting from Kat to Nirav and back. She had a restraining hand on Juni's collar.

"Lily, let go of Juni. Juni, come. Come here, girl."

The Lab hesitated, but then she stepped forward, sending stones cascading down onto Kat. Juni crouched low, and in only a few moments, she reached Kat, her head down and her tail tucked tight under her belly. Kat clipped one end of the double-length leash to her collar.

"What are you doing?" Lily called.

"Juni might be able to go where I can't." Kat patted the dog, then called down the hill. "Nirav, call Juni. Tell her to come."

But Nirav didn't seem to understand, and he asked what sounded like a question in Hindi, his English lost.

"Juni, go to Nirav. Go on." Kat pointed.

Juni whined and nuzzled Kat's pointing finger.

"Wait, I know," Lily called.

Kat turned to see her emptying the shoulder bag. Nirav's bowl, her wallet, her useless car keys. With a joyous shout, Lily pulled out one of Juni's tennis balls and held it up to show Kat.

"Give this to Juni," she called.

Of course. The game. "Throw gently." Kat twisted around as best she could.

Lily gave an underhanded toss that threatened to fling the ball all the way to the bottom of the slope, and Kat leaned far to the side, reaching with outstretched fingers. She bobbled the ball once, but then got a firm grasp. She held it out to Juni.

The Lab took the ball in her mouth, and then Lily called to her. "Take it to Nirav, Juni. Take it to Nirav."

The children had played this simple game a dozen times, trading off turns at throwing the ball. Juni gave a feeble wag to her tail. She once again crouched low and began picking her way down the slope, sliding and skidding a bit, but heading straight toward Nirav. The leash tumbled with her as she went, and Kat held her breath as the dog crept ever closer. Seven feet to go. Five feet. Two. At last she made it, and Nirav grabbed the end of the double-length leash with his good hand.

"Juni, come. Come here." Kat used the most commanding voice she could muster, and Juni stopped and stared back at her, the ball still in her mouth. "Come here, girl, come on."

Juni looked back and forth between Nirav and Kat, but at last she turned around and clambered back uphill, scrambling more than she had on the way down, slipping once to land hard on her chest and then struggling to regain her footing. As she pulled, she dragged Nirav away from the edge of the drop-off. She stopped once, but Lily and Kat both called her. Juni again shouldered into Nirav's added weight and forged onward. *Almost safe.* Kat could breathe again. Between Juni's pull and Nirav's scrambling efforts, the two made steady progress.

When Juni reached her, Kat grabbed the leash and helped Nirav the rest of the way up. She paused to hug him hard for a moment, then urged him to move again. Nirav clung to Kat, his hand clutching her wrist so tightly it threatened to cut off the circulation to her hand, making it awkward to crawl uphill. Rocks stabbed her hands and knees. Together, they inched their way toward Lily. When they finally reached the boulder where Lily waited, Kat sagged against it.

"Good girl," Kat said over and over to the Lab. Juni wiggled ecstatically over all the attention, still hanging on to her precious tennis ball, and Tye barked, caught up in the excitement.

Nirav's face, arms, and legs were scratched and bruised, and his cheeks were tear-streaked, but his quiet voice joined in the chorus. "Good girl."

"Lily, you saved us with that tennis ball."

Lily straightened, and she gave a half smile, the first since they'd left the cottage behind. Sara used to smile like that, half pleased, half embarrassed, when anyone complimented her, and Kat choked down a lump at the resemblance.

She wiped her free hand on her shorts, leaving bloody streaks, and she glanced at a jagged cut on her knee that throbbed in time with her heartbeat. "Okay. Let's get off this rockslide."

She reattached Tye's leash to his harness, but this time she tied the other end to Juni's collar to ensure the two dogs stayed together and out from underfoot.

"Lily, grab that stuff, put it back in my bag, and hand it to me. Then you hold on to the end of Juni's leash."

Kat waited for everyone to get situated, then took the ball from Juni and tossed it into the greenery on the far edge of the rockslide. Juni started forward after her toy, taking Tye with her, and Lily hung on to the leash and followed. Kat gripped Lily's hand and pulled Nirav in her wake. Rocks still tumbled out beneath them, each step precarious, but Juni's forward pull helped them keep their balance. When they finally stepped onto ordinary dirt, Kat pulled both children into her arms and hung on tight, her body shaking in relief at making the crossing. Too close to disaster. Far too close. She'd probably been wrong to even try to bring them across.

She turned them loose reluctantly.

Lily glanced down. "Oh no—Kat—your feet." She pointed to Kat's sandals. Rocks had torn their soles ragged, and blood oozed from the edges to stain the ground.

Kat kicked off one shoe and hung on to Lily's shoulder to peer at the bottom of her foot. Cuts crisscrossed the sole, dripping steadily, and the blisters that had formed under the straps had ripped wide open. She had hardly felt the damage while trying to reach Nirav, but now that she could see her shredded foot, the pain exploded. She slipped her sandal back on and didn't bother to inspect the other foot. No water to clean the cuts. Nothing to wrap her feet in. She didn't even have enough energy left to freak out over the blood.

"You can't walk. You're bleeding." Lily's voice trembled in a mix of sympathy and fear.

"Give me a minute." Walking would be torture, but as they stood there, a shift of wind carried a particularly dense cloud of smoke and cinders toward them. Kat and Nirav both coughed, a needless reminder that the fire still chased them.

Kat reached into her back pocket and pulled out her cell phone to see if that first hard fall had inflicted any serious damage. She held her palm over the screen for a moment, afraid to look. Then she uncovered it.

Countless cracks distorted the phone's screen. The icons were gone. Nothing happened when she pressed the *on* button. A black, blank screen. Kat licked her lips, her mouth suddenly desert dry.

Shit. Shit. Shit.

She pushed each button on the phone repeatedly, holding her breath until waves of dizziness rocked her, but nothing changed.

When she looked up, both Lily and Nirav were watching her. She dropped the phone into her shoulder bag without comment.

Lily opened her mouth for a moment as if she were going to ask, but she glanced at Nirav and remained silent. Kat suspected Nirav had tuned in to the problem as quickly as Lily had, but she couldn't speak the bad news out loud. She would break down completely.

"Time to get going." The threat of tears echoed in her voice.

Nirav came close and took her hand gently in his. Lily picked up the shoulder bag and the end of Tye's leash and for once started out without complaint. They waded into the tangled grasses of the old roadbed—their only path forward—as Kat concentrated on taking one unsteady step after another. A few yards in, she turned back for a final look at where they'd been. Her red hat sat forlorn on the landslide where it had landed when she fell, the only spot of color against the deserted patchwork of rocky brown and gray.

CHAPTER SIXTEEN

Where's Kat's car? The question reverberated in the cabin, and Malcolm looked again at the flaming scene below him. Scott was right. Steel wouldn't burn. He should have thought of that—would have done so if he hadn't been so twisted with worry. He had to get hold of himself, stay focused on the task at hand.

"Well done." He clapped Scott on the shoulder, and Scott looked startled. "Lou, we followed the road the whole way up, right?"

The pilot nodded. "The smoke's been heavy, but we would have seen a car if it was there."

Scott seized the possibility. "Maybe they got out before fire blocked the road. Made it to town. Missed us somehow?" As he said the words, his face fell. Even he knew the idea was absurd.

Malcolm peered through the smoke. No hidden trail up the mountain, but what was that at the far end of the gravel patch? "Look there. That band of shorter scrub that's burning. Is that the outline of a road?"

"Could be." Lou eased the helicopter along the route Malcolm indicated.

He'd been at Kat's cottage. Had there been an old road there? He couldn't remember. He'd been talking to Nirav. Enjoying normalcy. The last thing he'd been thinking about was vetting escape routes, the hard-earned lessons of Afghanistan and Iraq set aside to enjoy some time off.

"It's a path of some sort," Scott said. His voice rose in excitement, and although Malcolm wanted to share his confidence, he reined in the impulse.

But it *was* a path, a definite path, where the fire burned grass and underbrush, a path leading from the gravel road into the deeper forest.

They followed the route slowly, four pairs of eyes searching for signs of a car and four sets of anxieties dreading the prospect of finding it in flames. A half mile. Three-quarters of a mile. They hit a short stretch the fire had ignored so far, and Lou dropped even lower, the landing skids almost brushing the treetops.

"There are definitely tire tracks down there." Malcolm pointed. A line of crushed undergrowth marked the route where something large had forced its way through. *Good job, Kat.* Better than good. Nirav could be around the next bend. "Keep going." He leaned forward.

They continued their slow progress, flying over flames again, straining to see through the haze.

"There." Pete pointed ahead and to the right. "There's the car."

It stood, dented and forlorn, with two doors standing wide open, its way forward blocked by an enormous downed tree. The car appeared untouched, but the fire burned only thirty yards away.

"Where are they? Why can't I see them?" Scott had his forehead pressed to the side window, his fists clenched.

No one appeared.

Abandoned. They'd gone ahead on foot. A woman and two children trying to flee this fire on foot. Malcolm wanted to keep going to find them, but first he had to confirm the car was truly empty. What if Nirav was down there, unconscious?

There was no space to land. He pulled back from his position between the pilots' seats. "I need to go down and check, make sure no one's there. See if there's a message." It was the rational, one-step-at-a-time decision, but his gut ached over a delay that might prove pointless.

Scott gave him an incredulous look. "What do you mean, *go down*?"

Malcolm ignored him. Pete abandoned his copilot seat and scrambled between Scott and Malcolm, crouching low in the limited head space. He pulled the canvas cover off the equipment that bulked in the center of the cargo hold, exposing a large motorized cable winch bolted firmly to the deck. Big enough to lift machinery—plenty strong enough for anything they would need.

Pete tossed Malcolm a black webbed harness. "You've done this before?"

Malcolm nodded. "Special Forces."

"That would do it." Pete sounded impressed, and Scott's eyes widened.

Malcolm put on the harness and adjusted it for a snug fit.

Pete worked quickly, turning on the motor, unwinding a dozen feet of cable from the winch, checking various switches.

Scott shifted toward the front of the cargo space, then moved off to one side by the door, underfoot and in the way no matter where he was. Pete clipped a remote-control unit to his belt and slid the right side-door open. Ribbons of smoke blew into the helicopter, carrying visible flecks of ash that clung to every surface. The air temperature jumped twenty degrees, the air conditioning overwhelmed by the fire's heat.

Pete reached up and out through the doorway and pivoted a heavy-duty pulley outward to position it above the open door. It extended out about two feet from the side of the helicopter. He fed the free end of the cable through the pulley and let the clip end hang free. A bit jerry-rigged compared to some systems Malcolm had used, but feasible.

Malcolm unclipped the sat phone from where it dangled on his belt and set it aside on the folded canvas winch cover. He shifted past Scott to sit by the open door and clipped the cable to his harness.

"All set?" Pete asked.

"All set."

"Leave your headset on—should work fine at this distance."

Malcolm swung his feet out, rested them on the landing skid, and took a careful breath, cautious of the smoke. Wind slight but steady from the east. Fire moving closer, but he'd have enough time to search before it arrived. Lou brought the helicopter lower over the old roadbed, and when they were about thirty feet above ground, Malcolm stood up and stepped forward off the skid. He dangled now below the pulley, suspended by the cable, the vibrations of the helicopter transmitted to his chest through the steel fiber.

"Ready."

Pete activated the winch and began lowering Malcolm down. Lou held the copter steady.

Malcolm landed gently a few yards behind the car. "I'm down."

He detached the cable from his harness, and the helicopter rose a little, released from his weight. Scott was leaning out the door, watching, one hand no doubt keeping a death grip on his hand strap.

No time to waste. Malcolm moved.

Car—empty. No bodies, and although Malcolm had expected none, a wave of relief buoyed him. "No note. They headed on." He heard an inarticulate noise in his headphones that must have come from Scott.

Front seat—nothing of value. A scrap of white turned out to be a blood-stained tissue, and he slipped it absently into his pocket. No car keys, wallet, or clutter. Kat might have a bag with her.

Back seat—two day packs. He glanced in Nirav's. It held only his overnight things. The other bag, pink, had to be Lily's. A glint of metal on the floor caught his eye, a small bracelet. He added it to his pocket.

Surrounding area—a quick scan. Three apple cores. An empty wine bottle, a few remaining drops of water clinging to its sides. Malcolm's opinion of Kat went up yet another notch. She'd thought about supplies before she left. The rotting log that had blocked the car showed obvious marks where several people had scrambled over its top. The old roadbed stretched ahead, unquestionably the easiest path. They would stay on it.

Malcolm grabbed the day packs and walked behind the car. The smoke thickened; the fire closed in. Heat parched his face, and rivulets of sweat soaked his shirt. "All clear."

"Roger." Pete lowered the cable.

Malcolm caught it, clipped it on, acknowledged. In seconds, he was back at the helicopter, reversing his steps to get back into the cabin.

"They're all together." He unclipped the cable but left the harness on. "Three apple cores. Packs from both children."

Scott seized Lily's day pack, opened it, and pulled out a fuzzy red nightshirt. "Thank god. They made it this far." His hand smoothed the fabric over and over.

Pete rummaged in a canvas duffel and handed Malcolm a water bottle. Half the contents disappeared in a single long swallow, his throat screaming for relief after only minutes below. The thought of Nirav, down there with the fire, was a knife in his chest.

"I could see where they climbed over the top of that downed tree." He pointed.

Scott peered out the open door as if he would be able to see anything. "At least it gives us a direction."

"Keep following the roadbed?" Lou asked. The helicopter started forward.

"Seems like our best bet." Malcolm took a smaller sip and glanced at his watch. 0842. Less than three hours since he woke. "The road lets them move fastest. So far, Kat is making smart choices." If Nirav had to be caught in all this, at least he wasn't trapped with a fool.

Scott tucked Lily's nightshirt away, folded the pack with exaggerated care, and put it into the corner of the cabin where it wouldn't be stepped on. He seemed reassured by such a simple thing, but Malcolm's tension ramped ever higher. Minutes were ticking away.

Pete returned to the copilot seat, leaving the cargo door open and the winch-and-pulley setup ready. Scott scooted back from the open edge. He saw Malcolm watching him and gave an embarrassed shrug. "Don't know how you do it. Makes me dizzy. No glass between me and the ground."

Great. Afraid of heights. Just what they needed. Malcolm shifted forward to take his place looking ahead, but then he remembered the bracelet and pulled it out of his pocket. The stained tissue tumbled to the deck.

He held the bracelet out to Scott. "I spotted this on the floor of the car."

Scott grabbed it—silver, with dangling butterfly charms. "Thanks. It's Lily's. Her best friend gave it to her. She never would have left it behind if . . ." His voice broke, and he looked down. "What's this?" He picked up the tissue, the dark-red bloodstains brilliant against the white.

"I found it on the front seat. Lily and Nirav's gear was in the back." Scott's eyes were wide and horrified, and Malcolm hastened to reassure him. *Can't have him panic now.* "Only the one tissue. Not much blood. It looks worse than it is."

"Thanks." Scott tossed the tissue aside and clutched the metal bracelet tightly. Tight enough that the charms must have dug into his skin. "I keep thinking about Lily, hurt." He swallowed hard, holding himself together, but barely. A new recruit's fear, suddenly confronting reality and finding himself out of his depth. "I'll give this to Lily if we find her." He paled further. "No, no, no, I mean *when* we find her. *When.*" He turned away, blinking fast, and stared out the open door.

Malcolm returned his attention to the search. At least the fire hadn't reached this far yet. They moved more slowly now, inching along the old roadbed, no longer looking for a car, instead looking for people on foot. Images of Nirav crowded in, down there somewhere, scared and hurt, and he forced them out of his head.

Lou pulled back on the throttle, and the helicopter stopped its slow progress. "Which way?"

Malcolm peered ahead. The faint track they'd been following had disappeared, buried deep in an old rockslide. The mountain dropped precipitously here, and he searched both sides, looking for the most likely route someone on foot would follow. Downhill had steep drop-offs. Uphill—equally treacherous. Would Kat have tried to cross that rockslide? No way. Far too unstable. Far too dangerous. Surely she had more sense than that.

He shook his head. "They couldn't have gone downhill here. Unless they backtracked, left the trail at some point we've already passed." He pointed uphill. "Try that way."

Lou obediently angled the helicopter up the slope, but the farther they went, the rougher the terrain.

"Can't believe they came this way," Pete said.

"Agreed."

Lou turned the helicopter and retraced their route downhill, precious minutes wasted. Scott fidgeted, restless. "Where are they?"

A loud crackling and popping exploded in their headphones, startling and unexpected, followed by a man's voice. "Wolfpack two-seven-foxtrot. Wolfpack two-seven-foxtrot. This is Asheville Regional Tower."

Lou frowned and flipped a switch. "Asheville Tower. This is Wolfpack two-seven-foxtrot. Come in."

"Patching in a call from the Macon County fire chief. Over."

"Reading you three." Lou adjusted knobs, and some of the crackling improved.

More static followed; then the sharp voice of the fire chief Scott and Malcolm had spoken to came through the radio. "When I tell you to stay in phone contact, that includes answering the phone. Over." His pissed-off tone transmitted clearly through the crackles.

They may not have heard the sat phone ring, but its bright flashing signal should have caught Malcolm's eye, and he'd left it where it would attract attention. He looked toward the winch cover, where he'd placed it. The phone was gone.

"Roger that," Lou responded. "What's the issue? Over." Malcolm turned back to the conversation.

"Wolfpack, break off your search. Go immediately to these coordinates. Ready to copy." Pete grabbed pencil and clipboard and wrote down the string of numbers the chief repeated twice. "Four hikers. One injured. This can't wait any longer. The fire is closing in on their position. Over."

Lou glanced at Malcolm. This had been the risk from the outset, and here they were. No choice. The chief had laid it out. Malcolm nodded, the simple motion an ultimate betrayal of Nirav.

"Acknowledged," Lou said. "We'll evacuate to the landing site we used on arrival. Over."

"An ambulance will be waiting. Out."

The radio went quiet, and Lou flipped off the transmission switch.

"What are you doing? We can't leave!" Scott shouted the words, his face red. "We need to keep looking!"

Malcolm looked down at the mountainside, wanting with every fiber to continue the search. His jaw clamped so tightly his teeth ached, and he was having difficulty swallowing. "They have an exact location. We're still searching. We'll work fast and come back."

Lou altered the helicopter's course to align with the new heading, which brought its still-open side door directly over the landslide.

Scott took a deep breath, obviously ready to argue further, but he froze. "Wait, what's that?" He pointed down at the rocks below. "That red spot."

Lou held the chopper steady. Pete pulled a pair of binoculars from a compartment beside him, held them to his face and squinted through them.

"Looks like a piece of cloth."

Malcolm found it—a tiny fleck of red among the brown, about two-thirds of the way across the swath of tumbled rock. Pete handed the binoculars back and Scott seized them.

He fumbled with the focus knob, taking so long to adjust it that Malcolm was ready to rip them from his hands. Finally, he nodded. "Red with white flowers. It's Kat's hat."

"Are you sure that's what it is?" Malcolm asked.

Scott lowered the binoculars. "Positive. I saw her wear it when she picked up Lily for a walk." He was smiling, obviously pleased they were on the right track. But then his face clouded. "You don't think they tried to cross here and fell over that cliff, do you?"

Malcolm didn't answer, the same worry tightening his throat. Lou moved the chopper farther down the mountain and hovered over the sheer drop. They all scanned the rocky jumble.

"Nobody there," Pete said. "If anyone slipped over that edge, they wouldn't just stroll away. They'd be down on those rocks. We'd see them."

Malcolm could breathe again. "Good. The hat proves they were here, and it looks like they crossed the rockslide instead of doubling back. We're still searching the right place."

Lou nodded acknowledgment. As Malcolm fully expected, she put the helicopter into motion again, angling back uphill, away from the red hat and away from the old roadbed, obeying orders.

"What the hell are you doing?" Scott's clenched fist pounded the back of Lou's chair, but she didn't flinch. "They're here! They're close by!"

Lou glanced at Malcolm for an instant, got his confirming nod, and held her course. "We've got our instructions. It's my license on the line."

"Goddamn it! Turn this thing around!"

Her voice slashed like sharpened steel. "Calm down or I'll toss you off this bird when we drop these hikers."

Scott snapped his mouth shut, but after a moment he turned on Malcolm. "You asshole. You conjure up a helicopter like some magic act, and now you refuse to use it."

Malcolm held his own frustration in check. The last thing he wanted to do was abandon his son. "We'll be back." A firm promise. A promise he'd back with his life. "Fast as you can," he said to Lou, and the helicopter gathered speed.

Scott stared out the open door, watching until the rough tumble of the landslide disappeared. "We're heading the wrong way." He no longer yelled, but Malcolm almost preferred the shouts to the desolation that now dragged in Scott's voice. "We may have just killed them."

CHAPTER SEVENTEEN

Kat and the children walked in silence, Lily still in the lead, picking their path through a tangle of brambles. Kat focused on the small square footage of ground that lay between her feet and Lily's.

Her feet. Ten more steps, she promised herself, and she counted them off. There. That proved endurable. Now ten more.

The pain was insistent. She tried to distract herself by thinking of happier times—picnics, parties, vacations, holidays—but reality kept intruding. If only she could talk one more time with Sara, apologize for their disagreement, let her know how amazing she was. She set such an example to the world with her dedication to her animals. If only Kat could let her know one last time that she was loved. Her eyes filled with tears, and they weren't due to her feet. She had so much to say, now that she had no chance to say it.

She had counted dozens of sets of ten when Lily stopped and whirled to look behind them. She threw her head back and checked the sky, her body tensed and focused. "What's that noise?"

The forest still embraced its eerie silence. It took a moment for Kat to hear what Lily meant. An engine. Up high. An airplane, or maybe a helicopter.

Nirav pointed back the way they had come. Kat squinted, searching for anything that moved. The smoke cloud didn't hug the ground here, but it hovered close to the treetops, cloaking the sky, thick and impenetrable. Trying to find an airplane in its shifting mass was like trying to glimpse a straight-pin in a wad of gray-black cotton.

Lily waved her arms over her head. "Over here! We're here!" Even as she shouted, the engine noise faded and disappeared. Lily's arms dropped and her shoulders shrank. "They didn't see us. We have to go back. We need to signal them."

Kat seized Lily's arm. "We can't go back."

"How will they know we're down here?"

"We can't signal unless we can see them."

Lily glared.

Kat shifted her weight uncomfortably. "We need to keep going, Lily."

Nirav looked back and forth between them and then pointed in the direction they were headed. "We are walking now." He waved Lily forward with both hands.

Outnumbered, Lily spun on her heels and stomped ahead, her back unyielding.

Kat started counting steps again. Maybe there really was someone out there, looking, but if she and the children couldn't spot the airplane from the ground, they were equally invisible to anyone searching. Assuming anyone even realized they were out here. Assuming Scott or Malcolm had escaped the flames, hadn't been trapped, too. If they were alive, they must be frantic, but believing in a sensational rescue from the sky was as hopeless as believing in a miracle cure for her cancer.

Lily checked the sky at frequent intervals, but none of them heard any more engine noise.

They kept walking. Trees. Shrubs. Vines. Tangles of dead branches. An occasional scramble over a rotting log. A rabbit, munching greenery, froze as they passed. A lone squirrel scolded from a tree. After another half hour of slow progress, they reached a more open spot. A web of laurel and rhodo-dendron still fenced them in on the left, but on the right, a huge slab of ancient granite angled up and out of the moun-tainside, overhanging the valley below.

"Wait here a minute." Kat's whole body ached, and more than anything else, she wanted to sit down and rest, the con-stant fear more exhausting than the distance they'd traveled. She needed to close her eyes for a moment's escape. But if she stopped moving, she'd never be able to force herself back onto her feet again. "Let me see if I can tell where we are."

Lily and Nirav collapsed to the ground where they stood, and the dogs both flopped on their bellies, panting. Kat gin-gerly picked her way up the rugged incline, placing each dam-aged foot with care to avoid a fall or a twisted ankle.

At the highest point of the slab, the rock leveled and smoothed, and Kat inched forward to the very edge of the natural overlook. On a day with no smoke, no fire, the view here would probably extend for miles. Today, gray haze masked the distant scenery, but the smoke swirled and shifted, allowing Kat to catch occasional glimpses of the terrain below.

Off to the right, where the fire must have started, blackened zones marked where everything worth devouring had already been eaten. Closer in, yellow and orange flames spiked high. Patches of deceptive green poured smoke into the sky, burning invisibly low to the ground, and narrow bands of fire stretched up the sides of the mountains in multiple places, grasping at the slopes like greedy fingers.

No sign of other human beings. Kat's insides twisted into a tight knot. She had almost believed they had a chance, but she could find no reassurance in what she saw. Dragging the children here had only delayed the inevitable.

She looked back and forth and tried to orient herself. A break in the smoke let her see the crescent lake far below her, and she rocked backward, dismayed. They should be farther north by now, the lake well behind them. She focused on the area to her right, and in a flash, she understood where they were and how they had traveled. She fought down a panic-driven wave of nausea as the truth battered its way through her last shred of optimism.

They had followed the road, and the road followed the ridge. But the ridge wasn't straight. Kat recalled the persistent right-hand bends she'd noticed—they had traveled in a long U-shaped curve. Her cottage, the cottage where they'd started, the cottage with the great view, stood at one end of the curve, and Kat now stood at the other. Even though they'd traveled a mile by car and thrashed through another mile, perhaps two, on foot, Kat could see their starting point, far less than a mile away. Smoke billowed from that stretch of ridgeline, thick and angry, and Kat pictured her little cottage in flames. Her photographs, her plans to create something lasting for Sara, gone with all the rest.

She and the children were better off than they would have been if they'd stayed at the cottage, but they hadn't escaped. Far from it. Kat brushed her hair away from her face, her hands trembling. Even as she stood there, the fire quickened forward—standing dead trees flaring like Roman candles, the hot dry breeze nudging the fire ever onward, nibbling its way toward them.

Footsteps crunched on loose rocks behind her, and Kat turned. Lily scrambled up the last few feet to join her. She saw the fire, gasped, and took a hasty step away from the rocky edge. "I thought we left the fire behind us."

"So did I."

"We're going to die, aren't we?" Lily's voice was adult and strangely matter-of-fact, and her face looked oddly calm, as if she were so numb the danger no longer felt real.

"No. We're not going to die." Kat choked on the words. She couldn't let these children die. But they were running out of options. What they needed was water and lots of it. The one place flames couldn't go. But the fire lay between them and the lake, an effective blockade. "With the drought, all the water up here on the mountain has disappeared. The crescent lake is down there and it has all the water we'd ever need. If we could only get there . . ."

Lily's eyes were fixed on the flames, mesmerized, but then she turned to Kat. "What about the beaver pond?"

It took a moment for the words to sink in. "What beaver pond?"

"I told you at dinner. The one Dad and I hiked to."

Kat restrained a sudden soaring hope and tried to recall the details. "Think back to that hike. This could be important. You said you started at the big lake."

"Yeah."

"You were the one who read the map."

Lily nodded.

"You hiked uphill and reached a pond. You looked down and saw the lake where you'd started."

"No smoke like this. A pretty view."

"Close your eyes. Think about the way the lake looked when you saw it from above." If Lily could only remember . . .

Lily raised her eyebrows, thought, then bit her lip. "I can't remember." Her voice was shaking. "The fire. It's coming now. I can't remember yesterday."

Kat stifled a sudden urge to scream and instead forced her voice to sound patient. "Focus. Please. A pretty view. You probably took a picture with your phone."

"My phone is with Dad. I knew it wouldn't work at your place."

"I know, Lily. That's okay. Think about the way the picture looked. The shape of the lake. We need to figure out where the beaver pond is, and if you can remember the way the lake looked, that will help figure it out."

Lily glanced again at the fire. "I said I can't remember."

"Lily!" Kat's patience snapped, and she suspected her face was as savage as her voice. She reined herself in. "Try again. Please."

Lily frowned and fidgeted, but at least this time she closed her eyes. "We ate a snack. Walked to the overlook. Dad told me to take a picture so I could show Mom how far up we had climbed." Her eyes flew open, and she grabbed Kat's arm. "I remember! I can see it."

"Good. Look down at the lake now. Wait until the smoke shifts so you can see its shape."

They stood side by side, silent, and at last the smoke thinned briefly over the lake, and they could see its distinctive crescent through the haze.

"It's not the same. We're not at the right angle. I think we were more over that way yesterday." Lily pointed to the left, the direction they were already heading on the road, and a small bubble of hope jostled some of Kat's fears to the side.

"Were you higher on the mountain or lower? Did the lake look bigger? Or smaller?"

"Bigger. We must have been lower down, but not much lower." This time, she said it with confidence.

Kat tried to work up enough spit to swallow. She had wished for plenty of water, and perhaps this offered them their chance. If Lily was right, then the beaver pond should be below them. The fire had cut them off from the big lake, but hopefully Lily's pond was high enough on the mountain that the flames hadn't reached it yet.

"How big was the beaver pond?"

"Pretty big."

Kat maintained eye contact and said nothing. Lily mangled her lower lip with her teeth again and considered the question further.

"If we were standing at one edge, then the other edge would be at that big tree."

Kat gauged the distance to the fir tree Lily indicated. Assuming she could believe the recollection of a twelve-year-old, that meant a pond about the size of a football field. Would that be big enough to protect them from the fire?

Lily turned her back on the view and took Kat's hand. "The fire is coming."

"I know."

Kat looked toward the valley once again, a fire-driven miniature hell. She inspected the forest where Lily had pointed, but she found no sign of a pond. They couldn't force their way through the trees at random, hoping to blindly find water. For the moment, all they could do was continue to follow the old road. If they found a stream, or even a dried-up gully, leading downhill in the direction of Lily's pond, then she would need to decide the direction they'd take.

A decision. A major one. She had come here to the mountains seeking a respite from decisions, but the weight of this one pressed down with a force that made her knees buckle.

CHAPTER EIGHTEEN

It took two endless forevers for the chopper to reach the coordinates where the hikers waited for rescue. Malcolm stopped watching their progress, chaffing at the delay, anxious to get back in action. Sitting still, doing nothing while they headed in the wrong direction, only gave him time—too much time— to imagine Nirav trapped below. Lost. Frightened. Injured. He forced himself not to visualize anything worse. Life could not be so cruel—to let this child into his life and then snatch him away so soon. Malcolm swallowed the lump that had cemented in the back of his throat.

He knew they had reached the fire when the helicopter began bucking again, protesting the hot updrafts, and he shook himself back to the present moment.

"There they are." Lou slowed. Malcolm looked through the cockpit windshield, and Scott shifted out of his corner to look out the open door. They hovered over a steep uneven slope, and at its base four small figures waved frantically, their arms semaphores of panic.

"Fools," Scott said. "Of course we see you. That's why we're hovering right above you."

He had a point. Two women and one man stood clustered together, and nearby a second man lay stretched on the ground beside a heap of large backpacks. Lou slowly pivoted the helicopter, and the fire came fully into view, the flames only fifty yards from the hikers. Their panic became understandable. Smoke swirled in all directions, and hot air gusted through the open helicopter door. Malcolm tried to avoid it, but the moisture in his eyes and nose evaporated in an instant, and his eyelids scraped across his eyeballs like steel wool.

"I don't see anywhere to land," Pete said.

Lou gave Malcolm a hasty look. "You win another trip down."

Not as simple as he'd hoped, but he couldn't fault their assessment. No place to land. They'd need to bring people up one at a time, and the guy with the leg fracture was going to have a rough transit. "Anything we can use as a splint?"

"First aid stuff is in back."

Malcolm crouched low and inched around the far side of the winch to reach the back of the cargo space. He should have anticipated better, gathered supplies well before they arrived. These thoughts of Nirav were throwing him off his game.

First aid had been part of his training, and he rummaged through the contents of a bin marked with a giant red cross to assemble what he might need. Bandages, a pair of gloves, and a small squishy packet labeled *inflatable leg splint*. No morphine, which wasn't surprising, but that wasn't going to make broken-leg guy very happy.

Pete got out of his chair to run the winch. Scott shifted away from the open door and then back again, once again in the way no matter where he was.

Malcolm came forward and sat at the open door. *Get down. Pick up these hikers. Get on our way.* That was the mission.

Pete handed him two additional harnesses, and Malcolm ran through his mental checklist: wind gusting at five to ten here, cable under greater strain but should be able to take it, fire splitting off into two arms now, both getting too close. "Ready."

The helicopter bounced and rocked back and forth. Scott looked a little green and clung to his strap.

"Rougher ride this go-round," Lou said. "Don't waste time."

Malcolm grunted. *Yeah, no kidding.* He stepped out, Pete let out cable, and Malcolm dropped.

They were higher up now than when he'd gone down to investigate the car, and the cable—a slender steel thread—jerked and twisted on the way down. Malcolm landed hard only ten yards from the group of hikers, disconnected the cable, and hurried over to them. He was still in headset range, so he left it in place. "Everyone okay?" The three standing hikers began talking at once—*thought you'd never get here, fire is getting closer, didn't know what to do*—and Malcolm let the jabber wash past him. He knelt by the silent figure on the ground.

"What's your name?" he asked quietly.

"Trip."

How appropriate. Midtwenties and fit, but the taut strain in his voice evidenced his pain. Bad tibial fracture—jagged ends of bone stuck out horrifically through pierced skin. No serious bleeding. Major blood vessels intact. A serious cut above his right elbow showed bloody mangled muscle and oozed steadily. Malcolm ripped open packages even as he inspected the damage. He looked up and picked the person who looked the least panicked, a small blonde woman in too-new hiking boots. "You. Help with this splint."

She flinched but obeyed. One of the advantages of years of giving orders was that people knew at once that he meant it. He handed the deflated splint to her—an elongated version of the sort of water wings he'd seen children use in swimming pools, designed to encase the leg from foot to hip. He spoke to Trip. "This isn't going to be fun."

He lifted the injured leg, trying to keep the fracture as stable as possible while the woman slid the plastic sleeve in place. Trip moaned, and by the time the task was done and the leg rested once again on the ground, he was unconscious.

Malcolm pointed at the standing man, a tall redhead with a serious sunburn. "Blow up the splint. I'll work on this arm." The man gulped but knelt and got to it. By the time Malcolm had slapped a bandage on Trip's arm and strapped him into one of the spare harnesses, the leg was immobilized, rigid in transparent plastic that unfortunately did nothing to mask the ghastly break.

"Pete."

"Roger."

"Ready for the cable."

"Roger that."

The helicopter dropped closer, the cable flailing. "Watch it, all of you," Malcolm said. "Don't get hit."

The hikers pulled back. Lou dropped lower, letting the cable coil on the ground so Malcolm could snag it safely. "Okay, we need to lift Trip together. Keep that leg from hitting anything that would puncture the splint."

The four of them lined up, two on each side, and Malcolm attached the cable. Pete took up the slack, and they lifted Trip, supporting the leg. He ended up dangling in the air, his face bloodless, his head lolling, his injured leg rigid in its splint. As soon as he rose out of reach, Malcolm quit watching. Trip was Pete's problem now. He glanced at the fire—getting closer, smoke thickening—and then he turned to the girl who had helped with the splint. "What's your name?"

"Melissa." Her eyes were fixed upward, where Trip was being dragged into the helicopter.

Malcolm held out the second spare harness. "You're next." He helped her adjust it, then went to grab the cable, which Pete had lowered again along with the harness Trip had worn. Malcolm pulled the cable back toward Melissa and discovered she had put her bulky backpack on. "Leave the pack here."

"What?" Her voice was an indignant screech. You would have thought he was asking her to leave behind her firstborn child.

The others joined in, a cacophony of complaint, and Malcolm threw up his hands. He had no time and no patience for this crap. "Okay, okay." He clipped on the cable. "Pete, take her up."

Melissa whisked into the air.

"Who's next?"

The red-haired guy, who said his name was Brandon, stepped backward, so Malcolm fitted the second girl—Vi, Di, something like that—into the other harness and sent her up next, complete with backpack. The fire was making steady headway, a trailblazing flame only twenty yards away now with the smoke steadily thickening. He and Brandon both wiped their streaming eyes and pulled their shirts up to cover their mouth and nose. The updrafts must have been getting worse, because Lou was muttering an admirable breadth of profanity into her microphone as the helicopter bounced around unsteadily above them.

One more to go. Malcolm had interpreted Brandon's step backward to let the girl go first as chivalry, but when he tried to hand him the harness, Brandon shook his head and backed away, his hands extended in a keep-back gesture. "No. I can't. There's no way. Not dangling like that . . ."

Unbelievable. This guy thought there were options? "So, you want to stay here and burn?" Brandon looked toward the fire—fierce and threatening—and shook his head again, gulping in fear. Knocking him unconscious was a serious temptation, but Malcolm resisted the impulse. "Then close your eyes and do it." Brandon nodded, but he was shaking so hard, it was difficult to adjust the harness and lift on his backpack. At last he was ready. "Take it up, Pete."

Brandon, tense and pale beneath his sunburn, shook his head. "No, no, please, no."

"Tell him to get braced," Pete said. "This one's going to break speed records."

The cable tightened. Brandon lifted off. The instant his feet left the ground, he freaked. Arms flailed. Legs thrashed. His head twisted back and forth like something out of *The Exorcist*. His spastic movements set him swinging on the end of the cable, and Malcolm stepped forward with the vague idea of calming him down somehow. Big mistake. One of the frantic kicks slammed hard into Malcolm's arm, Brandon's heavy hiking boot hitting directly on the point of Malcolm's bent elbow.

A faint cracking sound and a distinctive internal popping sensation hit a millisecond before the searing pain reached his brain. He rocked forward for an instant, pulling his arm in tight against his chest, fighting the agony. *Stop it. Stop it now.* With enormous effort, he straightened and focused on Brandon's progress.

The guy had embraced full panic mode. He spun in circles in midair and swung back and forth in short pendulum arcs the whole way up, jerking at the end of the cable like a human worm on a giant hook. Pete leaned out of the helicopter, yelling, his words ringing in Malcolm's headphones. "Hold still. Hold still and let us pull you in. Hold still." It did no good.

Brandon reached the level of the helicopter door. The winch stopped, but instead of calming down to let them help, he lunged frantically toward the interior of the chopper, which only sent him spinning in circles on the shortened cable.

"Shit." Pete had pulled the microphone away from his mouth now, but Malcolm could still hear him yelling. "Stop. Put your hands on your chest. Hold still. We'll get you in."

Malcolm used his left hand to pull his injured right arm tighter against his chest. The fire was so near now that sweat flowed in rivers down his face, his chest, his back. *Come on, get this idiot in. We're wasting too much time.* The fire crept closer every minute.

As if he'd heard Malcolm's thoughts, Scott leaned out from his perch beside the open door and foolishly reached for the hiker while he still flailed. In a convulsive jerk, Brandon seized Scott's wrist, pulling him off balance.

Scott tipped forward toward the open door, forward toward nothingness, and his shriek transmitted clearly. Even at this distance, the panicked look on his face was obvious, and Malcolm could well imagine Scott's terror as the ground—jagged boulders, dark earth, aggressive fire—loomed into view too far below. Scott teetered, shifting outward farther, much farther, too far, the hiker's weight too much to fight against, his feet scrambling for purchase. Then, as suddenly as he had fallen forward, Scott was jerked backward, breaking the hiker's hold.

"Oh my god," Scott said. It sounded as if he could barely speak. "Thank you. I thought that was it."

"No problem," Pete said. Even through the headphones, his calm voice was steadying.

At last, Bandon quit thrashing. By the time he finally disappeared into the helicopter, Malcolm was ready to cheer. "Okay, you two," he said to Pete and Scott. "Good job. Now, if you're done playing around, I'm ready to get out of here." He made it sound light, but the truth was that he was about to melt in the heat, every breath scalding. What if, right this

minute, Nirav was fighting heat like this? This whole operation had taken too long. They needed to get moving again.

He looked at Trip's backpack, but there was no way he
could deal with it with his arm. Trip would have to live without it.

In only a moment, he was back up at the helicopter. Pete
helped pull him in, and Malcolm cursed inwardly over his
one-handed awkwardness.

"You okay?" Pete asked.

Malcolm shrugged his uninjured shoulder. No point in
answering. "Let's get these people where they're going." He
leaned back against the bulkhead and tried to hold his arm
still. The cargo space was jam-packed, with Trip and the
women smashed against the bins in the back, the winch hulk-
ing in the center, and Brandon, Malcolm, and Scott squished
with several backpacks into the space between the winch and
the pilots' seats. Scott still looked slightly green from his near
escape.

Pete swung the overhead pulley inward, freed the cable,
and crashed the cargo door closed.

"Move it, Lou," he called. She nodded, and they quickly
left the rescue site behind.

"We're heading on to search again, aren't we?" Scott's
anger came through loud and clear. "We can't screw around
anymore."

Lou and Pete both shook their heads at once. Lou never
shifted her focus from her controls, but Pete answered as he
finished retracting the cable. "We keep searching only if you
want to crash." He wasn't being flip. "This chopper is rated for

eight people, total. We've now got eight, plus the winch, plus more than a hundred pounds of backpacks. Three more people are a no-go. We've got to unload."

Scott spit out a stream of profanity, which Lou and Pete both ignored.

Malcolm said nothing. He had known from the start that success in picking up the hikers meant additional delays before resuming their search. Unless he pitched a few bodies out the door, they were stuck taking these people the rest of the way to safety before they could head out again. More delay. More risk. He checked the time. Already after ten. Every passing minute tasted more and more bitter. *Hang in there, Nirav. Hang in there.*

Pete clambered over Brandon to get back to his chair, and the helicopter swooped down the mountain, heading back to the field where they'd begun. Scott still looked pissed, but he handed Malcolm a bottle of water. The air conditioner started to make some headway now that they'd closed the door, and Malcolm could swallow without the sensation of choking on grit.

The hikers made no effort to talk, trapped on a noise-filled planet without headphones.

Malcolm cautiously shifted into a more comfortable position, his injury screaming every time he moved his arm. His elbow had swollen, already turning a dark blue-black, and it pulsed with every heartbeat. A fine coating of ash filmed every inch of his skin, hair, and clothing, and his face radiated heat as if he'd been sunburned. He needed to get back on track. Fast.

He closed his eyes. Forced himself to take five slow, deep, breaths. Focused on the pain. He visualized compressing the agony into a neat package and setting it aside on a high shelf—still present, still hurting like hell, but an object separate from himself. He selected a mantra—*Nirav, Nirav, Nirav*—and concentrated on his breathing while consciously relaxing the muscles around his injury. He took a few final breaths, rolled his head in a slow circle, and composed his face. Not as effective as morphine, and not as effective as using this technique in a quiet, comfortable space, but when he opened his eyes, he could cope again.

Brandon turned to him. "Thought we were done for." His voice shook as he yelled above the engine noise. "Couldn't abandon Trip, but, damn, that fire was getting close." He reached out as if he intended to clap Malcolm on the shoulder but pulled back, belatedly zeroing in on Malcolm's swollen arm. "Thanks, man, for coming to get us." He stammered it awkwardly and turned away.

Scott hadn't appeared to notice Malcolm's damaged arm yet, and his growl reverberated through the headphones. "Yeah. Right. *Thanks.* We rescue a bunch of strangers while our own children are trapped down there."

Malcolm tried to shift his arm into a more comfortable position. He didn't often find himself on Scott's side, but for once, he agreed.

CHAPTER NINETEEN

Onward, one step at a time. There was simply no other option. Every step sent bolts of jarring pain through Kat's feet, and her attempts to roll her weight to the outside of each foot made her stumble.

"Kat, should we pray?"

Lily's question caught Kat off guard, and she dragged her thoughts from her own discomforts to give Lily a close look. Tension radiated from the girl's face, and her hands twisted together fretfully. At the overlook, she had asked about dying in an adult voice, but at the moment she looked very young, very tired, and very frightened. Kat wrapped her arm around Lily's shoulder and gave her a hug.

"Yes. If you feel like praying, that's a great idea."

Lily nodded, and her lips moved silently for a time as she walked.

Kat's religious background was decidedly moth-eaten. Mandatory services at the boarding school where her father taught had meant itchy tights, starched dresses, and the embarrassment of being on display as she sat with her parents in the front pew reserved for faculty. The soaring music spoke to her, but she had never been able to accept the expected leaps of faith. Cancer had not resolved her ambivalence, but there were times when Kat envied those who believed. Surely life would be simpler if one could hand over trust to an outside force.

Kat considered asking Nirav if he, too, would find some comfort in prayer, but the boy was so withdrawn into himself, she let it go. Despite her personal doubts, the idea of prayers floating around them reassured her. She wasn't sure who or what she spoke to, but she whispered a quiet request under her breath regardless. *Please, keep these children safe.*

She hobbled on. Lily carried the shoulder bag and helped Kat over logs and rocks, and Nirav stuck close to Kat's side, holding tight to her hand to keep her from falling when she tripped. Tye lagged, tugging backward on his leash, and Juni walked beside Lily without making any effort to forge ahead. They couldn't keep going like this much longer.

They reached a level stretch, and Juni lifted her head high, her nostrils quivering, more alert than she'd been since they left the rockslide. She moved forward a few steps, looked back at Kat, and whined.

"Juni, it's okay. Come here." Lily snapped her fingers.

Juni ignored her and gave an imperious bark. Tye perked up and pulled forward on his leash, and Kat tried to pick up the pace. Maybe the dogs knew something she didn't. Juni dashed ahead and disappeared into the knee-high weeds. Tye followed, dragging Nirav with him.

"Wait for us," Lily called.

Nirav and the dogs disappeared around a bend, the first time the boy had been out of Kat's sight since they'd left the cottage, and she hurried as best she could. What if she couldn't find him again? She flashed back to the years when Sara was young, that constant parental watchfulness and the fear that a moment's distraction could be serious. What if Nirav got hopelessly lost? She'd been saturated with fear for so long, this overlay of new panic startled her. They had covered twenty or thirty yards when Nirav shouted and raced back toward them, alone.

"Water. Juni, Tye, are finding water. Come. Come."

He waved them onward, and Kat redoubled her efforts. Perhaps Lily was wrong and the pond was right here, not lower on the mountain. Perhaps they had already arrived. They rounded the final curve in the road, and Nirav swept his arm in a grand look-at-this gesture.

Water, yes, but not much of it. Not the pond. The ruts they followed crossed a narrow gully here, and a rivulet trickled down its center, forming small, dinner-plate-sized puddles as it curled in a thin line around rocks and boulders on its way downhill. At some point in the past, this had been a proper stream, but months of drought had shriveled it into this poor imitation.

The dogs wasted no time. Juni stood beside one of the deeper puddles, lapping water steadily, and Tye sprawled in the center of the dribbling flow, his fur thoroughly soaked as he drank. Nirav picked his way upstream a few yards to reach water the dogs hadn't yet churned to mud. He cupped his hands into a clear puddle and brought them, dripping, to his mouth.

"Can we really drink this stuff?" Lily sounded half wist-ful, half incredulous, but she rushed toward the water even as she asked the question.

Kat hesitated, but worries about parasites seemed ridicu-lous at this point. "Go up where Nirav is."

Lily set down the shoulder bag, and Kat pulled out the empty iced-tea bottle and limped her way up to the children. Lily was already drinking from her hands, but Kat sat on a rock, the first rest she'd permitted herself since abandoning the car. She angled the bottle in front of a trickle and waited as it filled. Seen through the clear glass, the murky water turned her stomach. She closed her eyes and swallowed it down in huge gulps, the same way she'd forced down cough syrup as a child.

The cold wetness left a gritty residue on her tongue, but at least it soothed her mouth and throat, and it didn't taste as bad as she'd expected. She finished the bottle and filled it again, sipping more slowly this time. She splashed water on her face to rinse off some of its grime, then slipped off her sandals and put her feet in one of the deeper puddles, the cold water instantly soothing.

"Lily, did you see the stream that fed your beaver pond?"

Lily thought for a moment. "There was a footbridge. Dad and I stood on it and looked at the pond. Not much water under the bridge, though."

Kat gestured to the meager flow at their feet. "You mean, like this?"

Lily nodded and peered downstream. "Do you think this is it?"

"I don't know."

Here it was—the decision she'd dreaded at the overlook. Keep going on the road in the hope they could outflank the fire. Stay here and wait for rescue. Or try for the pond.

The pond that might or might not be above the fire, might or might not lie along this stream, might or might not be large enough to protect them. A choice that gambled with death.

This time she couldn't run away for a month to debate the question.

She tried to ignore a wave of queasiness that radiated from her belly. It was hard to concentrate. Her newest round of cancer had destroyed her hopes for the future, but the decisions she made now would live on, one way or the other, even if she wasn't around to know it. Choose wrong and these children were doomed.

"There's some granola and one last apple in my bag," she said. "Go ahead and finish it while we have the chance."

Lily and Nirav shared it out, passing the apple back and forth, sneaking bits to the dogs, the smoke-filled sky behind them a backdrop of malevolence. They didn't talk. Their bodies drooped in exhaustion, and they both glanced again and again down the mountain, as if they expected fire to erupt in front of them at any moment.

If Kat had been alone, she suspected she would simply sit here, her feet in cool water, and let the fire take her, but she had to make a choice. At their current pace, the fire would inevitably catch them no matter which direction they went.

Getting to water—real water, not this whisper of a stream—was their only realistic chance of safety. Until now, they had simply been running away. If they tried to find the pond, it meant they would be seeking a specific destination, which felt intentional and reassuring. But it also meant heading toward the fire, not away from it.

Lily and Nirav finished the food. They were waiting. Waiting for someone to make the right choice.

If only she knew what that was. Kat took a slow, smoke-tinged breath. "We're going to the pond." She forced herself back to her feet.

Lily looked downhill at the smoky red sky, and she shuddered. "The fire's there."

"I know, but we can't stay here."

"I'm tired."

"We'll rest when we get there."

"I'm scared."

"Me, too." Exhaustion made the two simple words sound more despairing than Kat had intended.

Nirav looked down at Kat's feet as she shifted her weight from one to the other. He frowned, took one tentative step toward the trees, then one step back to where he started. "I am coming back," he said, as if trying to talk himself into it, and he headed again for the trees.

The boy probably sought some privacy to pee. "Make sure you can still see us."

He nodded, and he looked back at them every two or three steps.

"We won't leave you," Kat said.

He glanced around one more time, then stepped behind a tree, his head down, studying the ground.

Kat and Lily waited, and in a few minutes he returned. He had left empty-handed, but now both hands were heaped with rhododendron leaves. He set them down beside Kat.

"For feet."

Kat shook her head, puzzled.

Nirav called Tye toward him and began unwinding the bulky mass of vet wrap she had used on his most recent bandage. Now Kat got it. "Great idea."

Nirav tore the long bandage, leaving enough on the dog's neck to keep the wound covered, and he helped Kat press the stiff leaves over her cuts, binding them snugly with the stretchy wrap to hold them in place.

Leaves and used dog bandages. Kat tried not to think about it. She wedged her sandals back on and stood up. Her blue-wrapped feet were bulky, and the strap between her toes still ground in painfully, but the huge improvement might make more walking possible.

"Thank you, Nirav."

The boy's eyes crinkled for an instant and his mouth twitched, but a full smile never reached the rest of his face. He picked up Tye's leash and took Kat by the hand again. "More water now." He tugged her to follow him downstream.

Lily gave Kat one last pitiful look as if hoping for a change in plan, but she followed. Tye shook himself, spraying them all with muddy water.

The only path available lay along the stream itself, and it didn't take long before Kat missed the relative luxury of the roadbed. Low tree branches smacked her in the face, loose rocks turned underfoot, and sometimes the only way forward meant splashing directly through the shallow water. She stumbled and jammed her big toe into a boulder, and it swelled in seconds. Its throb provided a new counterpoint to the rhythmic pulse of her cuts and blisters. The dogs didn't seem to mind the rough terrain, but Lily and Nirav walked ever more slowly, their feet dragging in water-soaked socks and tennis shoes.

The smoke thickened noticeably as they moved downhill, no longer just a vague nuisance. Kat tried to breathe through her nose to filter the worst of it, but when she tried to talk, she tasted ash and started coughing. They could now hear the fire again, a low indistinct roar, punctuated by the snaps and crashes of damaged trees.

Lily stayed close, and Nirav clutched Kat's hand in a painful grip. Tye continued to lag, and Juni grew increasingly nervous, whining and nosing Kat's leg. Once, Juni turned around as if intending to head back uphill, and she returned reluctantly when Kat called her back. Kat clipped her leash on, and Juni walked by her side with her tail tucked.

Juni wasn't the only creature who thought they were headed in the wrong direction. They were seeing animals again, all headed uphill, not down. They glimpsed a doe with twin fawns moving through the trees, and a possum disappeared into weeds when they got too close. Even a bobcat approached, trotting openly toward them up the stream bed, ignoring the excited whines of the dogs.

Kat let go of Nirav, stepped back, and picked up an apple-sized rock, but Nirav seized her wrist. "Stay."

Kat let her arm fall to her side, but she didn't loosen her grip on the rock. The cat leaped into the trees with an arrogant glance and disappeared. The entire animal kingdom seemed to be scoffing at her decision to head for the pond.

A particularly loud crash sounded directly in front of them, and Lily froze. "We need to go back." Her last word disappeared into a coughing spasm.

Kat stopped, indecisive, and Lily dropped to her knees, her head drooping. She was near exhaustion. They should have reached the pond by now, if it was even there. The fire roared louder ahead of them, an ancient monster heralding its impending attack.

A patch of reddish-brown to one side of their route caught Kat's eye, and she stepped closer. A small rabbit. Dead. Its coat was a hideous patchwork of burns—singed hair, blackened skin, raw muscle. One ear was only a ragged strip of cartilage. All four feet were black and harshly blistered. Instead of finding peace in death, its lifeless eyes looked wide with terror.

Was this the fate that awaited them? Hair burning, then skin, then flesh. Horrific pain, immeasurable fear, and a panicked attempt to run across a flaming landscape. A foolish, hopeless attempt that was doomed from the outset.

Kat's heart ricocheted off her ribs, beating fast enough to propel her on a race of her own. In her head, she could hear the children's screams, their desperate pleas, but she could do nothing to help.

She had made a horrible, irretrievable mistake. There was no way to outrun the fire now—they were its prey. They should have stayed on the road.

She turned her back on the rabbit. Her feet refused to move closer to the fire, but they also refused to retrace their steps.

Nirav looked back and forth between Kat, immobile, and Lily, still huddled on the ground. He started downhill. His coughs rattled like an old man's, and he turned frequently to check on them, but he walked ahead with Tye to peer around a large boulder in the stream bed.

"Water," he called.

Lily ran, and Kat limped up beside them. Lily grabbed her by the arm. "Look, there's the bridge." She pointed.

Kat's heart slowed its efforts to flee, and she nodded, unable to speak. Ten yards ahead, two weathered planks spanned the gully. Beyond them lay the marshy margin of a pond.

CHAPTER TWENTY

Malcolm stared unseeing out the side window as the helicopter swooped down the mountainside, retracing their path, erasing their progress. They flew high over the forest, above the smoke, and they made good time, but the additional delay weighed intolerably. The hikers had indeed been at risk. Trip could never have walked out or been carried by his companions, and any rational person would label this rescue a good deed. He'd done the right thing, but in doing so he might have failed Nirav when his son needed him most. The caustic thought ate away at his insides, far more painful than his damaged arm.

The helicopter lost altitude. Two new fire engines and a half dozen additional pickup trucks now lined the roadway below them. Firefighters were unloading two Bobcats from a flatbed truck, and a bulldozer belched smoke of its own, already busy carving a rough firebreak. Despite the additional equipment, the small cadre of volunteers looked hopelessly outmatched by the endless expanse of flames. They had protected the road, but beyond that frail barrier, the fire burned viciously.

The chopper hovered over the landing field and settled with a hard bump to the ground, returning them to the exact place where they'd started. Malcolm checked his watch. 1037. Time moved too fast, and they moved too slowly.

An ambulance waited on the road next to the clearing, and two attendants in white uniforms pulled a stretcher out of the back and jogged toward them as soon as the rotors slowed. Good. Now they could dump this extra weight and get back out there.

Malcolm slid the side door open and eased himself slowly to the ground, trying not to move his bad arm, which hurt like hell. Scott followed out of the cramped space, bracing his back as he stood up straight.

"Your patient's in the back—broken leg," Malcolm said to the medics. "We need to leave as soon as possible—there are other people trapped in the fire."

The first medic, a tall guy with a shaggy haircut and bleary eyes, waved the three uninjured hikers out of the chopper and crawled into the back with Trip.

Lou and Pete clambered from the cockpit to stretch, and they came over to join the others. Now that Lou had emerged from her pilot chair, she turned out to be of medium height, lean and wiry. When she pulled off her thin leather gloves, she revealed bright red fingernails, and when she brushed her hair out of her face, each ear held three or four different pierced earrings.

The medic with the stretcher looked pointedly at Malcolm's arm. "Are you coming with us?"

"I'm fine." Malcolm hadn't intended to bark, but his words sent the guy back a few steps. There was no time to waste. "Get them out of here."

"We'll hurry," the medic said, but when Malcolm glanced into the cabin of the helicopter, the first guy was checking Brandon's blood pressure. This was a hurry?

Lou looked closely at Malcolm's elbow, even more black and swollen than it had been in the helicopter. "That looks bad. Could be a fracture."

"Later." Malcolm cupped the injury again in his good hand. *Let's go.*

Lou turned to the waiting medic. "Aren't you Jill Olsen's brother? She and I were in the same year at Franklin High." When the guy admitted the connection, Lou touched his arm and gestured across the field. "Let's go get some supplies from your ambulance."

The medic gave one more glance at his associate, still piddling around, shrugged, and followed her.

Scott started pacing, his impatience radiating. "This is crazy. We jerked this guy off the ground at the end of a steel cable, and now they can't even shift him three feet?"

Malcolm glanced at his watch every twenty seconds. "We need to go," he said to Shaggy-Hair Medic in the chopper, who was now drawing up some sort of clear liquid into a syringe, every movement in slow motion, as if he forced his arms through heavy syrup.

"Almost there," the man replied. He didn't look up, and he didn't alter his deliberate pace.

Malcolm exchanged frustrated glances with Scott. Once again, they were on the same side.

Lou came jogging back. She held up a roll of tape and a long strip of cloth that looked like it had recently been a pillowcase. "I can make your arm more comfortable until you get it checked out properly."

Malcolm started to shake his head, his *I'm fine* reflex primed and ready, but he stopped himself. It might help. "Thanks."

Lou worked swiftly, fashioning a makeshift sling from the cloth and using a half dozen yards of tape around his chest to pin both the arm and the sling tight to his ribs. The exposed elbow still looked dreadful, but at least it couldn't move. "Thanks. That helps a lot."

"No problem," Lou said, back to her no-nonsense self. "Got to keep a winning team in action."

Scott glanced at his cell phone. "Is that whole mountain a dead zone? Lily knows my number. Kat should have her phone with her. But there's no message. No missed call."

Lou's lips tightened, and she nodded. "They'd have to go a long way to pick up a signal. If you need to reach anyone, you'd better do it here."

Scott frowned and looked at his phone for a long minute, but then he put it back in his pocket. "I should call my ex. Let her know what's going on. But what the hell should I tell her?"

No one answered.

Malcolm had no one to call about Nirav. He was Nirav's entire family. But if there had been someone else, he would have let them know. He would have called Kat's daughter if he'd known her number. As it was, he would worry on her behalf. It was his job to make sure Kat got home safe.

Scott looked off to the distance. "I keep thinking *if only*. If only I'd woken up sooner. If only we'd made it to Kat's before the road was blocked. If. If. If." His fist thudded against his thigh, and he walked away from the others.

The same self-accusation churned Malcolm's insides. If only he hadn't let Nirav out of his sight.

Brandon, Melissa, and that Vi-person stood off to the side with their mountain of gear, and Malcolm caught snatches of conversation as they revisited their escape.

"Thought we'd be burned alive . . ."

"My mother is going to freak . . ."

"That rescue was worse than the fire . . ."

Rescue worse than the fire? Easy for Brandon to say, standing in safety with his friends, smoke and flames and terror already a fading memory. Nirav and the others were in mortal danger, and these hikers were already practicing stories for their next keg party.

Scott stomped back to where Malcolm and Pete waited. "Broken leg or not, I'm going to drag that fool out of there."

Malcolm gave his watch yet another glance. "One more minute and I'll help you."

"Count me in," Pete said.

"Okay. Ready." Shaggy-Hair Medic waved to his companion, and at last they shifted an unconscious Trip out of the helicopter and strapped him onto the stretcher with exaggerated care. The three other hikers surrounded him, half dragging, half carrying their backpacks, and the little huddle of people moved toward the ambulance. Malcolm erased them from his head as soon as he turned toward the helicopter; finding Nirav was the only thing relevant.

He hurried on board with Scott close behind, and Lou had the engine turning over before they'd even closed the cargo door. Unloading the backpackers had taken an agonizing fifteen minutes. Malcolm slipped his headset back into place as they lifted off.

"Back to the rockslide?" Lou asked.

"Yes. Fast as possible." Malcolm moved toward the map that was still clipped to the console between the pilots' seats. There were no agonizing howls of protest from his arm this time—the sling and tape definitely helped. The edge of his foot hit something, and he looked down. The missing sat phone. It was half hidden under Lou's chair—it must have been fully hidden when that first call came in from the fire chief. Weird that it had moved clear across the cabin from where he had left it.

He picked it up and pivoted to one side to clip it to his belt, awkward with only his left hand. He would have thought nothing more about it, but he happened to meet Scott's eyes, and Scott immediately hunched forward and looked down, the personification of guilt. *Damn.* Scott hadn't wanted to detour to pick up the hikers, but Malcolm wouldn't have expected him to be quite that sneaky. He couldn't decide whether to be impressed or irritated.

He turned back to the map. "We spotted the hat. They must have crossed that rockslide." His finger tapped the spot. "We should keep following the old roadbed. It's the most likely path."

"Makes sense," Pete said.

Scott crouched behind Lou, braced against the right-hand cargo-hold wall. "Are there any hiking trails intersecting the old road?"

Pete shook his head. "None shown."

"Good." Malcolm tried to make his voice sound confident. "That will keep Kat and the children on the roadbed. Follow it, and it should lead to Nirav."

Lou flew a straight line to the rockslide, staying high above the fire, but when they arrived, she dropped low to the ground. The relentless flames had edged uphill in their absence, and thick dark smoke snaked in all directions, buffeted by gusts of wind. Malcolm could glimpse only random patches of landscape through the shifting swirls.

He stepped back into the cargo space. "Scott—you take the door on the right, looking downhill. I'll take the left." If Kat had detoured off the road, it was most likely she would head uphill, away from the fire, and he trusted his search capabilities more than Scott's. "Pete—you're in charge of looking out front. Lou—take it slow. Don't want to miss them."

Scott opened the cargo door on his side, taking a firm grip on his grab-loop before he inched carefully to the brink. He acted even more hesitant now than he had earlier, and when he pulled his glasses off to wipe them clean, he did it with one hand, refusing to let go of his handhold. Malcolm wondered whether he was remembering the moment when Brandon had jerked him off-balance, almost dragging him out of the helicopter. At least Scott was still functioning.

Malcolm opened his door, too. With both doors open, smoke poured in, adding more ash to the film already gumming every surface inside the helicopter. His eyes watered, and his throat stung as if scalded.

He was used to conducting search-and-rescue operations with drone and satellite support. With a slew of experts at his side and specialized equipment lined up and waiting. Now, in the most important search operation of his life, he was leaning out of a helicopter, trying to glimpse his son through hazy smoke by simply looking. He tried to hang on to some shred of hope, but every heartbeat pumped only despair.

CHAPTER TWENTY-ONE

The bridge consisted of two shaky weathered boards, but it provided a way for hikers to cross the gully when water filled the stream. Kat bent double to duck beneath the planks, and when she straightened on the other side, the beaver pond, an actual pond full of actual water, stretched in front of her. They'd made it. Kat's spirits lifted slightly from rock bottom, where they'd been anchored.

A rough tumble of logs and debris along the opposite end of the pond dammed the creek, creating a pool at least thirty yards across at its widest point. Bigger would be better, but if the fire got this far, it might offer them a fighting chance.

"Lily, we wouldn't have known this was here without you." A surge of gratitude added emphasis to her words. If the children hadn't been with her and she had somehow headed out on her own, she'd be up on the mountain right now, alone.

"Are we safe here?"

"Yes." Kat hoped. For now. With luck.

"No fire here." Nirav patted Tye. "No fire is good."

Kat shared Nirav's outlook. The pond lay in a hollow, protected on all sides by steep surrounding hills. Here, her eyes didn't water, her nose didn't burn, her tongue didn't taste like pine sap. Maybe she'd done the right thing after all in bringing the children this way.

But maybe not. Tall green grasses grew at the water's edge, but beyond them, dead plants formed a drought-stricken tangle that looked ready to blaze at the first spark. Dead tree stumps, left by the beavers, and dead standing trees, far too many of them, ringed the pond's fringe. If the fire got close enough, this tinder would flare in an instant. Their only chance of survival would lie in the water.

"I'm going to see what the bottom's like," Kat said. The children straightened, watching her. "Wait here."

Kat waded into the cold, mucky-looking water and sank deep into slimy mud that worsened with every step. She bent and wrestled her sandals off, but without them, her makeshift bandages slipped and slid, and she kept stepping on sharp hidden lumps. Submerged vines and branches grabbed and scratched at her ankles and legs. She'd imagined some sort of smooth, sandy place to stand, but what she'd gotten was a treacherous quagmire.

She struggled back toward shore and lurched out of the water, her legs coated in mud and green slime, her bandages hopelessly wet and sagging. She pulled the wraps off and tossed them aside.

"Gross." Lily wrinkled her nose. "We don't have to go in there, do we?"

"We'll see. Does this trail loop around the pond?"

"Yeah, that's the way Dad and I got here." She pointed. "It goes along this edge and then leads down into the valley."

Kat bent and scraped off the sticky mud with a twig, but two oblong strips of brown clung like glue. She reached down to peel the gunk off with a fingernail, but her hand leaped reflexively away from her skin, and she yelped. The slimy patch of brown had moved—had flattened itself against her skin—when she touched it.

"Oh my god." She gagged, the constant fear she had carried all day instantly replaced by nauseous revulsion. Leeches were something you read about—a carry-over from the dark days of bloodletting or a plot twist out of *The African Queen*—not something that lurked in the mud of a North Carolina pond. Kat sank to the ground and covered her face with her hands. This was too much. Far too much. After everything else, undone by a blood-sucking parasite. If she had only been a spectator, she might have found some ironic humor in the situation, but this was too gross for laughter.

She couldn't leave them attached.

"Kat, what's wrong?" Lily sounded freaked-out, and Kat shifted her legs to block the children's view of what she was doing.

"Nothing. Just trying to get my legs cleaned off." Kat's breath came too fast.

Ticks repulsed her, but these slimy creatures made her want to amputate her leg. She bit down hard on her tongue, swallowed a deep groan, and grabbed the first leech around its middle. Her fingers slipped on the slick body, and she tightened her grip, the leech stretching as she increased the tension, its mouth still embedded in her skin. When it finally loosened, she flung it far into the pond. She ripped off the second one fast, before she could stop to think about it. A pair of small red welts marked the bites, oozing thin rivulets of blood. Kat peered into the mucky pond water and shivered.

She got up, stepped back into her battered sandals, and picked up her shoulder bag. Her fists clenched so tight, her fingers ached.

"Let's see how things look from the other side." She prayed she'd find a more solid bottom at that end. Surely the water-soaked dam would provide some safety, the wood too wet to burn.

"What did you throw into the water?"

"A gooey chunk of mud." If she ever said the word *leech* to Lily, she'd never get her into the pond.

Lily seemed to buy it. She groaned, but she started moving. Nirav got to his feet, took Tye's leash, and headed down the trail. Juni came to Kat, nudged her with her wet nose, and whined.

"It's okay, girl. It's okay." Kat picked up the dangling leash and patted the Lab, unsure whether she was trying to convince the dog or herself.

They followed the trail from the bridge, splashing through additional small trickles of water that fed the pond. When they reached the beaver dam, Lily gestured toward a sturdy log beside the trail.

"Dad and I sat here and had a snack." Her voice wavered, and Nirav patted her awkwardly on the arm.

At least people had been here recently, and they stood now on a real trail, a trail marked on a map somewhere. The thought made Kat feel less adrift.

The abandoned beaver dam spanned the gap between two massive granite slabs, which helped explain how the dam's thirty-foot barrier could create a far larger pond. Long logs formed the original dam, their pointed ends gouged with dozens of teeth marks. Broken branches and random debris had piled up against the original dam, but the basic structure looked solid.

The pond itself was clear enough at this end for them to see a rocky bottom. Toward the middle of the dam, where the water was deepest, a few boulders looked large enough to stand on. "This will work. We can go into the pond here if we need to."

"What about the dogs?" Lily asked.

Kat had a sudden vision of cowering in the deep part of the pond while Juni and Tye burned on shore. "We'll help them onto the dam. They'll be okay."

Nirav bent low and said something in Hindi to Tye, and he gave the dog a hug. The scarred area on his arm glistened, and Kat admired his ability to stay calm—or at least hide his fear as well as he did. He had more firsthand knowledge of fire than she could even imagine.

"When is Dad coming?" Lily asked. "How is he going to find us?"

"They'll find us." Rescue seemed an unlikely dream, but she certainly wasn't going to admit it.

"But *how* will he find us?"

Kat pulled a leaf from her hair and pretended she hadn't heard. "Didn't you say you could see the valley from somewhere near here?"

"There's a clearing with an overlook that way." Lily pointed farther along the trail, which zigzagged up to the low ridge that bounded this hollow.

"I'm going to go check things out. See if the fire has calmed down." Fires could burn out on their own, couldn't they? Exhaust themselves. Or the wind could change direction. She didn't believe in fairy-tale endings about cancer—or fairy-tale solutions for forest fires—but maybe just this once she would see good news. "Do you want to come with me?"

"Closer to the fire? No way." Lily shook her head. Nirav took Lily's hand, and after a moment, Lily stepped closer to him.

"Stay right here. I'll be back fast." Kat took a step down the path, but the sound of running footsteps on the trail above them froze her in her tracks. She and the children spun to face the noise. Someone or something was coming downhill, coming toward them, coming fast.

A tentative surge of hope caught in Kat's chest. A fireman? A rescuer? A miracle?

But the man who burst into the clearing and skidded to a startled halt in front of them didn't look like a savior. He was in his early forties, dark-haired, lean and fit. Dressed in jeans and a frayed yellow T-shirt, not a uniform. Carrying no equipment. Despite his rapid approach, he wore heavy hiking boots, not running shoes.

"What the hell are you doing here?" His incredulous tone underscored their danger. He gave a quick inspection of the three exhausted humans and two bedraggled dogs and zeroed in on Kat. "Turn back! You can't get out uphill—the fire has spread too fast up there. It's blocking the trail." His breath came in rapid gasps, but he spoke as if he expected instant obedience.

Kat abandoned any idea that this man's arrival meant instant rescue. "We weren't heading uphill. That's where we came from."

The man bent forward and braced his hands on his knees for a moment's rest, but after a few seconds he straightened and glared at Kat. "If you're not heading up, then why are you standing still?" He glanced uphill as if the fire was close on his heels, and both children looked as well, their fear obviously escalating. "Come on. Now. You've got children to think about. Let's go."

"Go where? We saw the fire from higher up. It stretches along the entire mountainside. There's no way past it."

"There has to be a path through." His tone implied that by saying it with emphasis, it had to be true.

Lily turned to Kat, her face anxious. "You said we should stay at the pond. What if he's right? What if Dad's down there?" Nirav straightened, his eyes fixed on Kat.

Kat hesitated. Fairy tales were out, but maybe this guy was right. Maybe they should keep moving. "I was just heading up to the overlook to see. Come with me."

The man nodded and glanced at the children, but Kat shook her head. "You two, wait here. Rest up. We'll come back for you right away if there's a safe path down." Lily looked doubtful, but both children nodded. Kat told Juni to stay. "We won't be long."

She started up the path, the stranger right behind her. "What's your name?" she asked.

"Kevin. Kevin Harris. I was on the Appalachian Trail when I saw the smoke, and I saw this path down the mountain on my map. Dumped my pack—it slowed me down." He came up beside her, his long strides hurrying her along faster than she liked. Every stone slashed her feet like razor-edged sheet metal, but she forced herself onward.

"I'm Kat Jamison. The children are Lily and Nirav. Do you have a phone?"

"No signal." He tossed the words over his shoulder and forged ahead.

Kat followed, trying to keep up. The arrival of someone new had injected new energy into the situation, but it wasn't yet clear it had actually changed anything.

If life were fair, she would be sitting on the front porch of her little cottage right now, a book in her hand and a glass of iced tea beside her, enjoying the view and avoiding all topics she didn't want to deal with. Her biggest decision would be whether she should go into town for groceries next or take a walk. Her biggest challenge for the day would be extracting the cork from the wine she planned to have with dinner.

Instead, here she was, tottering her way uphill, hoping for miracles.

The higher they climbed out of the hollow, the more the smoke thickened. Kevin started coughing. The smoke permeated the forest with a new smell, too—a harsh, acid odor that stung Kat's nose and irritated her eyes. Kevin slowed at the base of a rocky ten-foot scramble, waited with a look of tense impatience on his face for her to catch up, and helped her up the slope. They had reached the overlook—a swath of rough granite with a view of the entire valley. They stepped to the edge and looked down.

There was no fairy-tale ending here. Flames consumed undergrowth, flames crept up tree trunks, flames leaped into dry upper branches. Distant trees burned like torches, tossing fire into the tops of the trees beside them. The wall of noise struck Kat as a physical blow, and her mouth tasted like singed evergreen. The tall tulip poplar in front of her, still unscathed, stood in eerie silhouette against the glowing red expanse behind it.

Hell is empty, and all the devils are here.

Kevin scanned the valley, his face tense. "There has to be a way through."

Kat looked, too, but fire owned the entire mountainside. Death wasn't a black-hooded creature with a scythe in its hand, but a red demon, shrouded in a billowing cloak of tar-black smoke, devouring everything in its path. It was coming for them now, its jaws gaping, hungry for anyone in its way.

There was no sign of life—no firefighters, no helicopters, no airplanes. Any animal that could flee had already fled. The fire was racing this way, and the hollow that cupped their pond wouldn't remain protected for long.

Kat's heart clamored against her ribs, trying to escape her chest, and she fought a wave of dizziness and the irrational urge to turn and flee, a pointless attempt to outrun a fiend.

"It's worse than I expected. It's going to reach us soon." She hated the note of panic in her voice, but she was glad Kevin was with her. Just having someone else there to confirm her assessment was a profound relief.

He pointed off to the left. "There's a rocky stretch over there that leads downward. The fire has already burned it. We could work our way in that direction, follow it downhill."

Kat looked at the swath of tumbled rock he indicated and couldn't believe he would even consider it. "The fire is too dense between here and there. How do you propose to get through? With two children in tow? And there's no way to tell what it's like at the lower end of that rockfall." She and the children had already seen how treacherous those steep stretches of loose rock could be.

"I don't see any other option."

"The pond. That's the other option. I thought . . . if the fire . . . when the fire . . . the water . . ."

She let the rest hang unspoken, because Kevin was looking at her as if she'd completely lost her mind. "Are you kidding? That pond wouldn't even save a fish, not the way this fire is sweeping along the ridgeline."

His words amplified Kat's fears. Would the pond be big enough to protect them? A heavy tiredness made it hard to think, and she swallowed against a throat filled with gravel.

Maybe he was right. Maybe the pond really was hopeless, and they were all doomed to die.

She wasn't sure whether to argue more or give in. "We need to get back to the children."

Kevin nodded. "Come on." He led them downhill at an even faster pace. They arrived at the dam, and Lily and Nirav rushed toward them.

"Did you see anyone?" Lily's words were clipped and anxious. "Are they coming? Is the fire out?"

Kevin snorted and began pacing back and forth. "Don't waste time. Come on. We need to give it a try."

Kat knelt and pretended to adjust the strap of her sandal as she struggled to find the right choice. These children had believed in her when she led them here. Of course. She was the adult. *Come on*, she had said. *Turn here. This way. Don't stop. Keep going.* And she had led them to this pond, this teaspoon of water.

She looked up from her shoe. "It's too far to see the firemen."

"The smoke is getting worse." Lily's voice cracked. "We need to go."

"Papa needs to come now." Nirav sounded as freaked-out as Lily did, the composure he'd maintained all day suddenly gone.

Keven stared at them, his jaw tense, his body poised to take off.

Kat pulled both children into quick, tight hugs, but such gestures meant little at this point.

"It will be okay." She spoke the slick lie with hardly a tremor, but she was shaking as hard as the children were. "It will be okay." They clung to her for a few silent moments, and Kat flashed back for an instant to the long hug she'd shared with her daughter.

Sara. Be happy. Have a good life. I'm so sorry I'll miss it.

Kevin threw up his hands. "It's not going to be okay. You're wrong. We have to keep moving down the mountain. Come on." He stepped toward Nirav and grabbed him by the waist, lifting the boy as if he intended to carry him away. Juni growled. Nirav yelped and wiggled free, clinging to Kat's side. Lily backed up, her eyes on Kevin as if she expected him to grab her next.

"Stop that! What are you doing?" Kat put a protective arm around the boy.

Kevin backed off, no longer trying to drag someone with him, but not at all apologetic. Impatience sharpened his tone. "We have to move—it's our only hope."

He took two steps down the trail, waving them to join him, expecting them to follow. He sounded so certain. So confident. So commanding. The overwhelming temptation to fall in line was a physical force that threatened to draw Kat forward down the trail. So much simpler to follow than to fight. After all, this was what Kat had wished for—someone else to make decisions and face the consequences. Someone else to take the blame if they failed.

It was painful to lock her knees and stiffen her resolve, to force herself not to move. She'd just seen what lay below, and no matter how desperately she wanted to hand off responsibility, she couldn't ignore deadly facts. Not when the children's safety hung in the balance.

"There's no way out downhill. You saw it. We both saw it. The whole valley is in flames."

The children flinched, their dismay at this news obvious, and she regretted her blunt words. But she had to convince this man. He might be in great physical shape and he might be accustomed to being right, but if he kept traveling downhill, he'd be killed.

Uncertainty hovered over all of them as thickly as the smoke.

Lily and Nirav stood together, even more frightened now. "Kat, what should we do?" Lily's voice was a plea.

Kevin took another step along the path. "I'm leaving."

"I can't stop you. But when you realize there's no way down, come back. This pond is better than nothing." It was at least better than being burned like that poor rabbit.

He was already yards along the path, and her words bounced off his back. Perhaps he hadn't even heard.

"When I make it out, I'll let them know you're here." With that, he started jogging up the steep incline that led out of the hollow, his boots triggering small cascades of loose stones.

Lily grabbed Kat's hand. "Are you sure? Maybe we should go with him." Her face was pinched, her lips white.

Nirav looked at Kat, at the spot of yellow shirt that marked the disappearing Kevin, and back at Kat again, his eyes wide and frightened.

Kat took a deep smoke-tinged breath. She pulled up the scene she'd seen from the overlook and examined it one last time. The mountainside had been a solid expanse of flame. "We're staying here. There's no way forward. He'll be back."

The rock-scramble sounds of Kevin's progress up the slope faded away. They were left only with the noise of the fire itself, its terrifying growl growing louder and closer.

CHAPTER TWENTY-TWO

Lou kept the helicopter hovering over the rockslide, then inched ahead along the path of the old roadbed. Malcolm leaned out as far as he dared, searching the area directly below and uphill.

Trees. Rhododendron. More fucking trees. Patches of rocky gravel. Two dried-up creek beds. Nothing moving. Nothing alive. The fire was closing in, and thin fingers of flame were already grasping sections of the old road. Malcolm's fear and frustration escalated with every fruitless minute.

The smoke flowed and eddied, and the bright yellows and reds of the fire flared at the edges of his vision, tinting the smoke cloud an eerie orange. They dipped down into a valley, where fire had already engulfed the old road, and Lou hovered in place for a few moments. Malcolm searched the burned area foot by foot, praying to find no sign amid the flames. He didn't realize he was holding his breath until it escaped his chest with a whoosh.

They rose slowly up the hill on the other side, once again traveling over terrain not yet burned. When they reached the crest, Lou hovered in place. "I can't see any more road."

She turned the chopper in a slow circle, and Malcolm seized a safety strap and leaned out even farther, coughing now, trying to find a path Kat and the children could have taken. The roadbed had given their search a defined direction. If they had to search the whole ridge . . .

Malcolm blinked smoke out of his eyes and redoubled his efforts.

The roadbed stopped dead here. A dense wall of rhododendron blocked it, impossible to penetrate on foot.

Pete unclipped the folded map and peered closely. "No help here."

He handed the map to Malcolm, who tried to spread it flat on the deck one-handed. Scott reached over and helped. Malcolm leaned on it with his left hand and right knee to keep it from fluttering in the backwash that gusted through the open doors. His eyes darted back and forth, inspecting and reinspecting every detail of the map.

"We've been careful. We should have found them if they were still on the road." The shreds of hope he clung to were growing more and more tattered. If Kat and the children weren't on the road, the odds of finding them plummeted.

They couldn't give up. Below them, acres and acres of national forest. Peaks and valleys. Gullies and hollows. Ravines and chasms. A full-scale army could hide down there. An instant of panic swelled through his chest, and he forced it aside. *Focus.*

He turned and looked at Scott. "Where the hell are they?" The anguish and frustration he thought he had just suppressed came through loud and clear in his voice.

Scott's whole body tensed. "What do you mean, *where are they*? You said they would follow the road!"

My decision. My fault. The knowledge was acid. If they failed, he would never forgive himself.

Malcolm traced his finger on the map along the line they had traveled. "No way Kat and the kids could have climbed uphill—it's too steep. The road stops here. I doubt they could have made it this far this fast anyway." He turned again to Scott. "Could we have flown over without seeing them?"

"This engine is loud, and we were flying low. They should have heard us."

Malcolm agreed. "Pete. Lou. What do you think?"

Pete answered at once. "We took it slow. With four of us searching, we should have seen them, even with the smoke."

"Agreed." Lou sounded unperturbed, a pilot doing her job. Malcolm envied her emotional distance. Usually he was the dispassionate one. She kept fine-tuning their course, holding over the point where the roadbed ended.

"So where the hell are they?" Malcolm asked again, this time addressing them all. "No way to go forward beyond this point. No way to go uphill without rock-climbing gear. Stupid to head down the mountain, closer to the fire, and so far, Kat hasn't acted stupid."

No one answered. Scott sagged against the cabin wall.

They couldn't give up. They couldn't. Malcolm wadded the map into a badly folded clump with his uninjured hand, unsure of the next move. He prided himself on always knowing what action to take. Such indecision was agony.

Scott stared at the crumpled map, his face desperate. Then he straightened, galvanized, his whole attitude suddenly purposeful. "Our hike. Water. Lily was the one with the map. She checked it every two seconds."

"What are you talking about?"

"Hand me the map." Scott flattened it again on the vibrating floor. Malcolm shifted across to look over his shoulder.

"Which trail is it?" Scott spoke under his breath, but the words came through clearly in the headphones. "Which trail?" He put his finger on the crescent lake. "We parked here." His finger traced a dotted line. "Not this trail—it just goes around the lake. Here. This one. We hiked this one." He traced a dotted line that left the lake and switchbacked up the side of the mountain.

Malcolm resisted the urge to shake him. *Come on, man, get to the point.*

"Here." Scott tapped a small blue circle on the trail. "A pond. Lily's been here. She might remember. They might head for water." He took a deep breath. "Where's the rockslide where we saw the hat?"

Malcolm pointed to a spot on the map only inches from Scott's pond. "Here."

Scott slid his finger uphill, across the topographic markings, following the thin line of the stream that fed the pond until it intersected the path of the old road. "We flew over a rocky gully here."

Malcolm nodded, a fizzing hope building. "I remember." He clapped Scott on the shoulder and got a startled look in return. "Lou, retrace our course. We're looking for a stream—more rocks than water—a hundred yards or so this side of the rockslide."

"Got it." The helicopter accelerated forward.

Malcolm inspected the map again. A pond. Big enough to show on the map. Kat would have had to turn toward the fire, but if they reached water in time, it could have bought them the time they needed. "I hope—" He broke off, startled by a vibration on his hip. He reached back and unclipped the sat phone from his belt. The phone vibrated in his hand, the light on top flashing to signal an incoming call.

"You're not going to answer that, are you?" Scott's voice was incredulous, the voice of someone who would have hidden the phone again if he'd had the chance.

Malcolm hesitated. He didn't want to be ordered away from their search, but maybe, just maybe, some miracle had occurred, and Kat and the children had already been rescued. "It could be good news this time." Malcolm clicked the speaker button and thumbed the volume knob to max. "Yes."

A squawking voice filled the cabin, audible even over the engine noise. "This is USFS Director Ted Mitchell. You are flying in a fire zone without authorization. Air support is en route. Clear the area."

"No. Hell no." Scott's protest echoed.

Malcolm met his eyes and mouthed *wait*. Not the right time to piss this director off. He spoke into the phone. "Have you located our children?"

"Rescue operations will be implemented. Clear the area."

"We have a strong lead. We're going to follow it."

"All civilian flights are required to clear the fire zone. Now."

Scott grabbed Malcolm's arm. "You can't do this. Not again."

Malcolm shrugged him off, but he didn't say anything into the phone. Mitchell had jurisdiction. Chain-of-command dictated that Malcolm should obey the order, and twenty years of military training conditioned him to comply. If others had obeyed orders, he wouldn't now have a ravaged face.

But this wasn't the military and this time there weren't hikers' lives at risk. He glanced at his watch. 1121. More than five hours since he'd wakened to the fire. They had run out of time. Another rescue team, directed back to where they hoped the children were, would be too late.

The phone blared again. "Acknowledge." Malcolm said nothing. A pause. "Confirm."

Malcolm clutched the phone with whitened fingers.

Nirav. My son.

With a casual flip of his wrist, he tossed the still-squawking satellite phone out the open cargo door. It smashed against the skid, bounced high, and tumbled out of sight.

"Lou." Malcolm snapped the single syllable, hoping a little attitude would tip the balance and get her to go along. "Turn off your radio."

Lou didn't respond.

Malcolm waited for her to protest. As she'd pointed out earlier, she was the one whose license was at stake; she was the one responsible. It had to be her call, but he willed her to go along. If they didn't keep going, Kat and the children would die. He held his breath, his heart pounding so hard, every beat pulsed in his fingertips.

A long, silent pause. Then Lou reached out with a slim gloved hand and turned a black knob on the dashboard all the way to the left. The tiny green light above it disappeared, and Malcolm took a slow, even breath. "Thank you."

Lou waved one hand in a broad it-doesn't-matter gesture. "I have nieces and nephews. If they were down there . . ." She paused. "But I sure as hell hope you know what you're doing."

Malcolm sure as hell agreed. They had only one slim chance left, and he clung to that single hope with all the desperate strength he could marshal.

CHAPTER TWENTY-THREE

Kat and the children waited, but Kevin didn't return, and the smoke grew thicker every second.

Nirav tugged on Kat's shirt and pointed up the trail toward the overlook. His voice shook, and his face paled. "Fire here now."

He was right. Through the smoke, Kat could see the first tentative flames. The dry underbrush caught first, crackling merrily, deceptively benign. Nirav took two steps back, and Kat grabbed his shoulder, afraid he might simply turn and run. Lily, too, looked toward the fire and bleached white, perhaps realizing for the first time the consequences of what they faced. She shook her head over and over again. "I want my mother."

A pocket of sap exploded nearby. They all jumped.

"Time to get moving." Kat scooped Tye into her arms. Nirav still had a firm hold of the leash, and Kat gently opened his fingers to take it. She had marveled at his composure, but the sight of actual flames had stripped away any last pretense of calm. The whites of his eyes framed enormous pupils, his breathing raced, and he moved in mechanical jerks. He looked from the fire to the dog, shaking, his good hand tracing the scars on his damaged arm with trembling fingers. Finally, he seized Lily's hand.

Kat kicked off her sandals for the last time—no place left to walk to—and plunged into the water. "Lily and Nirav, come on. Juni, come."

Juni jumped into the pond at once and swam easily toward Kat. Lily splashed in behind her, and Nirav took a cautious few steps into the shallows. The logs Kat had eyed for the dogs looked inadequate now that the time had come to use them, but she wrestled Tye into place and knotted his leash around one of the branches to keep him there.

Lily reached the middle of the dam. She had to tip her head back to keep her nose and mouth above water, but she helped Kat boost the Lab onto the platform. Juni crouched across the branches, panting heavily and whining.

"Stay." Juni gave Kat a wild-eyed look, but she obeyed. Tye quit pulling at his leash and pressed his body tightly against the larger dog.

Kat helped Lily step onto one of the boulders she'd spotted, and Lily's tense face relaxed a bit once she stood on a solid surface, only waist-deep in water. She grabbed hold of one of the sticks that jutted from the dam to keep her balance, and she patted Juni on the head.

Two dogs and one child in place. Kat turned again to Nirav, who stood in the shallow water near shore, staring at the fire, making no attempt to wade any deeper. Her shoulder bag hung limply over his arm. "Your turn, Nirav. Come on, it's not safe there."

He shook his head and glanced her way. "Too much water." He added something lengthy in Hindi, his body visibly shaking and his face a mask of pure terror.

"Kat, I don't think he can swim," Lily's shrill voice telegraphed her panic.

Of course. No wonder he hesitated. Kat waded back to him and held out both arms. "I'll carry you. I promise."

"No. No." He kept shaking his head, the fire closing in.

Kat doubted he even heard her anymore. She lifted him and he thrashed hard against her, panicked. But when she reached deeper water, he clutched her shoulders and buried his face against her, too frightened to fight any longer.

Kat headed toward Lily, awkward with Nirav's weight. The shoulder bag he still held thumped against Kat's side, and she lost her footing and almost fell when she stepped into an unexpected hole, but she made it to the dam and found a thick branch a short distance from Lily and the dogs, strong enough to hold Nirav's weight.

She had to pry his fingers off her skin and hoist him up to safety, but once he perched on the dam, out of the water, a fraction of his rigid tension left his body. Her useless shoulder bag sat on the dam beside him.

Kat took a deep breath and took stock. She and Nirav were closest to the shore they'd started from. The dogs crouched unhappily on their logs near the midpoint of the dam. Lily stood beside them, perched on her rock, petting and reassuring them. Kat stood chest-deep in water and ankle-deep in mud. The cold seeped steadily into her legs even as the heat seared her face and neck.

"Kat, look." Lily pointed back to where they had entered the water.

Wisps of smoke rose from the log the children had used as a bench. Ash drifted toward them, coating their wet hair with a thick gray paste. Dark shapes plopped into the water, sending out rings of concentric ripples—frogs and turtles fleeing shore. A long black snake—six feet? eight?—slithered across a log and disappeared beneath the pond's surface. Kat's skin crawled.

A sizzling sound erupted behind her, and Kat turned and checked the opposite end of the dam. Flames moved ever closer to the pond on that side as well, not one fire, but hundreds of individual encroachers, a swarm of fires that surrounded and surged forward. Her adrenaline commanded her to run, but all she could do was stand frozen, her muscles cramping in knotted tension.

"Papa come now. Papa come now." Nirav spoke the wish in a fervent whisper. His eyes never wavered from the closest fires, and he was trembling so hard, it shook Kat's arm. A shrub burst into flames at the end of the dam, a patch of grasses and vines now smoldered, a towering oak had smoke streaming from its trunk and lower branches. Its leaves quaked in the hot updraft.

"All right, Lily?" Kat's parched throat seized up, the sharp pain piercing like dozens of individual needles. It was difficult to yell.

Lily looked at Kat, her eyes raw, her cheeks red. She nodded a yes but then buried her face against Tye's fur.

They waited. Minutes passed, every second prolonged into an eternity. They had staked their claim to safety, and the next move belonged to the enemy.

Kat kept looking toward the trail, expecting Kevin. But he didn't come. Had he been right? Had he made it out? Was he even now safe and rescued, leaving the children the victims of her deadly judgment?

She closed her eyes for a moment, trying to blot out reality. Over the years, there had been events that had been life-altering, and she'd known their impact at the time. Her wedding day. Sara's birth. Her decision to teach. Her cancer diagnosis. Jim's death. Some she had chosen. Some she hadn't. None had prepared her for this wait, a wait with little hope and few options, heavy with the knowledge that the choices she'd made that day had doomed these two precious children.

Sara would learn what had happened and know her as a failure. Malcolm and Scott would revile her. All she wanted was a chance to change the odds. But all she could do was watch the fire and wait.

Smoke swirled from every direction, and all of them, human and dog alike, coughed each time a deep breath sucked in too much gray. Heat seared the inside of Kat's nose and mouth. She and Lily ducked underwater often, the cold depths a welcome relief, and they all drank the scummy water, heedless of the unidentifiable floating bits. They tried pulling wet clothing up to protect their faces, but that made it even harder to breathe. Kat splashed water on Nirav, and Lily did the same for the dogs, but clothes, skin, hair, and fur dried again in seconds.

The noise intensified. Sharp explosions, loud as gunshots. A deep whooshing from the fire itself, a wind from hell. Crashes in the distance as branches and whole trees fell from great heights.

With a loud crunch, a flaming branch launched itself onto the dam, landing only a few feet from Kat and Nirav. They both cried out, and Kat recoiled. She jerked her hand from Nirav's. "Don't move."

She waded along the edge of the dam and grabbed a section of the branch that hadn't yet burst into flames. The bark scalded her hand and she yelped, but she held on long enough to drag the branch off the dam and into the water. The flames sizzled out, but twigs and leaves on the dam still glowed red.

She plunged her burned hand into the water for a moment, then cupped her hands and tossed water onto the embers. For every hot coal she doused, two more sprang up, her puny efforts overwhelmed.

Wet wood shouldn't burn. She had counted on that as an unquestionable fact, but this fire parched everything in its path. Once it caught, the rotted wood of the dam burned all too well, threatening to turn their safe retreat into a funeral pyre.

"Kat." It was Nirav's shout, the first time he'd ever spoken her name, and Kat startled, almost losing her balance as she turned. Nirav had snapped out of his trance, and he rooted around in the shoulder bag beside him. He pulled out his precious bowl and held it toward her.

Kat forced her way through the water, back to the boy, and took the bowl. *Damn. I should have remembered we had it.*

It took several long minutes to douse the smoldering areas with bowl after bowl of water.

Maybe they could do this. Keep the dam wet as a safe zone while the fire burned itself out around them.

"Kat. Over here." Lily's penetrating screech shattered her optimism.

Flames had advanced from the surrounding grasses onto the opposite end of the dam, and the section closest to shore burned as bright as a campfire.

Kat inched as close as she could, her eyes stinging from the smoke. The heat, intolerable for more than a few seconds, repeatedly drove her back, but she poured water over the flames, flinging it in a high arc, her arms tiring. The water hissed and sizzled and the wood smoldered, but then caught again. She needed a fire hose, not a bowl.

The dam was going to go.

In synchrony with this thought, a horrible cracking sounded behind her, and she turned to see the flaming oak tree begin to lean over Nirav's end of the dam.

"Nirav, look out!" Kat and Lily both screamed at the same moment. Nirav gave a frightened glance upward and leaped into the water. The tree gave way, falling with a crash, one of its flaming branches hitting the spot where he had been sitting.

Kat thrashed forward, thrusting the bowl at Lily when she passed her, moving toward Nirav as fast as she could through the deep water. Nirav's arms flailed, and he sputtered and coughed. Kat grabbed his good arm, and she pulled him up so he could hang onto her shoulders, his chest heaving against hers. She carried him back to Lily and the dogs, his fingers digging into her shoulders like claws.

Lily sobbed.

Nirav coughed and retched up foul pond water.

Kat's head pounded, and her burned hand throbbed.

"We're going to die." Lily clutched at Kat's arm.

Kat tried to take a deep breath to answer, but that only triggered an endless bout of coughing. Each hacking jolt stabbed deep, and her heavy, useless lungs clenched in spasms. The end of the dam where the tree had landed burned steadily, and at Lily's end, where Kat had tried to wet things down, the wood crackled with flames as if she'd never made the effort. Twenty feet of dam separated the two fires, and Kat and the children crowded together in the middle of the span.

"We need to move." Kat stopped to cough. "The center of the pond. We can't stay here."

Lily looked back and forth along the dam, and their danger seemed to sink in. She nodded, and her hold on Kat's arm relaxed a fraction. "Where?"

Good question.

"Follow close. We'll find a place." A place where Lily could stand. Kat hoped such a spot existed. Why hadn't she checked the depth of the rest of the pond in those moments before the fire hit?

"What about . . . the dogs?" Lily coughed between each phrase, the smoke worsening every moment.

Kat's arms tightened around Nirav, and she swallowed hard. The dogs couldn't stay on the dam, but they couldn't stand in deep water. She looked from the two anxious children to the two wet panting dogs. Her logical self argued that trying to save the dogs put the rest of them at risk, but she couldn't abandon anyone.

"We'll try."

If it came down to a choice of saving Lily and Nirav or saving Juni and Tye, the dogs would have to go, but perhaps they hadn't yet reached that disastrous moment.

"Nirav, get on my back."

"No fall." Nirav's voice shook.

"No. You won't fall."

With Lily's help, Kat got him to shift onto her back to ride piggyback, his arms wrapped over her shoulders. He abandoned her shoulder bag on the dam, but he clutched the now-useless bowl, its edge digging into her collarbone. What a shame he hadn't fixated on a tiny token that would fit in a pocket, but she didn't have the heart to make him drop it. She reached toward her chest without thinking, to touch the precious necklace that wasn't there, and the stab of its loss pierced her all over again. This bit of her history, gone, like everything else abandoned to the fire.

Nirav's weight settled better on her back, and Kat released Tye's leash from the dam and lowered him into the water, her hands laced under his chest. He hung in her arms, panting, a slow ooze of blood dripping from the wound on his neck, each drop creating an instant's pink on the ash-covered surface of the pond.

"Come on, Lily." Kat stepped away from the dam.

The water rose to her neck within two steps, the original path of the stream deep here. Lily started treading water.

"Juni, come." Juni yipped and leaped into the water, swimming strongly. Lily grabbed her collar as she swam past, and Juni towed her forward.

They inched ahead, and at last, halfway between the center of the pond and the shore, Kat cracked her shin against a large boulder. The new bruise was worth it. She stepped onto it, caught her balance as she slipped. "Here."

Lily let go of Juni, and Kat pulled the girl up beside her, Nirav still holding tight to her shoulders. The slick, uneven surface of the rock meant they were forced to stand shoulder to shoulder in order to fit, but at least Lily could touch bottom here. The wind, an enemy until now, became an ally, swirling occasional gusts of clear air around their perch as the hot fire sucked in the cooler air over the pond. They breathed the snatches of fresh air hungrily, desperate for each instant's respite. All too soon, the smoke returned, and Kat's head pounded again.

Juni whined and swam in circles around them. For the moment, she swam well, her head and shoulders high and her stroke strong.

How long could a dog swim? Kat had no idea.

Flames encircled the entire circumference of the pond now, and when Kat looked back at the dam, it, too, exhaled smoke along its full length.

Time passed. Kat's muscles weakened. Her knees threatened to buckle. The bodies of dead animals drifted past. A rabbit. Two frogs. A baby blue jay, too young to fly.

The flaming trees began to disintegrate, dropping more debris into the water. Crashes and splashes echoed from all directions, the noises even more frightening because they couldn't see what caused them. A claustrophobic terror, like being attacked while blindfolded. Juni kept circling them, but she swam lower in the water now, her movements choppy. The struggle to breathe, to stand upright, took all of Kat's energy. Coherent thoughts hovered just out of reach.

An explosive cracking sound echoed across the water, and an enormous dark shape plummeted out of the smoke. It fell at an angle, hitting the surface of the pond with a thwack that sent a wave of water into their faces.

Lily screamed. Nirav called out something in Hindi. Kat tried to blink pond water out of her eyes. They were all unharmed, but Kat's initial relief proved short-lived.

"Where's Juni?"

They couldn't see her. She had been swimming in the area where the tree fell.

"Juni!" Kat and Lily and Nirav called as loud as they could.

At last, what might have been a whimper came from the direction of the fallen fir. The tree lay steaming in the pond, its broken branches tangled one on top of another. Several jutted out of the water, still burning.

"Lily, stay here. Don't move. Hold Tye." Kat thrust the pup into Lily's arms.

She stepped off the boulder before she even thought it through. Nirav tightened his hold on her shoulders, and she forced her way toward shore. She sank deep in the clinging muck, a slow-motion nightmare. Walking got easier as the pond got shallower, but Nirav gained twenty pounds on her back without the water to support some of his weight.

"Juni!"

Another whimper, but Kat couldn't tell where it came from. The smoke thickened here, so close to shore. Everything looked hazy, and Kat couldn't tell how much was smoke and how much was the fault of her raw, streaming eyes.

"There." Nirav pointed left, and Kat headed that way, turning every few steps to make sure Lily still stood safely on her rock. Kat had promised herself she wouldn't jeopardize the children to save the dogs, but here she was, putting all of them at risk.

They found Juni at last. The main trunk and its branches had missed her, but as the large tree fell, it had taken down several smaller trees with it. Juni's back legs dangled underwater, a thick branch pinned her chest, and blood dripped from a gash at the base of her ear. She whined and struggled when she saw Kat, but she couldn't move. Kat needed to lift several large branches to free her, and she couldn't do it with Nirav on her back.

"Nirav. Stand in the water. It's not deep here."

He shook his head against her shoulder. *No.*

"Nirav, we need to help Juni."

There were a long few seconds of silence, broken only by Juni's whimpers.

"I help." Nirav's voice shook, but he slid down Kat's back to stand waist-deep in the water. One hand still clutched his precious bowl, the other the tail of Kat's blouse.

Kat grabbed the uppermost branch of the heap that trapped Juni and pulled it to the side. The second one still smoldered, and she took the bowl from Nirav and doused a handhold, handed the bowl back, then pulled the branch off the dog, clearing loose debris.

Another enormous cracking sound echoed over the pond, and Lily screamed. Kat froze. A giant splash echoed behind her. She whirled, fearing the worst, but Lily still stood safe on her rock. The tree had fallen somewhere out of sight, leaving Kat with an indelible image of what might have happened if it had struck Lily.

She turned back to Juni. With the top branches gone, she could see the trap more clearly. Juni had scrambled up so that her chest rested on one of the submerged branches, and the support held her partly out of the water. She couldn't move any farther because a broken branch arced over the main trunk and then over her shoulders with only an inch of clearance. The branch was big. It looked heavy. Kat took a deep breath and lifted, her arms shaking with strain. She managed to create only an extra three or four inches of space.

"Juni, come. Come here."

Juni tried, Kat gave her credit, but she needed to move sideways to get out, and she couldn't get traction.

Kat tried to shift the branch to the side, but it wouldn't budge. She needed to pull Juni out, but she needed to keep holding up the branch to do it.

It couldn't be done. A caustic wave of hopelessness burned her eyes and throat with an intensity that surpassed even the effects of the smoke. She was going to have to let go of the branch again, which meant abandoning the dog.

At that moment, Nirav let go of her blouse and forced his way through the water, pushing aside the remaining tangle of twigs and leaves, making a beeline for the trapped dog.

"Nirav, stop." Parts of the tree still smoldered. "Come back."

Nirav didn't pause.

Kat couldn't let go of the branch for fear of hitting him. "You can't pull her out. Too heavy." Her coughs made every word a challenge.

Nirav ignored her.

When he reached Juni, he spoke a few words to her in Hindi in a quiet voice, but he made no attempt to take hold of her. Instead, he reached over Juni's shoulders with the arm that held his bowl, and he wedged it under the branch Kat was struggling to hold up. It created a brace against the main trunk, holding the branch in place.

Nirav hit the bowl hard several times with the heel of his good hand, wedging it in securely.

"Yes." Kat couldn't manage to say more, the word of praise acid in her scalded throat.

She eased off on the branch. The bowl held. She waded forward, grabbed Nirav, and pulled him away from the path the branch would take if it slipped. Then she got a firm hold on Juni's collar and dragged her sideways out of the snarl. Blood smeared the dog's head, raw scrapes covered her back and side, and she could barely keep her head out of the water.

Kat hunched forward. Nirav climbed onto her back again, his weight oppressive, and she kept one hand on Juni's collar and slipped her other arm under the dog's chest to keep her afloat. They made their slow way back to Lily, leaving Nirav's bowl behind, still braced against the tree. The deep water was even more of a challenge now with Juni's extra weight. It was a relief to return to the boulder, where the smoke was a little less dense and the wind carried occasional puffs of fresh air.

Lily struggled with questions between coughs. "Is Juni all right?"

Kat didn't even try to answer. Lily gave up trying to talk and slumped against Kat's shoulder as she held Tye, Kat struggled to keep Juni's head out of the water, and Nirav clung to Kat's shoulders. Kat's arms and back ached; her burned hand throbbed; her feet and legs were dead with cold. They were running out of air, and they were running out of time.

She had spent a lifetime taking the future for granted, but now she wouldn't see the leaves transform in the fall. She wouldn't see sunrise or moonrise again. She wouldn't have a last conversation with Sara. In the past three weeks, Kat had thought a lot about dying, but it had all been distant visions of an abstract event. Now that death was real and immediate, she could only focus on taking one shallow breath after another.

CHAPTER TWENTY-FOUR

Lou retraced their original route, guiding the helicopter toward the thin stream Malcolm and Scott had noticed earlier. The roadbed itself burned along most of its length now, its flaming grasses a blackening path, easy to follow. Malcolm peered through his open doorway into thick smoke that clogged his throat and lungs. Scott clutched his precious handhold, fighting for balance as the chopper jerked and shuddered through shifting updrafts. He muttered under his breath, and it took Malcolm a few moments to make out the words. *Let her be safe. Let her be safe. Let her be safe.* His plea paralleled the one that had taken up permanent residence in Malcolm's heart.

"Slower." Malcolm shifted to lean forward between the pilots' chairs, searching the ground in front of them, anxious not to miss their landmark.

The helicopter eased back, but the dense smoke here blurred all details on the ground. Occasional gusts of wind revealed a patch of dirt or a random boulder, but they could fly over a hundred stream beds without seeing them. He strained to find anything at all that would give them a clue they were in the right place, but he failed. No landmarks. None.

At last, they reached a zone where the smoke thinned. The rockslide.

"We've overshot." "Too far." Scott and Malcolm spoke at the same time.

"Agreed." Lou held the chopper in place.

Pete held a pair of calipers to the trail map, the constant vibrations of the helicopter making exact measurements a challenge. He double-checked instruments on the dashboard and jotted down a few numbers. "Okay. Reverse course. I'll tell you when to stop."

Malcolm nodded approval. The stream bed should be close.

The helicopter turned and moved on again, but nothing was visible except smoke and fire.

"Stop." Pete said. "If this map is scaled right, the stream is right below us."

Malcolm leaned out the door on his side, straining to see through the swirling fog of gray. Pointless. They could have been hovering over a stream or a highway. Hell, they could have been hovering over a whole city.

"We're in a low spot between two hills." He gestured to the vague shapes on either side. "The map can't be too far off. Turn here. Calculate the distance to the pond."

Scott kept glancing at Malcolm, as if trying to gauge his level of confidence, but Malcolm was struggling to keep his face neutral. Too early for optimism. Too many challenges still ahead.

Pete gave a new heading, and Lou made the adjustment. Her hands shifted her joystick in micro-increments, her feet did something with the pedals, and the helicopter began its turn, smoothly at first. Then, without any warning, the chopper gave a sharp sudden lurch, dropped straight down at least two stories, and canted hard to the right.

Scott yelped, and he swung out through the open cargo door, restrained from plunging to the ground only by his death grip on the safety strap and the toes of his tennis shoes, scrabbling across the slick deck for traction. It was a slow-motion replay of the instant the hiker had dragged him out. Malcolm, thrown off-balance, reached out to try to grab Scott and pull him back, and a final jerk of the helicopter tossed him hard against the edge of Lou's chair. His injured elbow smashed against the chair's metal frame with a cracking sound, and Malcolm dropped to his knees in agony.

Lou and Pete fought the helicopter back level, and Scott pulled himself back into the cargo hold. The helicopter surged upward, regaining the altitude they'd lost. Scott clutched the back of Lou's chair, gasping as if he'd never get enough air again.

"Choppy thermals." Lou's tone was half explanation, half apology. "You two okay?"

Malcolm struggled to find breath enough to talk. What had started as a likely hairline fracture near his elbow had exploded after impact into something much worse. His elbow looked disjointed. Disconnected. A sharp point of broken bone poked up, tenting the blackening skin. Worst of all, a nerve must have gotten caught in the break somehow, and it sent electrified jolts of pain shooting up the full length of his arm. His sling still held the arm in place, but even without it, Malcolm doubted he would have been able to move it.

Scott seemed to pull himself together, and his gaze fell on Malcolm's arm.

"Shit, what happened?" Scott crouched beside him.

Malcolm tipped his head toward the metal frame of Lou's chair, but he made no effort to speak, his jaw locked tight in his effort not to moan out loud. He carefully moved his supporting hand away from his injured arm, and Scott's sick expression reinforced his own assessment.

Pete twisted in his chair to look. "Fuck." He inspected the damage, his eyes wide and worried.

"I'm okay." Malcolm heard the double-length stretch of the simple words and saw Scott's disbelief. Yeah, all right, he was definitely not okay, but that didn't matter. "Give me a minute." He turned his head to one side. "Can't lose my son. Can't."

He hadn't intended to say those last words out loud, but Scott reached out and briefly rested his hand on Malcolm's good shoulder. When it came right down to it, they were both just fathers, doing the best they could.

Malcolm closed his eyes, and he tried the same breathing trick he'd used before. This time, the attempt to get on top of his pain didn't work very well. His teeth no longer ground together, but the nerve in his arm—torn or crushed or whatever—still screamed its agony, and the fracture itself hurt like hell. If he'd been out in the field on his own with time to recover, he would have holed up for twenty-four hours before moving on. That was definitely not an option here.

Pete sat frozen. Lou held the chopper in a slow circle.

"Go." Malcolm gave himself points—his voice shook only slightly. "Go to the pond."

"Are you sure?" Lou asked.

"Go. Now." Malcolm used his legs to slide himself across the floor, and he wedged his body against the wall of the cabin. "Scott, you're my eyes. Tell me what you see."

Scott stared at him, slack-jawed. He licked his lips, but he didn't move.

Pete looked from Malcolm to Scott and tapped the map. "We're here."

Scott shook himself and shifted into the position Malcolm usually occupied between the pilot seats. He looked at the map. "We're still above the spot where the stream crosses the old roadbed?"

"Yes."

"Head toward the pond." Scott cleared his throat and squared his shoulders, but the tremor in his voice trumpeted his uncertainty.

Lou turned the chopper down the mountain, toward the valley. Toward the worst of the fire.

Malcolm stayed on the floor, but he watched their progress out the open door. His clothing, his arms and hands, every exposed surface of the helicopter, were flecked with soot. His eyes watered from the smoke, or maybe from the pain, but his tears dried instantly. As the smoke got thicker, every excruciating breath was a nightmare.

"Stop here," called Pete.

The tone of the engine changed, but there was no other way to know they were stationary—Malcolm tried to identify details below them, but he could find no point of reference. Smoke cloaked everything, a swirling shroud pockmarked by flames.

"There's nothing there," Scott said. "Oh my god, even if they're down there, how will we find them?"

Malcolm scanned the area he could see, trying not to let Scott's anguish overwhelm him. They had to find them. This was their last chance.

Looking. Searching. Hoping.

Please.

"Could that be the pond at ten o'clock?" Pete didn't sound at all certain. Malcolm twisted to see. "There. See it?" More insistent this time.

At first Malcolm saw nothing. Then he caught what Pete had noticed. The gray held scattered specks of yellow and orange where flames burned high enough to be seen, but a roughly circular area held only smoke. No fire.

"That has to be water. That's the pond." Malcolm looked at Scott, hoping to infect him with his certainty. "Do you see it, Lou?" It would be better to get up and see more clearly himself, but there was no way. "Can you go down?" The answer was obvious, but he needed to hear the bad news out loud.

Lou grunted something, but she shifted the helicopter until it hovered directly over the flameless space. It began to descend. Lower. Lower still. The smoke got worse, and the racking coughs of all four of them echoed through the headphones.

"That's as low as I go." Lou's tone left no room for disagreement. "The altimeter says any farther and we'll hit whatever is down there. Visibility sucks. Even if they're here, we'll never see them."

She regained altitude, and at least they could breathe again.

"The smoke is bad," Pete said. "Would they still be alive?"

"Stop," Scott said. "You can't say such a thing."

Malcolm straightened and looked directly at Scott. "We can't leave without knowing."

Scott's face cleared and he nodded. "Yes. Absolutely. We have to know for sure." He looked from Malcolm to Pete and back again, expectant.

Malcolm sat there. Looking at Scott. Waiting for him to understand. The only way they would know for sure was for someone to go down there. Scott was the only one who could do it.

Malcolm hated the very idea. Scott wasn't trained; he wasn't fit. Yes, he had been more helpful than expected—he had prompted them to look onward for the car, he had spotted Kat's hat on the rockslide, he had remembered this pond. All good. But go down into this pond and search it effectively? Scott was the last person Malcolm would choose for such a task.

The idea of putting his trust—putting Nirav's life—in Scott's hands made him want to punch something. The only way it would work was if they were in constant radio contact, and even then, Malcolm had serious doubts. But it was the only option they had. With his arm . . . impossible. Passing out from the pain on the way down wasn't the way to rescue anyone.

Scott froze, all blood draining from his cheeks. He got it. He looked at Pete, his question shaping on his lips, but Pete shook his head. "Can't do it. Needed here."

"Scott. You can do this." Malcolm forced certainty into his voice. The confidence of a commander could instill bravery in the most fearful new recruit, but Scott was no recruit, and Malcolm would not be at his side to help.

Scott grabbed hold of his handhold strap, as if the fierceness of his grip would make the prospect of leaving the helicopter disappear. "I can't. No way. I can't do it." He twisted to look down into the smoky morass below them. "When Brandon pulled me out . . . almost fell . . . I just can't."

"Scott. I'm out of play. You have to."

Scott stared at him. Slowly, he nodded.

Pete scrambled to get ready. He fastened a harness to Scott's unresisting body and adjusted the straps. He clipped on the cable. "Unclip it. Reattach it. Show me you can do it."

Scott obeyed like an automaton.

Malcolm thought through the steps involved, what gear would be needed. He gestured toward the back of the cabin. "Pete, I saw a couple hundred feet of rope back there. Tie one end to Scott's harness, and see if you can find something heavy to anchor the other end in the water. Scott, make sure the anchor's solid. The rope will guide you back to the drop-off point after your search. Without it, you'll never get back, and we'll never find you. Here, take this." He shifted awkwardly onto one hip, pulled out his compass, and handed it over. "Do you know how to use it?"

Scott looked insulted. "Hey, I was in Cub Scouts." He stuffed it into his pocket.

Pete scrambled to the back of the cabin and returned with rope and an old-fashioned metal toolbox. He opened it and pulled out a few small items that he stuffed into his pocket, but he left all the heavy things in place—a metal hammer, several large screwdrivers, a set of wrenches. He tied the rope as Malcolm suggested, one end to Scott's harness and the other to the rattling box. He rigged the box to Scott's harness so he wouldn't have to hold it. The weight of it hunched him forward.

"Fill this box with water when you're down, and with all that stuff inside, it should anchor pretty well."

Scott nodded.

Lou twisted in her chair and gave Scott a tense look. "Visibility sucks down there. A dozen feet at best."

Scott nodded.

"Don't screw around. The engine's running hot."

Scott nodded.

"Walk or swim an organized pattern," Malcolm said. "That's your best bet if they're there."

Scott nodded.

"We'll stay in radio range." Pete clapped him on the shoulder. "Don't let the headset get wet."

Scott nodded yet again.

Pete led him to the open cargo door, nudged him into a sitting position on the edge, and double-checked the cable attachment. "Whenever you're ready."

Scott looked down. He was visibly shaking. He turned and looked back at Malcolm. "I can't do this."

"You can. I know you can." Scott shook his head, and Malcolm kept his voice calm with an effort. "Think of what Lily means to you." His voice shook, thoughts of Nirav rushing in. Scott loved his daughter, and everything he'd done that day testified to that fact. Now, he just needed the strength to take this next step. "You plan trips for her every year. You make her animal pancakes for breakfast. You save bracelets for her. You came here, on this helicopter, to find her. It's time, Scott. Go."

At last, the words sank in. Scott slid his butt forward until his legs hung out the cabin door, dangling over nothing. Another six-inch shift and he'd be suspended, the cable taut, and Pete would start him on his journey down. If they were right, the pond lay below, and Scott would land in water. If they were wrong, he would come down in fire.

He paused, but then, in a convulsive movement, he used both hands to give himself a final push. His body left the chopper, and the cable snapped tight. Pete triggered the winch, and Scott dropped out of sight, disappearing into the smoke-filled hell below.

CHAPTER TWENTY-FIVE

Kat huddled with the children on their boulder in the beaver pond. She struggled to breathe, struggled to stay focused, struggled to stay upright. Nothing improved. Lily leaned against her, Nirav clung to her back, and Juni sagged in her arms, unconscious and heavier by the minute. Her shoulders ached. Her arms cramped. Her head pounded, the worst headache she'd ever had, their precious gusts of clear air less and less frequent, taunting them. Lily still held Tye, but several times her grip loosened. He thrashed each time to stay afloat, and she had to jerk herself back to alertness and grab him again.

Kat gasped for air between coughs. They no longer talked. They no longer jumped when branches fell and trees toppled. They no longer recoiled when half-seen creatures swam past or when the singed corpse of a rabbit or squirrel drifted against them. Their world had shrunk to a smoke-shrouded circle with a six-foot radius.

Coherent thoughts were rare. The words she needed hid from her, and she wasted precious seconds tracking each one down. Images surfaced, tinged with yearning and regret. Sara as a baby, asleep in her arms. Jim, smiling over a shared moment together. She kept visualizing clean, clear water. Water flowing down a river, water cascading in a mountain stream, water pouring from a tap. Unlimited, magical water. She could taste it for a split second, cool and sweet, slaking her thirst, but the imagined relief disappeared every time.

The fire showed no sign of burning itself out. Ash rained steadily, a filthy snow, floating to form a thick film on the water. No matter how much Kat drank, her throat burned. Her eyes were sandpapered. Her nostrils had swollen closed. Her chest shrank and her lungs shriveled, leaving less space for air in each breath.

No more. She'd reached her limit. She would have to let Juni go, in the hope that she could hang on to Lily and Nirav a little longer.

Ten more breaths, she promised herself, recalling her step-counting. Ten more, and she would let go. She tried to focus on the count and nothing else, but each breath triggered another soul-racking cough.

She made it to ten. Juni half floated, half sagged in her arms. The Lab's eyes were closed, her mouth open, her chest rasping so hard her rib cage vibrated. Juni had saved Nirav. She had stuck by Kat as she led them all to disaster. Sara had been right. Kat had needed a dog.

Juni must have sensed her look, because her eyes opened and focused on Kat's face. The soft double tap of her tail swished through the water against Kat's leg.

Kat tasted salt, and she forced her arms to tighten more firmly around the dog. Ten more breaths. Concentrate and count. She could make ten more.

Death hovered close, but not as frightening as she'd feared. They wouldn't write *cancer* on her death certificate after all. She'd had a good life, a good job, a good marriage. Time to wrap it up. Every actor takes a final bow, every script has a final line. *Life's but a walking shadow.*

At least none of them would die in flames; she could claim that as a minor success. When they couldn't get enough oxygen, they'd lose consciousness, slip into the water, and drown. Hopefully without even knowing.

Kat made it to ten. Convinced herself to try ten more. She made it to three, but all that noise kept making her lose track. The fire had changed tone. It rattled. Throbbed. Sounded almost metallic. It moved closer.

How was that possible?

Lily stirred and lifted her head. "What's that?" Her scraped voice was inhuman.

Kat tried to restore some order to her muddled brain. The fire made countless noises, and this was just one more. No, wait. That made no sense. Something else sounded like this.

An engine? The heavy curtain in Kat's head lifted enough to allow coherent thought. "Helicopter."

Lily gave her a startled glance. They both looked up, but they were trapped in their smoke-lined prison. They wouldn't see a helicopter unless it landed directly on top of them. That meant nobody in a helicopter could see them.

Kat tried to yell, but it came out a croak. Pointless. No one could hear over this noise even if they screamed at the top of their lungs.

The sound came closer. Firefighters searching for a way in? They might not even know there were people down here. People in trouble. Kat's hopes sank as quickly as they'd gone airborne. It wasn't here for them. It would leave.

As if driven away by her skepticism, the noise faded.

Their last hope had just abandoned them.

Nirav still clung to her back, but he hadn't moved in ages. Hadn't spoken. "Lily. Check Nirav."

Lily twisted, let go of Kat, and grabbed his shoulder. She shook her head. "His eyes open, then close again." She coughed her way through the sentence.

Pointless to rouse him now.

Pointless to keep hanging on as well, but giving up was too overwhelming a decision. Kat locked her knees, reminded herself to keep standing, keep breathing, keep her tight grip on Juni. Her concentration skittered and slipped. She had been trying to do something important, something she had to complete, but she could no longer remember what.

CHAPTER TWENTY-SIX

Malcolm shifted carefully across the cabin to join Pete by the open cargo door, the pain in his arm escalating with each tiny motion. The cable spooled downward and the two of them stared into the smoke. Futile. There was nothing at all to see.

"Scott, how's it going?" Pete asked into the headset.

There was a long pause, and then Scott coughed. "Smoke bad. Getting worse."

Malcolm and Pete exchanged glances. If Scott landed safely in the pond but couldn't breathe, they'd have to bring him right back up.

The cable reeled out farther, the winch engine working smoothly. Malcolm held his breath. At last, Scott's voice came through. "Okay. I'm down. Water. Waist deep."

Malcolm breathed again. One hurdle down. "How's the air?"

"Better." Scott coughed hard, which wasn't very reassuring, but at least he wasn't gasping for breath. "Lily! Lily! Where are you?" Scott's shouts ended in another coughing fit.

Malcolm waited, hoping it would be that easy—someone would answer, and all would be well. "Anything?" he asked after a moment.

"Nothing."

Not that easy after all. "What about the fire?"

"Can't see any flames. Hotter than hell. Visibility sucks. Which way do I go?" Scott's panic-edged voice provided little reassurance.

Malcolm organized his thoughts. What would he be doing if he were the one down there? "Okay. Step one. Disconnect the cable." The tension on the cable eased, and Pete began reeling it in. "Good. Now fill the tool chest with water and let it sink. We have this position, and this is where we'll pick you up." Pick *all of you* up. He wondered if he still even believed that was possible. At this point, hope seemed a hallucination.

A pause. "Done. Seems solid. I've uncoiled the rope." Scott's voice had calmed. He was better at following directions than winging it.

"Take out your compass. Find north. Walk that way. See if the water gets shallower or deeper." Malcolm had no clue where in the pond Scott had landed, but it wasn't all that big. They would figure it out.

"Okay. Heading north."

Lou had taken the helicopter higher after Scott disconnected, staying in communication range but giving them better air. Scott had no such luxury. Malcolm tried to imagine the conditions down there—no way to orient, smoke-filled air leading to muddled thinking, enough fear to keep the adrenaline pumping and the heart racing but not enough experience to remain logical. He would rather face those conditions himself than force them on Scott.

If he only had more faith in the guy, he'd be more optimistic about their chances. They'd assigned Scott an impossible task and given him no equipment, no training, and no backup. He needed to tap into strength he didn't even know he had to seize even a remote chance of success.

"Getting shallower. Getting hotter. Seeing flames now."

Malcolm pictured it in his head. Scott must have landed off center, closer to the north shore than the south if the water was getting shallower.

"Oh my god." Scott sounded stunned. "Fire everywhere on shore. No way could anyone survive there. They have to be in the pond." Scott's sentences were interspersed with spasms of coughing.

It was what Malcolm had expected based on the uniform carpet of smoke below them, but hearing the words out loud chilled his soul and made the risk that much more real. If Kat hadn't taken the children into the pond, they'd lost them.

"I can't go any closer. Too hot." Scott's voice rose again, panic creeping in.

Pete and Malcolm exchanged glances, and Pete shook his head. "Not good."

Malcolm forced his voice to stay calm. "Kat wouldn't stay that close. Turn to your right and follow the shoreline but stay far enough away to be safe."

"Yeah. Okay. The dam should be here somewhere."

Things got very quiet. Malcolm leaned forward, trying to pick out clues as to what was happening through the static, but there was nothing. "Keep us posted."

All they heard for a long while were periodic coughing spasms. Scott called for Lily every few minutes, but his shouts grew weaker. Malcolm doubted anyone would hear them unless he was right on top of them, and his despair deepened. He should have gone down, arm or no arm.

Finally, "Okay. The dam." Scott's voice had gotten progressively hoarser, almost a croak now.

"Good job. How're you doing?"

"Uh . . . eyes bad . . . smoke . . . chest . . . hurts."

Pete gave Malcolm a worried look and covered his microphone so Scott couldn't hear. "He sounds confused."

He did indeed. But as long as Scott could hang in there, they couldn't give up. "Turn right. Keep going along the dam."

"Getting deeper."

That was good; he must be crossing the midpoint of the pond.

A sudden hoarse shriek came through.

"What's wrong?" Malcolm's heart rate skyrocketed. Maybe Scott was injured.

A coughing fit lasted a few moments before Scott answered. "Dead raccoon. I'm okay."

Malcolm's tension didn't ease. It had to be pure hell down there. *Come on man, keep going. It's our only shot.*

"Something . . . on the dam . . . burned."

Malcolm swallowed his irritation. Scott needed to stay focused; he shouldn't go haring off after nothing. He bit back the comment that rose to his lips. Scott was the one down there; he was the one with eyes on.

"Wait . . . let me get it . . . it's canvas." A pause. "It's part of Kat's bag!" The energy in Scott's voice came through clearly.

"Are you sure?" Malcolm remembered the bag. Some sort of school name on its side, with an eagle logo. Kat had been there. She and the children must have made it to the pond. "Are you really sure?"

"Positive."

"Okay. Keep . . ." Malcolm had to stop, clear his throat, pull himself together. The possibility that this insane search might actually succeed overwhelmed him more profoundly than even his fears of failure. He tried again. "Keep along the dam, then when you see the shore again, follow it." This would let Scott complete the circuit of the pond. If he didn't find anything, then he would need to cut across the middle. Assuming he could stay down there that long.

Scott went silent for a spell. Twice they heard splashing, and Malcolm pictured him losing his balance. Things couldn't be easy down there.

"Nothing." Scott's voice dragged. "They're not here."

"Keep going," Malcolm said. "You're doing great." He fervently hoped that was true. What the hell was really going on down there? Scott could be traveling in circles, for all he knew. So close, so close to success. What if Nirav was really there and Scott missed him?

"Head . . . hurts . . . hard to think."

The bad air must be taking its toll. A wave of utter hopelessness forced Malcolm to lean hard against the cabin wall. This wasn't going to work. They were too late to save them. *Nirav, I'm so sorry.*

Desperation must have shown on his face, because Pete reached out to squeeze his shoulder. "Still time." But even he sounded doubtful.

"Anything yet?" Malcolm finally asked. Scott was getting more and more confused, less and less likely to be able to continue. If he got much worse, they would need to have him return to the pickup point, or they would lose him, too.

No answer. Malcolm repeated it. Still nothing. Then a long, drawn-out spell of coughing. "Something . . . here . . . deeper water." Scott's voice was so hoarse, his words were almost indecipherable.

Malcolm leaned forward. "What? What is it?"

"Hang on . . . a shape . . . it's moving . . . oh my god . . . a person . . . Lily." The last word was a hoarse shriek. There was garbled noise at that point, nothing that could be understood.

"What's going on?" Malcolm tried not to scream. Was Lily really there? Was Scott hallucinating?

A choking sob came through the headphones. "Here. Alive. All three."

CHAPTER TWENTY-SEVEN

Kat turned to see what could sound so human, what new threat approached. An upright ash-coated creature—a bear?—struggled toward them. Kat tried to focus, think, react.

The animal lurched closer, waving its front legs, grunting strange sounds.

Lily gasped and leaned toward the animal, not away. She croaked the words, *Dad, you came*, but Kat still didn't understand. The creature kept coming, only a few feet away now, and then it registered.

Human.

A man.

Scott?

Kat's knees gave way, and she pitched forward. Juni disappeared underwater, thrashing in her arms, and Kat forced herself upright, pulling the dog's head back into the smoke-laden air.

Scott. His hair streamed water and ash, his reddened face looked scalded, and he stumbled with each step. He splashed toward Lily and swept her to his chest, squashing Tye between them. "You're here."

"How?" Kat couldn't manage to say anything beyond the single word. Had he followed them somehow? Was he as trapped as they were?

Lily pulled back from her father and shifted Tye so she could hold his harness in one hand. "Can we get out?"

Scott nodded.

Nirav moved on Kat's back, half awake at last, and he reached out and touched Scott's arm, his shoulder, his face, as if confirming he was real and not imagined. "Papa?"

"In the helicopter." Scott made it sound like such rescues arrived every day, but Kat fought against a wave of dizziness and disbelief. Nirav's hands tightened on her shoulders, and for the first time in that endless day, he gave a choking sob.

"Can't land." Scott gestured toward his webbed harness, and Kat made the vague connection to the noise they'd heard.

Scott's headphones squawked, and Kat jumped. Voices, invisible people out there, people here to rescue the children. *The children will be safe.* The words filled her, soaking their way into her exhausted body the way liquid saturates a sponge. *The children will be safe.* Nothing else mattered.

Scott listened to the static-filled noise and nodded. "Yes." He coughed, appeared to listen again. "Yes . . . no." He glanced at the three of them. "Bad shape . . . two dogs." A long spell of squawking came from the headphones. "No, dogs. *D-O-G-S.*

Dogs. Two of them." He shook his head. Shrugged. "Will do . . . yes."

He turned to Lily. "Can you walk?" He gestured to the rope tied to his harness. It floated in long curls on the surface of the water and disappeared off into the smoke.

Lily nodded, but she leaned against him. "I can walk."

Kat was forgetting something. Something important. The piece she groped for fell into place. "Scott. Another man. He was here."

Scott looked around at the surrounding smoke. "Here? In the pond?"

"No. He went downhill. Down the trail."

Scott shook his head. "Toward the lake?" Kat nodded, and Scott reported the fact to the helicopter. He listened. "Yes . . . yes. Agreed . . . no chance at all." He turned to Kat. "They're radioing it in to the fire teams. They'll search. Here, let me take the boy."

No chance at all. The blunt words seemed to seal Kevin's fate, and in that moment, Kat didn't want to let Nirav go, didn't want to lose the tight grip of his hands on her shoulders, the badly needed reassurance that he was still okay. But she couldn't carry him any farther.

Nirav reached for Scott, and Kat straightened as his weight left her, the relief unspeakably wonderful. The next moment, a wave of foul water splashed her face. When she cleared her eyes, Nirav was completely underwater, hardly struggling. Scott grabbed him, pulled him out, and held him as he coughed up the foul liquid he'd inhaled. He finally got the boy settled on his back. Nirav's head sagged forward, but Kat saw that he held on this time with both hands.

Kat tightened her hold on Juni. Almost there. She could do this.

Scott looked at Kat. "The dogs . . ." He shook his head.

Lily gasped and gave her father a horrified look.

Kat met his eyes. Abandon the dogs? After all this. "We've come so far." The hoarseness of her voice didn't hide her pleading tone.

Nirav leaned forward over Scott's shoulder so he could look him in the eye. "Dogs are coming. They . . ." He appeared to grope for his next words; then his voice disappeared in a long spasm of coughing.

Scott let out an audible sigh and shook his head one more time. "We'll try. No guarantees."

He stepped forward and tried to lift Juni out of Kat's arms. He pried her stiffened fingers one at a time from their taloned hold on the dog's fur. Juni didn't even open her eyes, but her chest still rose and fell. At least she was alive.

Kat rubbed her aching shoulders. No dog in her arms. No child on her back. A wave of dizziness threw her off-balance, and she grabbed Scott's arm for an instant to recover.

"Not far. Stay together." Scott shifted Juni onto one arm and used the other to pull the floating rope toward him until it tightened into a straight path. "This leads to the pickup point." He placed it in Lily's hands. "You first." His voice rasped as hoarsely now as everyone else's. "Kat, stay close. Watch the boy."

Kat nodded. *Follow Scott. Don't let Nirav fall.* She repeated it to herself. She stepped off the boulder and forced her way through the water, an amazingly easy task without added weight.

Focus on Nirav's red shirt. One foot in front of the other. Ignore the heat, the smoke, the fire. The water got deeper, the bottom rockier—they were crossing the middle of the pond. Kat's bare feet were numb with cold, and she slipped again and again on the uneven bottom.

Focus on Nirav's red shirt. Concentrate. Keep going. The water got shallower closer to shore, the smoke thicker, the fire louder. The red shirt got smaller. Kat stumbled, smashed her bruised shin against a rock, fell forward, dropped the rope, sucked in foul water, and retched it back up.

The red shirt. Gone. The rope. Gone. Kat opened her mouth to call for help, but then she stopped.

The children were safe.

The dogs were safe.

If she stopped, if she stayed right here, she wouldn't burn. She would simply fill with smoke, embrace it, and become part of it. She would slip into the water and drown. A far less daunting fate than fighting forward one more time—only to wait for her cancer to take her.

Here it was at last. A final decision. Exactly the reason she'd come to these mountains, to accept her inevitable future, the approaching endgame. She waited for a sense of relief to envelop her. Waited for calm. For peace.

Instead, every aching muscle, every cut, scratch, and burn, shrieked their damage. Her eyes were dried raisins, her throat so raw and swollen she could no longer swallow. Every nerve in her body reminded her she was still alive.

A flood of memories rocked her. Jim, at the little bistro on King Street, down on one knee, promising a life together. Sara, toddling through her first steps. Jim, the morning she rolled to his side of the bed to tell him he was running late, only to find his body cold and stiff. Sara now, her love for her bewildering succession of dogs, her determination to have Kat fight on as long as possible. Malcolm. Lily. Nirav. The sickening fear of failing them.

Scene after scene tumbled through Kat's head, the random pattern of a life. She would miss it. All of it.

Something brushed against Kat's side, and she hesitated before she looked down, afraid to see another dead animal, or worse, another live one.

Not an animal. The slack coil of Scott's rope floated beside her. Kat picked it up. Heavy, wet, slimy with the ash that crusted the surface of the pond. A lifeline that would lead her to Scott, Malcolm, and the children.

A chance.

A chance, if she wanted to take it.

Malcolm's deep rasping voice echoed in her head. *I finally decided to embrace what life handed me, even though it wasn't what I was seeking.*

In the end, the choice was surprisingly easy.

CHAPTER TWENTY-EIGHT

All hell broke loose in the helicopter the instant Scott found Kat and the children. Pete and Lou let out shouts of delight, and Pete pummeled the deck with one fist, his face ecstatic. "Fucking unbelievable!"

All Malcolm could do was sit, frozen. Stunned.

Scott had done it. Nirav was alive.

His relief left him deeply shaken. If things had worked differently—if he'd lost his son—he wasn't sure how he would have faced the next day.

But they still had a way go. Scott was leading the group to the pickup point, following the guide rope back to the anchor. Malcolm wanted details on Nirav's condition, and he wanted to talk to him, but he forced himself to be patient. He couldn't risk distracting Scott and perhaps prompting some sort of mistake.

Pete sat by the open cargo door, ready to lower the cable as soon as Scott reported in. "I can't believe they have two dogs with them."

Unbelievable indeed. "Do you have anything they can use to bring the dogs up?"

"No. They'll have to make do with the regular harnesses."

Maybe that would work. Malcolm tried to picture anything else that could go wrong. "They may have trouble finding the cable in all that crap. Do you have any sort of flare we could use?"

Pete nodded and opened a small compartment. "Good idea." He dug out a handful of flares and duct-taped one near the free end of the cable, ready to light.

That should help. Their positioning wouldn't be exact. They'd heard nothing from below for a good long while. "How's it going, Scott?"

"Okay." Scott's comments had grown shorter and his coughing spells longer. "Should be almost there."

"Dad! Where's . . ."

Malcolm tried to make out the rest, but Lily's voice wasn't strong enough for Scott's microphone to pick up everything.

"What's wrong?" he asked. "What's happening?" So many things could still go wrong.

The pause that followed was endless. "Kat's not with us."

Malcolm turned away, staring sightlessly at the winch to avoid meeting Pete's eyes. He didn't think he could mask his distress. He had promised himself he would save Kat along with Nirav. If they lost her now, it meant failure.

Exhaustion. Poor visibility. Lack of oxygen. There were an infinite number of reasons for Kat to get confused or lost. The last thing he wanted was to save the children and lose her. She'd done a phenomenal job, but they needed to get the children out before they could consider any additional search. "Keep going," he told Scott. His voice gave no hint of the turmoil that scrambled his insides. "Let's get the children out, and then we'll see if there's anything we can do."

"Okay." The single word dragged with fatigue. "We're here. We're at the pickup point."

"Great." Pete's crisp voice spit from the headphones, all business. "We're coming lower. I'm sending down two harnesses. The children can come together. Clip both onto the single hook." He lit the flare, which spewed out an arc of brilliant yellow sparks as the winch dropped it downward. "Look for the flare."

"Send both children at the same time?" Scott's confusion was getting worse.

"Yes. The cable will take their weight easily. We can't waste time."

Malcolm started itemizing the millions of ways things could still go fubar, but he stopped himself. He needed to have faith. Scott had done the impossible; he'd found Kat and the children. Hopefully he could keep going long enough to get the children out and find Kat again.

"I see the flare," Scott said. "Okay, I've got the cable. Lily, you and Nirav go first."

Malcolm and Pete peered into the smoke, listening intently.

"No!" Lily's voice carried up to them clearly—she must be yelling close to her dad. "Not without you."

"Honey, you need—"

"No! No! I won't." Her voice squeaked in panic.

"Okay. Okay. Calm down. Your mother—"

Lily didn't let him finish. "No. You take me."

Malcolm tried to picture what he would do in Scott's place. It made the most sense to get the two children out first, but Lily's fear was understandable. He'd be tempted to simply order her to behave, but that was probably an impulse born of his lack of understanding of twelve-year-old girls. Scott was going to have to figure this one out on his own.

He waited through a long silence but finally couldn't stand it any longer. "What's happening?"

"Sending your boy. And the big dog. If I can manage it."

Pete shook his head, but at least a decision had been made. Malcolm would have Nirav with him in only moments, but they were adding the risk of a freaked-out dog as it was lifted through the air. Special ops used dogs all the time in parachute drops and rappels, but those dogs had tons of special training. "Muzzle the dog. It might panic."

"Are you kidding me? With what?" Scott's exasperation made it sound like he was at the end of his endurance.

Malcolm let it drop. He'd have to just hope for the best. The minutes dragged on, and he tried to be patient. It would take time for Scott to fit the harness around Juni, adjust a separate harness for Nirav, and then attach the cable to both Nirav and the dog. Why didn't Nirav say something loud enough to be picked up by microphone? Then again, he was usually soft-spoken. That was probably why his voice didn't come through. But Scott wasn't reassuring the boy or telling him what was happening. He had to be as frightened as Lily was.

The horrifying possibility that Nirav couldn't speak forced itself into Malcolm's list of worries, and his chest compressed inward, his lungs full of concrete with no room for air. *Come on, come on, come on.*

At last, Scott gave the signal they'd waited for. "Okay. Take it up."

Pete started the winch again, and Malcolm leaned as far out of the helicopter as he dared, trying to see. Nothing but swirling smoke. Still nothing. Still nothing. Then, a vague shape, darker than the rest. It got bigger. More defined, but still hard to make out—an amorphous lump hanging at the end of the steel cable. Closer, then closer still, and at last it reached the helicopter's side—two inert bodies, Nirav and Juni. Neither was moving. Juni's tongue lolled out of her mouth, a sickly bluish gray. No wonder Scott scoffed at the idea of a muzzle.

"Nirav! Nirav!" His son didn't even flinch.

Pete guided the two in, and Malcolm slid over beside them, damning his injured arm and its relentless pain. He felt at once for Nirav's pulse, couldn't find it, then finally felt a few beats. Weak and irregular. Nirav's breathing was horribly shallow. His eyes were half open, but he didn't seem aware of what was happening, and his face shimmered sickly white under a coating of ash. Malcolm had gotten so used to coughing that it didn't register anymore, but Nirav wasn't coughing. Wasn't coughing at all. That had to be a bad sign. Malcolm's heart seized down hard. He'd imagined Nirav, rescued and safe. Now he could only pray they could get him to a hospital in time to save him.

Pete attached two more empty harnesses to the winch and sent the cable down with another brilliant flare. "On its way," he said to Scott. He turned to Malcolm. "Is that dog even alive?"

Malcolm shook his head and checked Juni. Alive, yes, but cut, burned, and barely breathing. The surface of her fur was dry—the heat of the fire had vaporized all available moisture on the journey up—but her undercoat was soaking wet. How in hell had Kat managed two dogs in deep water?

He helped Pete shift Juni and Nirav off to one side, out of the way for the next rescue. Two more trips and they'd have everyone in the helicopter. They could head to the trauma center in Asheville.

Nirav clung to the dog like a limpet, his fingers twined in Juni's fur, and Malcolm tried to convince himself it was a good sign. "Hang on, Nirav, just hang on." He didn't think his son could hear him, but saying the words helped. He whispered a fervent prayer and wished he knew which Hindu god Nirav would want him to address. "I'm here, Nirav. I'm right here. You're safe now."

Malcolm hoped with every fiber of his being that what he was saying was true.

CHAPTER TWENTY-NINE

Kat slogged onward, clinging to the guide rope as a lifeline, pulling herself forward hand over hand, too exhausted to focus on anything but the few feet of sludgy water in front of her.

Her legs shook uncontrollably, and a vise clamped her head as if trying to crack open her skull. Her shriveled lungs demanded more air than she could give them. The water slid up a little higher along her chest. Very peaceful. The crackling of the fire. Winter evenings when Jim would cook popcorn and she and Sara would play Scrabble. Hot chocolate. A good book. A nap. Just a short little nap.

A hand closed painfully around Kat's arm.

"Almost gave up on you." Scott's voice.

Kat lifted her head. She'd made it.

"This way." Lily gasped out the words. Kat meant to reply, but the intention slipped away.

"You're next." Scott said it as if he expected her to understand. *Next for what?*

Straps tightened around her body.

A clicking sound—a heavy snakelike cable clipped onto the straps.

"Okay, Pete. Ready."

Scott talking, but no one named Pete here.

The cable tightened, and the straps pulled snug. Kat rose into the air, drawn upward, away from the water. She could fly.

The surface of the pond disappeared below. Her hair, skin, and clothing dried fast, all exposed skin parched and crispy. The water of the pond had provided some relief, but now the heat reached up to envelop her, as if she were being tugged upward through a working chimney. Smoke choked her, and ash clogged every breath.

A noisy roar came from above her, louder and louder, then an open door, hands reaching, a stranger pulling her into a cluttered space. Relief flooded her body like water released from a burst dam, but she had no tears left to cry, no voice left to speak her gratitude.

A scarred man, familiar, one arm in a sling, gently unfastened her harness and pulled it off. No name to go with the voice. Kat fell forward and buried her face against his chest, blue cotton streaked with soot. A strong arm closed around her, kept her from falling. Blackness telescoped inward and the blue shirt shrank as if it moved far away. *Follow the shirt*; that much she remembered, but she couldn't remember why such a task was so important. She fell toward it, such a blessed release, such a restful letting go.

CHAPTER THIRTY

Two people safe, plus a dog. Two more to go, plus the puppy. Even the grinding pain from his arm couldn't temper Malcolm's buoyancy. Against all odds, they were almost there.

Pete swore under his breath. "Need some help here."

Malcolm reluctantly let go of his optimism and dropped back into the urgencies of the moment. "Coming."

He eased Kat onto the deck beside Juni and Nirav. His son's breathing had improved slightly, and he acted somewhat aware of his surroundings, but Kat remained in bad shape. She had drifted out of consciousness, and there were long pauses in her breathing that didn't bode well. The faster they got Scott and Lily up here, the faster they could get to a hospital.

He climbed awkwardly over the inert bodies and joined Pete at the open cargo door. "What's up?"

"I'm trying to get the cable down to them again, but it keeps sticking. Take this remote while I check the motor."

"Got it." The yellow flare hung only a few yards below the helicopter. An empty harness hung from the hook, flapping and twisting in the helicopter's backwash.

"Can't see anything yet," Scott said from below. Malcolm and Pete exchanged glances.

"Stand by," Malcolm said.

"Stand by? What the hell? Send now. Smoke worse."

"Roger that." Malcolm tried to sound calming. Pete removed the engine cowling and poked at something unseen with a screwdriver.

"It's all this crap in the air," he said. "It's gumming everything up. Almost have it." He worked for another minute, then nodded. "Okay, try again."

Malcolm hit the down arrow on the remote, and this time the flare disappeared smoothly into the smoke. "On its way."

"About time." Scott's irritation came through loud and clear.

The now-familiar sequence played out. Scott reported in when he spotted the flare and retrieved the harness and cable. A long pause followed, and Malcolm pictured him adjusting the harness for Lily.

"Face me," Scott said. Good, he was giving Lily instructions. "Dog between us."

A quiet mumble came from the girl. If she was in as bad shape as Nirav and Kat, Scott had his hands full.

"He'll be fine. I've threaded the straps of your harness through his." He must be talking about the dog.

Another garbled comment came from Lily.

"Close your eyes. Don't look when we go up. I've got you."

Finally, Scott gave the word. "Okay. We're ready."

Malcolm's thumb started for the up switch, but Scott spoke again.

"Wait. Wait. Not yet." A pause. "Okay. Ready now. I had to untie the toolbox."

Yes, that would help.

Malcolm pushed the switch and the winch came to life. Pete hovered over the motor, making adjustments, and the cable spooled upward for ten yards. Fifteen. And then it froze.

"Shit." Pete worked frantically.

"What's happening?" Scott asked. "What's wrong? We've stopped." His coughs—and Lily's—came through clearly. They were hanging now in the densest smoke, down where the air looked thick enough to scoop with a spoon.

"Hang on. Winch is binding again."

"Dad. We're stuck." Lily's voice was pitiful and shaking.

"Not stuck, Lily. Just a pause." Scott was obviously making every effort to be reassuring, and Malcolm hoped the confidence wasn't misplaced. The cable twisted slowly, which meant Scott and Lily were swiveling through a 360-degree view of nothing but smoke.

Malcolm's headset suddenly went silent, the background static gone. Lou pivoted in her chair. "I cut off the audio—they don't need to hear this." She was yelling to be heard. "We need to get out of here. Engines are overheating."

"Damn winch is frozen solid. I'm not making headway." Pete gave Malcolm a pleading look.

"Sorry, engines aren't my thing. Can we pull them up by hand?"

Pete shook his head. "Not with only the two of us." He glanced at Malcolm's worthless arm.

"Will the cable hold if we pull them along with us?" Malcolm asked. Pete nodded. "Lou, can you get to an open spot and get them down to the ground safely?"

There was a lengthy pause that didn't inspire confidence. "Don't think we have any choice."

"Okay. Turn the headsets back on."

Lou reached out and flipped a switch, and Scott's voice came through. "Anytime now," he said.

"Scott." Lou had sounded doubtful when she agreed to the plan, but she didn't let Scott hear that now. "The helicopter engine is overheating. The filters can't handle this smoke. We think the winch has the same problem. It's frozen. I'm going to move away from the fire."

"Move? What the hell do you mean? Move with us outside? Hanging here?"

Scott's voice was a shriek, and Malcolm didn't blame him one little bit. Scott's face had been a mask of pure terror when he almost got pulled out of the helicopter, and that was nothing compared to what they were proposing.

"The cable will hold. It's good for thousands of pounds. Just hold still."

"You are fucking kidding me." Scott's comment dissolved into a coughing fit. "Lily, hang on. Keep your eyes closed. Don't look down."

Malcolm thought he heard a small whimper, but he couldn't tell if it came from Lily or Tye. They were so close—so excruciatingly close—to success. They couldn't lose them now.

The helicopter surged forward, gaining elevation as they went. Pete abandoned the winch, and he and Malcolm peered down into the mass of gray. The cable began to angle backward as Scott and Lily were dragged sideways through the smoke, two marionettes on the end of a fragile string.

The helicopter picked up speed, but the smoke was still so thick that nothing was visible. They needed to get Scott and Lily to fresh air.

At last, the helicopter broke free of the clinging smoke. Sunshine, patches of blue sky, clear air. Malcolm breathed in deeply—cool fresh air that didn't scald his throat—and his chest loosened. Seconds later, the distant end of the cable also left the smoke bank. "There they are!"

Scott and Lily were being pulled behind them like water skiers skirting the wake of a motorboat. The two hung face-to-face, their arms wrapped tightly around each other. Tye was barely visible, a bit of fur squashed between them. Lily had buried her eyes in her father's shoulder, probably too scared to even try to look, and Scott stared only at the helicopter, as if actively avoiding any view of the distant rocky ground.

"Get us up there!" Scott yelled a complete sentence without a cough. At least that was an improvement. A spate of profanity followed. He was definitely getting more air.

"The winch is fried," Malcolm said. "We're going to land. Get you inside."

"Land? Are you crazy?"

"Going down now," Lou announced.

The helicopter slowed and lost altitude. The cable, instead of dragging Scott and Lily behind them, returned to vertical.

Below them, a stretch of dirt road, away from the fire. Enough open space for the chopper.

"Lily, we're going to land." Scott's voice came through the headphones shrill and pinched, and Malcolm wished there was something he could do to help. "Wrap your legs around me. Hold on tight."

"No. No. No." Lily sounded completely freaked-out.

"It will be fine," Scott said. "They do this all the time."

Not quite. The only time Malcolm could recall seeing anything like this was in a James Bond movie. With a professional stuntman. And this was no movie.

Without the smoke in the way, he could see Scott clearly. He had clamped both arms even more tightly around Lily. With her legs wrapped around his waist, he would take the brunt of the landing impact. Very sensible. Now they needed to get them down without any damage.

The helicopter sank lower. Lower still. The road inched closer. Tire tracks became visible, then rocks, then pebbles. Scott and Lily were five feet off the ground. Three feet. One. Scott's knees hardly flexed when his feet hit, the impact less violent than if he'd stepped off a chair.

"Beautiful job, Lou. Beautiful." Malcolm said. If Scott had any sense, he should fall to his knees in thanks for her skill.

"Made it." Relief was audible in Scott's voice. "Lily, you okay? Let me get you unhooked."

Lily wasn't moving, still clinging to her father, and Scott fumbled with the cable, trying to detach it. They were standing in the center of the only possible landing site. Pete hung out of the side door of the helicopter and yelled. "Unhook and get out of the way."

The chopper dropped even lower, and yards of cable coiled on the ground. The hook end finally fell free of the two harnesses.

"This way." Scott gave Lily a shake, grabbed her by the arm, and half led, half dragged her off to one side. He'd lost a shoe somewhere along the line, and he limped heavily across the rocks. The helicopter settled to the ground behind them, kicking up a massive cloud of dust and dirt.

"Come on." Pete began pulling the cable in hand over hand, waving them in.

"Almost there," Scott said to Lily. He boosted her into the cargo hold, and Pete slammed the door closed behind them.

"Oh my god." Scott reached out to touch the vibrating wall of the helicopter as if he couldn't quite believe it was real. "Oh my god. We made it. No pond. No fire. No smoke." He wrapped Lily in an enormous hug, then turned to Malcolm and Pete. "Thank you. Thank you so much. I thought we were done for."

"All set?" Lou called.

"Head for the nearest hospital." Malcolm settled back beside Nirav and Kat, a sharp spasm in his arm reminding him of its damage.

The helicopter sped over the landscape, and Lou issued terse details over the radio—*smoke inhalation . . . fractured arm . . . emergency.*

Emergency was the right word. Injured people and dogs filled every square foot of open space in the cargo hold, making it look like a poorly equipped field hospital.

"Twenty minutes to Mission," Pete said.

Twenty minutes. With these three in such bad shape, twenty minutes sounded like eternity.

Lily sagged against Scott's side. Dirt layered her face, dried pond scum stiffened her clothes, and soot sludged her orange hair into a knotted tangle. Cuts and scratches and bruises covered every inch of exposed skin. She coughed steadily and took short quick breaths, even though the air in the helicopter had cleared and the air conditioning was making headway on the heat.

Scott unfastened Lily's harness, unweaving its straps from the puppy's. Tye wiggled out of Lily's arms as soon as he realized he was free. He crouched unsteadily on the vibrating floor and lifted his head to sniff the air. Blood dripped from the raw wound encircling his neck, but he stumbled forward in a straight path, directly toward Nirav.

Nirav lay still, apparently oblivious to everything around him, but when the puppy crawled beside him and buried its nose against his side, he let go of the Labrador and wrapped his arm around the little dog.

Kat lay curled on the deck. She hadn't even lifted her head to look when Scott and Lily arrived, her eyes closed and her body slack. She took two shallow breaths close together, followed by an endless pause that had Malcolm mentally rehearsing his CPR, but then her chest finally gulped another lungful of air.

Lily tried several times to say something, but her weak voice couldn't fight the engine noise.

"Don't try to talk." Scott put his arm around her. "Pete, we need oxygen."

Pete gave Lily a worried glance but shook his head. "Sorry, no oxygen—we're not equipped for major medical." He rummaged through his supply duffle, pulling out water bottles and handing them around. "Drink slowly," he advised.

Pete shifted forward and peered at a raw oozing burn that covered the palm of Kat's right hand and extended up along her wrist.

"Looks like she must have grabbed hold of something actively burning," he said. "Wish we could do something, but these injuries need more than a slapped-on bandage."

Malcolm shifted forward to give him more room, and for the first time, he saw the soles of Kat's bare feet. Even through a layer of drying mud, he could tell they were riddled with deep cuts. One of her big toes stuck out to the side at an unnatural angle, swollen and sickly black.

When he looked away, he met Scott's eyes.

"She did an unbelievable job," Malcolm said.

Scott nodded. "Down there. In that pond. I can't even tell you how awful it was. She walked out on feet like that to save two kids who aren't even hers. Not to mention bringing along two idiot dogs."

Malcolm glanced at Juni and Tye. "Lou, radio ahead and ask for transport to take these dogs to a vet. I'll cover costs." He shrugged at Scott. "After all she's done to get these dogs out, it's the least I can do."

Pete scrambled over the tangle of bodies and wedged himself into the copilot seat. The engine roared on.

"Lou, are you going to get in trouble for turning your radio off?" Malcolm asked.

The pilot's chuckle came through clearly. "Turn my radio off? I think you're mistaken. Two trips out. Seven people rescued. That's not the track record of a crew that would screw around with a radio."

Malcolm let a micro-smile escape. "I stand corrected." He glanced at Scott. "A shame that satellite phone fell out in the turbulence."

"Nothing we could have done," Scott said with a genuine grin. "A real shame."

Endless minutes later, Lou requested landing instructions from the hospital, and Malcolm looked out the window. They were hovering over a sprawling complex of buildings with a landing area on one roof. A cluster of people wearing blue scrubs and white coats stood beside a line of wheeled gurneys at the edge of the marked landing zone. They turned their backs and shielded their eyes from the chopper's backwash.

"I hope everything turns out all right," Lou said.

"I can't thank you and Pete enough." As far as Malcolm was concerned, they both deserved medals. "My office will transfer funds." With a spectacular bonus added in.

Lou brought the helicopter down in a gentle landing, then turned around in her chair and surveyed her grubby passengers. "All in the job description." Even though her voice had been business-as-usual, her face struggled to stay composed.

"More exciting than hauling executives on business junkets," Pete said. He unlocked the cargo door and clapped Scott on the shoulder, which sent him teetering off-balance. "We'll wait here for the dog transport."

Someone outside flung the door open with a bang, and a half dozen medical people leaned in to survey the mess. The man in front—close-cropped beard, bushy eyebrows, a stethoscope around his neck—assessed the crush of bodies. His inspection passed quickly over Scott and Lily, paused at Nirav, who watched the activity through half-open eyes, and lingered longest on Kat, who hadn't stirred.

"The woman. How long was she trapped in the fire, breathing smoke?" His New Jersey accent clipped every word short.

"Hours," Malcolm said. "The two children the same."

The team moved fast, helping Scott and Lily out first, who were closest to the door and who at least were sitting up. A nurse eased Lily onto one of the rolling stretchers, slipped an oxygen mask over her face, and pressed a stethoscope to her chest. One of the waiting men took hold of Lily's stretcher, and the nurse gave cryptic instructions. They whisked away with Scott close behind.

Kat was next, and three attendants carefully eased her onto the next stretcher in line. The same routine—a quick check and an oxygen mask—before they jogged toward the elevators at the far end of the roof.

"Now the boy," New Jersey said.

"Nirav, we're at the hospital." Malcolm could at least talk to him now that the helicopter engines were silent, but Nirav didn't seem to hear. "Tye needs to stay here." Malcolm eased the puppy out of Nirav's grasp and placed him in Pete's arms. Eager hands lifted Nirav onto the remaining stretcher, and Malcolm scrambled out behind him. One of the remaining nurses started Nirav on oxygen, her movements fast and urgent, and they started off.

For the first time that day, Malcolm wasn't responsible for anything that was happening, and the rigid control he'd maintained since he'd awoken to smoke crumbled as he walked at Nirav's side and they took their turn in the elevator.

A new, desperate fear swamped him. Nirav was safe now, wasn't he? He looked heartbreakingly small and helpless in the midst of all this bustle. Malcolm held his hand, but Nirav didn't hold back, his fingers slack. His eyes were open, but they had sunk deep into his skull, and he still didn't seem to be taking in anything that was going on.

The elevator whisked them down to a cavernous white room with desks and monitors in the middle and curtained-off cubicles along the edges. One with partially open curtains held Trip, lying there with his leg propped on pillows and multiple fluid bags hanging above him. The attendant rolled Nirav into an empty cubicle a few spaces down the row and gestured Malcolm toward a chair crammed next to the bed.

With that, the medical whirlwind began. Oxygen, blood draws, IV lines. Heart monitors, chest X-rays. Multiple people wielding stethoscopes, thermometers, blood pressure cuffs, and those gadgets for looking at eyes.

"You need to get that arm looked at."

Half a dozen people said it as they bustled in and out, but Malcolm shook his head every time. "Not until I know more about my son." The throbbing pain from his arm was background noise compared to the agony of his worry.

This place had all the bells and whistles, but except for the high-tech, it wasn't all that different from a field hospital. Intense, hardworking people, moving fast, making choices. As a patient in the field, he had known he was in good hands. As a parent, he had more doubts. "It's okay, Nirav. I'm right here. It will all be okay." His son had to be all right. Simply had to.

* * *

Malcolm stepped out of the cubicle to stretch. It had been a challenging few hours. Tests. Medical history. Conversations with the doctors. Nirav's breathing continued to ease, and he'd fallen into a deep sleep. He lay cocooned in warm blankets with the steady reassuring beep of the heart monitor serving as an unlikely lullaby.

Scott stood at the nurse's station, hanging up the phone, and Malcolm walked over to him.

"How's Lily?"

Scott made an I'm-not-quite-sure face. He still wore stiff, mud-caked pants, but someone had given him a clean scrub shirt, and a pair of hospital socks had replaced his one-shoe-on-one-shoe-off tilt. It looked like he'd doused his head in a bathroom sink, but there were still traces of muck in his hair. "Sleeping. They say she's as good as can be expected, but then the next minute they start talking about pneumonia and hypoxia and all kinds of awful-sounding shit. They're even talking about parasites from drinking the pond water. Did they tell you it would be two or three days before they know whether complications are going to set in?"

"Yes. Same thing for Nirav. All of it." Well, not exactly the same. Nirav's chest X-rays had shown significant scar tissue in his lungs, probably a result of exposure to chemicals in the train accident fire when he was younger. The doctors were ultra-cautious in everything they said.

Two or three days before Nirav would be out of danger. Two or three days of waiting and watching and worrying. Not fair. Rescuing Nirav was supposed to be the win. Malcolm hadn't realized fatherhood could tear into his soul this way. He wasn't sure he could face it.

Scott ran his hand through his hair. "I don't know what I'm going to tell Jennifer. I just tried to call. Ended up leaving a message, telling her to call me here. My cell phone was in my pocket when I went down to the pond. It's trashed."

"You'll find the right words when she calls."

Scott snorted. "Right words? I never have the right words. It's why we got divorced." His voice dragged, sad and discouraged. His face looked tired and worried.

"Scott, you found them. You."

Scott's head came up, his attention focused.

"Kat worked a miracle, but if you hadn't found them in that pond . . ." Malcolm couldn't even think the rest of that sentence. He held out his good hand for an awkward left-handed handshake. "Thank you. Thank you for saving my son. If your ex gives you a hard time, you send her to me."

Scott seized his hand in a tight grip. "You were the one who knew what he was doing. I was scared shitless every minute." He turned Malcolm loose. "It took all three of us. Do you know how Kat's doing?"

"Apparently still unconscious. They're trying to find her daughter. The doctor wouldn't say anything more than that." Kat had come to these mountains believing her biggest challenge would be a decision about cancer treatment, and instead she had saved these children. Walked out through a fire. Done an incredible job. She'd done all that even knowing she herself might not have much of a future.

They both turned toward the cubicle where she lay, but all they could see was a steady parade of blue-scrub hospital people, hustling in and out.

She'd saved his son. It was a debt he'd never be able to repay.

CHAPTER THIRTY-ONE

It was a full seven days before Malcolm saw Kat again.

That week would forever remain a blur, a hospital circus staffed by a dizzying swirl of strangers, all focused solely on helping his son. Pediatrician, pulmonologist, parasitologist, radiologist, hospitalist. Nurse, physician assistant, respiratory therapist, nurse's aide, transport assistant. All dressed alike, all coming on shift or going off shift, far too many to keep straight. They were each incredibly kind, but they moved fast, logging in data, checking off checklists, hustling onward. Malcolm gave up trying to keep track and simply categorized them all as *them*.

In the early days, Nirav drifted in and out of consciousness. He looked like a shrunken doll, helpless and lost in the white expanse of his tall hospital bed, too frail for all the equipment that surrounded him. Malcolm held his hand. Talked of quiet nothings. Most of the time, he just sat and watched his son gasp his way through each ragged inhalation.

"I'm here, Nirav. I'm here." He would never take that for granted.

In the midst of it all, Malcolm had surgery that meticulously pinned the puzzle pieces of his shattered elbow back together. A sling and pain meds kept him functional, the discomfort inconsequential compared to his other worries.

Finally, around day three, Nirav turned the corner. The change was slow at first, but then visible progress came in leaps and bounds. His son was back, alert and talking, restless in the confines of the hospital room, eating everything in sight. The constricting band that had strangled Malcolm's heart eased with each bit of evidence that they were on a solid path.

"Papa, is Lily okay? Kat? The dogs?"

Malcolm offered what reassurance he could. Just hearing the word *Papa* again was an indescribable relief.

Still, nightmares haunted Nirav, and Malcolm, sleeping on the recliner in his son's room, woke with each restless cry. The dreams were a confused mix of events, sometimes involving his parents, sometimes Kat and Lily, all of them heartbreaking. In his nine short years, Nirav had experienced more crises than anyone deserved in a lifetime.

At random moments, Malcolm paced the hallways, searching out news.

Lily was recovering well, and Jennifer, Scott's blonde, energetic ex-wife, who had swept in the day of the fire, kept the nursing staff on their toes. Sara, pale and drawn, came down each day to share updates on Kat—three days in ICU on a respirator with all of them worried, then breathing on her own at last, a moment to celebrate. Daily messages from the vet clinic assured him that Tye was doing well. Juni was improving more slowly, with fractured ribs, a fractured scapula, and a long list of injuries he couldn't keep up with.

Even the weather cooperated. The long-overdue rain arrived two days after the rescue, a full-day deluge that finally killed the horrific fire.

Along with the fire's end came the grim news that firefighters had found human remains, identified as those of Kevin Harris. Interviews with the man's heartbroken parents were broadcast on the local news, forcing Malcolm to turn away from the newscast. *That could have been Nirav. That could have been me, grieving for a lost son.*

At last, after a full week, they reached the day Nirav had been talking about nonstop—a picnic where he could see Lily, Kat, and the dogs again before everyone dispersed in separate directions. If everything remained stable, Malcolm and Nirav would be able to leave the hospital in another few days, a target that couldn't arrive soon enough, as far as Malcolm was concerned. A normal life was long overdue.

The picnic was Jennifer's idea, planned for the shaded patio the hospital used for outdoor events. Nirav was too excited to sit still, so they headed out early, oxygen tank in tow. The day was clear, and drifts of clouds floated lazily across a sky laced with jet trails. The leaves of a giant magnolia tree rustled in the breeze, and the air smelled like new life, damp and green.

Scott, Jennifer, and Lily were unpacking food and drinks at a long picnic table, but Lily raced in their direction as soon as she saw Nirav. She looked thinner, but compared to Nirav's fragile recovery, she acted like a poster child for good health.

"Nirav!" She pulled him into a giant hug that left him grinning but a bit out of breath.

"I am being better here," he told her. "Today we see Juni and Tye." He said it with the air of imparting top-secret knowledge.

"I know. Mom said." She grasped the handle of Nirav's wheeled oxygen tank. "Come see. We've got lemonade and cupcakes." She led him toward the table, chatting nonstop. A cluster of bracelets jangled with every movement, the result of Scott's careful rescue of the trinkets. How fitting that they had ended up back on Lily's wrist, an emblem of triumph.

Malcolm greeted Jennifer, and when she left to fetch more paper plates from the car, Scott stopped helping and joined the other man to talk. Malcolm shook hands left-handed, his sling a constant aggravation. "Lily looks great. How's it all going?"

Scott looked at his daughter, and his face lit up, his pride obvious. "So far, so good. She's a little too quiet sometimes, sort of lost in her own head, but she's young. She'll be fine. Jen is already making noises about taking her back to St. Louis." Lily had rebounded the fastest of the three, no question.

"A shame—I know you'll miss her. Nirav's doing well, too." Malcolm's spirits lifted every time he spoke his son's name. "Another few days and we'll be ready to head for DC."

"I'm glad he's recovering." Scott's voice was sincere, and he gave Nirav an approving glance. A far cry from the judgmental attitude he had radiated that first day. He looked

Malcolm in the eye, his face more serious than usual. "Listen, I want to thank you. For everything. Without that helicopter, without you there, knowing what to do . . ."

"Forget it. Success took both of us." Malcolm felt himself reddening, the conversation awkward. He had always assessed people by their rank and their training, putting his trust in those whose backgrounds matched his own. He'd considered Scott deadweight—judging him in a superficial appraisal just as Scott had judged Nirav. He'd been wrong, totally wrong. Scott had stepped up and proved his worth.

"If you or Lily ever need anything, let me know. Anything. I mean it."

"Thanks. If I can ever return the favor, give a shout." Scott grabbed a napkin, scribbled down his home address and email, and handed it over. Malcolm folded the floppy scrap into his wallet. He would log the contact in; he would stay in touch. Scott grinned, obviously pleased that the offer was taken seriously.

Malcolm turned to check on Nirav and saw Kat walking slowly in their direction. White bandages masked her burned hand, and she moved a bit unsteadily, but she looked far better than he'd expected—no oxygen mask, no IV line, and her color was no longer the forbidding gray it had been in the helicopter. He hurried forward, and as he got closer, he realized that what he had thought were white socks were actually more bandages, swathing her feet.

Seeing her here, alive and recovering, loosened a few strands of guilt. In that moment in the helicopter when he'd thought they'd lost her, he'd told Scott to take care of the children first. The right choice, but one that had plagued him.

"Kat, how wonderful. How are you?" He reached toward her, offering a stabilizing arm.

"Much better, thank you." She took his arm with a smile that reminded him of their conversations before the fire had thrown their lives into chaos. "Sara will probably fuss because I didn't bring that damn walker with me. She went out to pick up the dogs, so I seized the chance to escape my room." She caught sight of Nirav and Lily and gasped. The blood drained out of her face, and she leaned more heavily on Malcolm. "Oh my god. They're really here." She hastily wiped at her eyes with a tissue she pulled from her pocket.

The children saw her at the same moment and came racing over.

"Kat!" Lily hugged her with a fierceness that threatened to rock her off-balance, but Kat held her close. Malcolm quickly pulled up one of the metal patio chairs, and Kat sat, her unbandaged hand holding tight to Lily's.

Nirav hung back shyly, and she looked his way. "Nirav, I'm so glad that—" Kat's voice choked off, and Nirav launched himself forward. She held him tight, her face buried in his hair, and Malcolm thought of the hours she had held him in the pond. "You're both okay." She whispered it so quietly, Malcolm almost missed it. "I keep picturing you still back there in the fire. I had to see you myself to believe."

Nirav clung to her, the only time Malcolm had ever seen him trust someone else so completely, and a wave of gratitude threatened to break through the unruffled veneer he worked hard to maintain.

Kat had saved his son, and she genuinely cared for him. Throughout the stories Nirav had told him, what had come through most strongly was the absolute faith he had in her. *She said we are okay. She said Papa is coming. I am very scared. On the rocks. In the water. In the fire. She is keeping me safe.*

After several long moments, Nirav straightened.

"I'm glad you're feeling better," Kat said. She gave Malcolm a worried glance, and he knew she'd heard the raspy sound of Nirav's breathing. His oxygen mask still dwarfed his too-thin face, and he coughed too often for comfort.

"He's much better. Really." Malcolm hoped that reassured her. He couldn't tamp down his own concerns, despite the doctors' optimism. They predicted a full recovery; it would just take time.

"I am being better here." Nirav gave Kat an incandescent grin. Malcolm hadn't seen one of those since the fire. "Papa says I am seeing Tye and Juni today. In not even one hour. One." He held up one finger.

"Juni is here because of you, Nirav," Kat said. "I'm sorry we lost your bowl."

Nirav's smile didn't waver. "Juni is better than bowl."

Kat laughed. "Yes indeed. Sara is picking the dogs up now. They're doing so much better; they get to leave this afternoon when I do."

"You're heading home?" Malcolm asked.

"Not quite," Kat said. "The only reason they agreed to discharge me now was because I'll stay with Sara for at least another week and come back here to the hospital for outpatient visits. I'd rather go back to my own house, but this will work out well. It will give Sara and me more time together. Time I was afraid we wouldn't have."

Right on cue, Sara arrived with the dogs, and chaos ensued. Juni and Tye dragged her forward on their leashes, Tye bouncing and Juni hobbling, each tail wagging in a wild blur.

The puppy looked great—his neck neatly bandaged again—and he pulled against his harness with plenty of energy. The Lab looked more borderline. She had one front leg strapped to her chest, and a patchwork of shaved areas on her legs, chest, and neck showed dark bruises and uneven lines of sutures that looked straight out of a bad horror flick. Despite it all, she looked a hell of a lot better than she had in the helicopter, and she limped fast in lurching, three-legged steps. Malcolm was relieved she'd pulled through. Kat would have been devastated if Juni hadn't survived.

"Tye!" Nirav plopped down on the pavement and held out his arms, and the puppy galloped toward him, dragging a laughing Sara behind him. Juni came to sit beside Kat, who gave her a gentle pat, avoiding all the injuries.

Sara glanced their way. "Mom! No walker?"

Kat tried to look innocent, but she gave Malcolm a told-you-I'd-get-in-trouble glance. Sara shook her head in mock dismay. Kat was going to have a hard time getting away with such things when she stayed with her daughter.

Jennifer had been waiting on the fringes, but once initial greetings were over and Sara, the dogs, and the children moved to the far side of the patio, she came over to Kat and knelt in front of her. She took Kat's hand and held her gaze. "You saved my daughter. You will be in my heart and in my prayers every day for the rest of my life."

Kat's face crumpled. Tears streaked her cheeks as she took Jennifer in her arms, and Malcolm had to turn away for a moment. Jennifer's simple words tore into his heart like shrapnel. They tossed him back to that mountain road, blocked by flames, prevented from reaching his son. Back to that helicopter, imagining Nirav dead in the forest below him. Back to that fiery pond, convinced their search would fail. Jennifer had found the words he hadn't been able to find himself.

When he turned back to the group, the emotional scene had dissolved. Jennifer, Scott, and Sara spoke on one side, and Kat watched Lily and Nirav roll tennis balls to the excited dogs. Dark circles shadowed her eyes, and her face was tense, drawn tight. A garbage truck backing up in the street gave a strident series of beeps, and she jumped. More of a reaction than the sound deserved.

He pulled up a chair beside her. "I hope we aren't tiring you out too much."

"Oh no. I'm glad I could see everyone. If I could get some real sleep, I'd be fine."

"Nightmares?"

"Yes."

"Nirav, too." The flames had been doused, but the fire's impact lingered. "Are you having any flashbacks during the day?"

Kat looked at him, startled. "How did you know? My brain seems hardwired for panic. I'll be thinking about something else entirely, and then the littlest thing launches me back there. The other day, I heard flames crackling at my bedside, and I was halfway to the door before I realized it was just a nurse opening a package of bandages." She looked down at her hands. "Night is the worst. I see Nirav falling off that rockslide. I watch Juni take a last breath. Lily slips unconscious into the water. I try to save them, but I fail no matter what I do." Her voice shook, and she swallowed with a visible effort. "Those failures feel more real than what I know is the truth."

Malcolm reached out, took her hand, and gave it a reassuring squeeze. She was carrying too much, no question, and she had no background to help her deal with it. "That kind of trauma rearranges your brain. Nirav has told me quite a bit about what happened, and his story included some pretty scary stuff. But he has a child's perspective, without the responsibility you carried. He had faith you would take care of him. You didn't have that luxury."

Kat's eyes widened. "How do you understand all this?" The words came out sounding close to a sob, and it took her a minute to pull herself under control. "I was so frightened. Of the fire, of course, but mainly I was terrified of making mistakes."

"You were afraid that if the children died, it would be your fault."

She nodded.

"And even though I can look you in the eye and tell you that you did an amazing job, and that the children are only alive because of what you did, you don't really believe me."

That got another nod. A slow one this time. "Sounds like you know an awful lot about all of this."

It was Malcolm's turn to stare at his hands. If he gave her a superficial, dodge-the-issue response, she would accept it. Usually, that was exactly what he would have done. But this wasn't a random stranger, this was . . . Malcolm straightened, startled. *Family.*

He examined the word. It was the only one that fit. The events of the past few days had intertwined their lives—his, hers, and Nirav's—in a way that was too intense to shrug off casually. He needed to honor that and tell her the truth.

Memories of blood, pain, and desperation flooded in, fierce and immediate. He took a deep breath. "I know it from personal experience. It's a bit of a long story."

"I'm not going anywhere. Tell me."

He nodded, looked off to one side, and tried to pull himself together to sort out a cogent narrative. "I run a security business, working mainly with companies who do business in the Middle East and Asia." He waited for her nod of understanding. "Before that, I was in the Army, enlisted straight out of college. I wanted to see the world, and I ended up making the service a career, got accepted into Special Forces. That put me all over the world, wherever we were needed."

He paused again. "After nine-eleven, my unit got very busy overseas. We were high up in isolated mountains when we got caught in a mix of mortar fire and hand-to-hand fighting. I got cut up pretty bad"—he gestured to his face, and to the right side of his chest, where his shirt hid a complicated patchwork of scars—"and I ended up coming back cross-country with two others who were even worse off than I was."

He chose each word carefully, wanting to let Kat know he genuinely understood what she was wrestling with but not wanting to describe the full horror. This was a story he never shared. Lewis and McKenzie. Blood-soaked. Battered. Both so young. Lewis with a wife and child at home. It had been Malcolm's responsibility to lead them to safety, and the weight of that had been crushing.

"We had no supplies. I packed my wounds with snow every hour to stop the bleeding and kill the pain. More than once, I thought we weren't going to make it. The only thing that kept me going was knowing that if I curled up and quit, the others were done for."

He gave Kat a sharp glance, and she turned away, her emotions twisting her mouth. He knew what she was remembering. Those moments when it seemed no open path existed. The deep desire to stop struggling and simply give in, find rest and peace. The temptation of the easier path. He knew, because he'd been there. This, too, bound them together.

"Long story short, we made it. Eventually. All of us." The details of those three gruesome days struggling back to safety were something he never planned on revealing to anyone.

Kat clenched her hands. "All of us." She didn't seem to realize she'd spoken out loud.

"Those days in the mountains were a turning point for me," Malcolm said. "There was my life before, and my life after. The person I was before, and the person I am now. It was a change for the better. I no longer take my life so much for granted, and I realize now what I'm capable of accomplishing when I have to. It's hard to put into words, but I think you understand." Again, he paused and looked at Kat.

She found her voice. "I'm still trying to sort it out, but when I think back to what happened, what I did, it feels like a stranger took over."

"Exactly. As if a different person had been hiding inside, waiting for the right moment to put in an appearance. Eventually, I decided I needed to get acquainted with the stranger I'd become." Malcolm gave Kat's hand a reassuring squeeze. The stranger he'd become. Like dropping a handful of pebbles into a calm lake—the ripples had steadily expanded, ultimately giving him the confidence to strike out on his own. Start his own business. Adopt his son.

Not an easy process, this business of sorting oneself out, but Kat had the grit to do it. Of that he was confident. Now, she just had to convince herself.

CHAPTER THIRTY-TWO

THURSDAY, A WEEK AFTER THE FIRE, 3:00 PM

Kat sat back in her chair and enjoyed the bustle that surrounded her, happy to be outdoors. Much of her past week in the hospital had been lost in a drug-clouded haze, and it felt surreal to be here, safe and surrounded by people she cared for fiercely instead of fleeing for her life. Even the presence of the dogs, patched up as they were, brought her to the edge of tears. She wouldn't have thought she could grow so attached to two stupid dogs.

Malcolm's story gave her plenty to think about. He was right—being trapped in the fire had changed her profoundly, but she wasn't sure of the implications. It felt no easier to face the future and decide on the right path.

Malcolm had shifted over to the picnic table, where he was having an animated conversation with Sara, a reminder of the fact that they'd had a week to get to know each other while Kat was out of the loop. As soon as she learned of Kat's injuries, Sara had abandoned her competition in Florida and driven all night to get to the hospital. Ever since, she'd been faithfully at Kat's side, chatting with the nurses, calling in meal orders, fetching ice water, helping Kat to the bathroom. Sustaining her. Not arguing. Not questioning the treatment decision that still hovered between them.

Kat had spent days like that at her own mother's bedside, feeding her ice chips, swabbing her mouth when she could no longer swallow, helping her shift position when weakness overwhelmed her. All things she had wanted to spare her daughter. But for the first time, Kat also remembered how desperately she had wanted to hang on to her mother for one more week, one more day, one more hour. How they both treasured every moment of those last few months together, each day valued even more because they knew their time had a limit. Perhaps Sara felt the same. The possibility made it easier to understand Sara's side of things, and a surge of love for her daughter left her smiling.

Scott came over and sat in the chair beside Kat, and she set aside her thoughts. "Can I get you anything to eat? Jen brought enough food for an army."

"No thanks. It feels good to just sit here awhile. I'm still trying to come to grips with everything."

Scott nodded. He looked subtly different than he had before the fire—more certain in his movements, more confident in his attitude. He no longer seemed so boyish. Perhaps he, too, had discovered a side of himself he hadn't expected. They sat for a moment in peaceful silence.

Lily left the dogs, and she stood off to one side, staring into the distance. As Kat watched, her shoulders slumped forward, her chin trembled, and her smile wavered. Here, in the middle of a picnic, surrounded by friends and family, she looked frightened.

Scott must have noticed as well, because he called Lily over. When she got closer, lines of tension were obvious around her eyes. Her restless hands jerked occasionally with no purpose.

"You all right, kiddo?" Scott asked.

"I'm great, Dad. Those cupcakes are amazing, aren't they?"

It was a blatant evasion, and Kat's heart went out to her. They were all struggling, one way or another. She glanced at Scott and was relieved to see he wasn't buying it. She stayed silent, hoping this new version of Scott would say something.

"You didn't look fine," he said. "Standing over there, you seemed . . . scared."

Lily bit her lower lip and looked away. "I'm fine. Really. Mom says I need to be grateful and move on. Think about school. And friends. And fun stuff." She said it as if it were a dreaded homework assignment.

Scott snorted. "Well, if you figure out how to stop thinking about that fire, let me know the trick."

Yes. Kat was tempted to reach over and hug him. Lily needed more than a simple admonishment to think about something else.

Lily whirled to face him, her eyes startled. "You think about it, too?"

"Of course I do. It's scary stuff." He squared his shoulders. "Look, if you ever want to talk about it, let me know. Your mom wasn't there. I was. We can set up some Skype calls. Whatever you want."

Lily chewed on her lip again. "Yeah. Maybe." She scuffed the toe of one of her new tennis shoes along the concrete patio.

Sara used to do that when she had something to say but couldn't figure out how. It would be tragic if Lily and Scott didn't connect on this.

"If there's something you think might help," Kat said, "you should tell your father."

Lily looked interested, but she shook her head.

Kat tried again. "Lily, you were the one who figured out how to help Nirav on that rockslide. You were the one who got us to the pond. If you can do that, you can do anything you set your mind to."

Scott gave Kat a grateful glance, and after a moment, Lily took a deep breath. "Dad, you still have two weeks of vacation left, right?"

"Yeah. Claude is trying to talk me into starting back sooner, but I'm holding out."

"I don't want to go back home with Mom. I want to stay with you for the rest of our summer trip."

This was definitely not the same girl who had whined about her father's plans on that first walk. Scott made an obvious effort to act nonchalant, but his delight bubbled to the surface, and Kat found herself smiling along with him. "Really? That would be great."

"I guess maybe we can hike some more if you really want to, but not around here."

Scott's eyebrows hit an all-time high. Lily, trying to suggest something she knew would make her father happy? Amazing.

But he shook his head. "No, I don't think hiking's a good idea. You need to take it easy."

Lily had mentioned something in that first conversation with Kat. "What about New York City?" Kat asked.

Lily's eyes lit up. "Really? Could we?"

Scott at once rose to his feet. "Sounds like a plan. We can go tell your Mom."

Lily seemed about to agree, but then she shook her head. "That's okay. I'll tell her." She walked away, head high.

"*Though she be but little, she is fierce.*" Kat spoke the quote out loud without thinking. "Sorry, Shakespeare takes over sometimes." She must truly be getting back to normal.

Scott laughed. "Fierce is right. I'm so grateful we didn't lose her." He gave her a pointed look. "Thank you."

Kat turned away. First Jennifer, now Scott. They didn't understand. She was no heroine—she'd faked it every step of the way. Malcolm was right. Even though everyone kept telling her she had done an amazing job, it just didn't mesh with the person she believed she was. It was easy to give Lily a pep talk, tell her she could do anything. It was much harder to convince herself.

Malcolm came over to join them, his cell phone in his hand. "The landlord just called me. Amazingly enough, the house Nirav and I were in made it through the fire. She wants me to go up this afternoon and clear out our things so they can start making repairs. Nirav will be pleased—everything he brought to the States is in that cottage."

Scott looked momentarily disgruntled, but then he glanced toward Lily and his face cleared. "I got a call this morning, too, but not such good news—our stuff didn't make it. Oh well. I'm sure Lily will enjoy a shopping spree in New York to replace everything."

Kat stared at Malcolm for a long moment. Her cottage had been destroyed, and her stomach churned every time she thought about the fire, but the idea of going back up the mountain—seeing the damage for herself—was nonetheless tempting. Maybe going back would let her leave the horrors of the fire behind her. "Your car is still up there, isn't it?"

Malcolm nodded. "Sounds like it may be salvageable if I get it towed in."

"Why don't you let Sara and me give you a ride up? They're going to walk me through all of my discharge stuff right after we're done here, so we'll be heading out anyway."

Malcolm's brow furrowed. "Are you sure? It would take you out of your way, and it sounds like there's not much left up there."

"To be honest, I'm not sure at all." In the fire, her choices had been forced, with no time for inner debate. As hard as those decisions had been, they still seemed easier than the decisions she still needed to face.

She asked herself what Jim would have said about such a foolish trip, but for the first time, the question felt irrelevant. She had come back to the cottage they'd shared to recapture the sense of comfort she'd felt with him, but instead, she'd proven she had to move forward on her own. Jim had left the stage.

Malcolm waited patiently while she sorted herself out.

"Yes," Kat finally said, "I think I want to go see it myself. It wasn't until I saw the children that I truly believed they were safe. Maybe seeing the mountain again will help me believe all this is over."

"In that case, a ride up would be great. I'll arrange for one of the volunteers to keep an eye on Nirav while I'm gone."

The rest of the picnic flew past, including tearful good-byes to Scott, Lily, and Jennifer, with promises to stay in touch. They all might wish to forget the fire, but that didn't change the fact that their connections to each other remained.

* * *

A few short hours later, Kat waited in Sara's 4Runner while Sara walked the dogs and Malcolm got Nirav settled. Kat had been officially discharged, and countless instructions cluttered her head—apply this, inhale that, swallow the rest. Yet another disheartening reminder of the ways medical care could take over her life.

A tangle of hospital bills lay ahead, and she needed to figure out how to repay Malcolm for the vet bills. The list of everything she had to replace was long and intimidating. Cell phone, driver's license, credit cards, wallet. Clothing. Books. A car. That's what she should be working on, all those practical details, instead of offering to take Malcolm on a trip into the fire zone that was likely to be distressing.

Sara returned and helped the dogs into the far back of the car, both worn out after all the excitement.

"I'm not very happy about this." Sara plunked down in the driver's seat, leaving the door open. "You're already having nightmares; why make things worse?"

"I'll be fine. Honest."

Sara snorted, her disbelief obvious, but she pulled out her phone and started checking email.

This week in the hospital had been a much-needed break in their argument. They'd talked, but only about innocuous things—Sara's job, her fostered animals, her vacation plans. Kat drank in the details of her daughter's life with an insatiable thirst, wanting to absorb it all while she could.

The urgent, unspoken messages she'd considered in the pond flared brightly. *Tell Sara I love her. Tell her I'm proud of her. Tell her how precious she is to me.* She needed to say it all out loud, but she hesitated, cautious about the risk of undermining a calm that still felt so fragile.

She was relieved when Malcolm arrived and her chance for serious conversation with Sara passed. "Everyone all set?"

"Ready," Sara said.

Malcolm settled into the back seat, and Kat twisted around so she could talk to him while Sara drove. A bright blue sling still immobilized his right arm, and dark bruises were visible around the edges of its fabric. He moved a bit slowly, but otherwise he looked unchanged by recent events, as calm and composed as ever. It was a great piece of acting, but she'd seen the worried way he watched Nirav.

The scar that so defined him no longer disturbed her—she couldn't now imagine him without it. She dreaded the moment she would have to say good-bye to him. He and Nirav meant more to her than she would have believed possible only a few days ago.

"I'm not sure what we're going to find up on the mountain," he said.

Sara frowned, but she merely gave Kat a glance and said, "If you find it upsetting, Mom, speak up."

No way could this drive be more upsetting than the memories Kat already carried. "It's weird—despite it all, I miss that raggedy little cottage. The quiet. The birds in the morning. The view all the way to the horizon, with no buildings anywhere in sight. Hard to believe it's all gone."

Malcolm nodded. "There's something special about an unobstructed horizon, isn't there? The polar explorers discovered they could even see things beyond the horizon—something about the frigid temperatures causes images to reflect into the sky from enormous distances. Like seeing into the future."

"That sounds like magic." Kat liked the idea of seeing beyond expectations. The sky functioning like a giant crystal ball. "Speaking of the future . . . does this new house you're moving into have room for a dog? Tye needs a home, and he and Nirav were inseparable at the picnic."

Malcolm tipped his head to one side. "We'll have plenty of room, and Nirav would be happier than I can even find words for." He paused. "You know, Nirav and I will be living in Falls Church, near my office."

"Falls Church? That's right around the corner from me."

"That hadn't escaped me. Kat, listen, regardless of what you end up deciding—treatment, no treatment, whatever—I want you to stay a part of my life and Nirav's. By saving Nirav, you saved us both. We can help you in return. I know we can."

Sara glanced in the rearview mirror and gave Malcolm an appreciative smile. Kat turned away, afraid she was going to break down and start crying. She'd been dreading a good-bye, and her relief at not yet having to navigate that moment took her by surprise. Malcolm's steady support had already been a lifeline. It had been the memory of his words that had given her strength and tipped the balance for her in that moment of decision in the pond. "That would be wonderful. Thank you."

"Good. One condition, however. You have to stop thanking me."

Kat laughed. It felt like it had been a long time since she'd laughed. "Okay, it's a deal. And I'm glad you'll take Tye. I've decided to keep Juni with me instead of handing her back to Sara."

No way could she give Juni up now. A nagging inner voice pointed out that this was a commitment she couldn't follow through with indefinitely, but she shoved the reminder aside. Sara had promised to step in when the time came. Kat reached over and squeezed Sara's hand.

The road got steeper, and at first, everything appeared unchanged—green trees, blooming wildflowers, unruly grass. The rains had vanquished the drought. Water flowed through every gully, now that they no longer needed it.

Robins and sparrows flitted by, and a squirrel dove into the underbrush as they approached. Small drifts of ash edged the road where the rain had washed past, the only visible evidence of the fire. But ahead on the mountainside was an unsettling contrast, a black swath of burned land at the higher elevations, a path wiped clean.

They reached the abandoned pastureland. "Over there is where we found Tye," Kat said to Sara. A week and a half ago? It felt like years.

They turned onto the gravel road, and Sara slowed to a crawl, dodging deep ruts left behind by heavy firefighting equipment. At the first bend, Kat caught her breath, her dismay taking her by surprise. The two sides of the road looked like they belonged on different planets. On the right, Malcolm's cottage stood intact—coated with ash and streaked with soot, but otherwise solid. His car stood in front, thickly shrouded in gray. On the left, where Scott and Lily's pretty cottage had been, there was only a blackened expanse, and the sight made Kat's skin crawl. A bulldozed trench of churned dirt paralleled the road in front of Scott's house, a firebreak that had saved one house but given up the other.

She reached for Sara's hand. Houses weren't supposed to simply disappear. The world needed to be more stable than that.

"Oh my god," Sara said. "It's all just . . . gone." Her face was sheet-white. Kat reminded herself that of the three of them, Sara had known least what to expect.

"It's like Scott's cottage was never here." Kat could make out parts of the stone foundation beneath heaps of ash and cinders, and the remnant of what might have been a stove hulked farther in. Those were the only identifiable bits.

The contrast between destruction on one side and survival on the other was stark. Kat's choices in the fire had been equally black and white: life on one side, death on the other. It was a blunt reminder that her final decision about cancer treatment still loomed. Her throat tightened, and she had trouble swallowing. Sara had been right. Coming here was going to make her nightmares more vivid.

But this was her only chance to face it.

"Can we go farther up the road? Stop on the way back to pack your things, Malcolm?" Maybe the destruction was not so complete higher up. She hadn't grabbed even a single photograph out of the boxes she'd brought up for the scrapbook. There might be something salvageable.

Sara looked startled. "I'm not sure how far we'll get."

"I'm curious myself," Malcolm said. "Worth a try."

Sara nodded and put the car in gear. They once again crept uphill. Both sides of the road had burned here, and it looked like a post-apocalyptic pen-and-ink drawing, all color erased along with all life. Charred tree trunks with jagged stubs of burned branches jutted from heaps of scorched debris, and a thick layer of powdery ash masked the ground. It looked nothing like the forest Kat had walked through.

She found it hard to breathe, the air clear but the smell of smoke and charred wood still seeping into the car. She grabbed her armrests as the road got worse, tossed back into that horrifying drive with the children down the abandoned road, her pulse racing.

The SUV struggled across the bridgeless gulley, their route roughly graded by the bulldozers that had passed during the firefight, and they zigzagged up the long series of switchbacks, dodging debris. Before Kat was ready, Sara stopped the car, her hands tightening on the wheel. She didn't say anything, and Malcolm, too, was silent. The stone foundation and heaps of burned rubble to their left said it all.

"Oh, no." Kat got out, the slam of the car door sending eerie echoes over the dead landscape. She walked around the front of the car, her sneakers kicking up puffs of ash with each step. The smell of stale smoke rose from every blackened surface, and a flicker of fear clawed a path inside her chest. She wrapped her arms around herself, suddenly ice-cold in the midst of the June heat. If she and the children had stayed here instead of fleeing . . .

Malcolm came and stood beside her as she turned to inspect the valley, the view she had once thought perfect for a postcard. Ash covered the stone bench where she'd first seen Malcolm and Nirav, and a thick layer of soot caked the rocky tumble below her. Everything beyond it was black and twisted. Dead. "I can't believe I was down there."

Those moments when she'd known death was close came rushing back, and she fought against rising panic. She concentrated on a single curling flake of ash, rocking gently in the breeze, and tried to anchor herself.

Malcolm touched her gently on the shoulder. "It's okay. You're safe. You're alive."

He was right. *Focus on now.*

They all moved uphill to stand beside the remnants of the house. Kat stepped into the heaped debris, heedless of her aching feet and blackening shoes, her eyes cast down, searching for anything recognizable.

Sara picked up a deformed chunk of metal and glass that might once have been a living room lamp and tossed it aside.

Where the kitchen had been, the porcelain sink had cracked into three great chunks. The refrigerator, its outer skin cracked and peeling, lay on its side, its door open, its plastic drawers melted into shapeless blobs.

Nothing of Kat's.

Everything she had brought for her month here was gone. Most of her losses were inconsequential, but the scrapbook boxes were irreplaceable. Photos, souvenirs, memories. Logically, she'd known everything had burned, but seeing the hopelessness of salvaging anything filled her with regret. She had envisioned this gift to Sara so clearly, passing on history like handing off a baton from one generation to the next. All she could give her daughter now was a heap of ashes. The stale smoke that coated her tongue tasted like failure.

"Sara."

Her daughter stopped picking through the rubble and straightened.

"I'm so sorry. There's something I've been afraid to tell you." Here, amid such destruction, she could no longer avoid serious topics. She had to tell her it was all gone.

Sara blanched and came to stand next to her. "What is it, Mom?" The strain in her voice made her sound like a stranger.

"I thought since I had four weeks here on my own, I would finally sort through those boxes of memorabilia I've saved all these years. I brought them to the cottage. All of them. Your baby pictures. Your schoolwork. Your father's high school football clippings. Things that belonged to Oma and Opa."

The magnitude of what had been lost pressed down on Kat's chest. That snapshot of Sara at the lake when she was three and found herself face-to-face with a frog. The second-place ribbon from Sara's fourth-grade spelling bee. The program from her high school graduation, the one with photos of all her classmates.

Kat wiped her eyes with the back of her hand. She'd lost so much more than just boxes of stuff. "I wanted to take it all with us when the children and I left, but there wasn't time. I'm so sorry. I didn't grab a single picture. It's all gone. All of it."

Sara looked at her for a long moment, utterly expressionless. "That's what you were afraid to tell me? That boxes of photos were burned?"

Kat nodded, confused. Sara seemed puzzled, not upset.

Before she could sort it out, Sara started laughing. "Mom, I thought you were going to tell me the doctors had told you something awful. Burned papers? That I can live with." She leaned forward and kissed her mother on the forehead, an astonishing gesture of affection that delighted Kat. "You don't get it, do you?"

Kat shook her head. The scrapbooks. The path she had planned to use to strengthen her connection to her daughter. Sara acted like she didn't even care.

Sara took Kat's undamaged hand in hers and gave it a reassuring squeeze. "The only thing I needed from the fire is you. You, Mom. I know we haven't been seeing eye to eye lately, but when I got that phone call, saying you were here in the hospital . . ." She broke off, tears spilling down her cheeks, the first time Kat had seen her cry since Jim's funeral. Kat reached for her, and they clung together for long minutes. This was the same closeness they'd shared for a moment the day Sara brought Juni to her, and this time, Kat could believe it would last.

A screech caused her to pull back and look toward the bedroom, where Malcolm was lifting a long piece of twisted metal out of the wreckage. Part of a bed frame. "Stop," Kat said. "The fire has taken it all. It doesn't matter."

He set aside the piece of frame and rejoined them. "Not much left, I'm afraid. As bad as a bomb site. I did find this, however." He held out his hand, a blackened object on his palm.

"What is it?"

He placed it in her hand, an odd lumpy shape. Sara gasped, but Kat had to stare at it for a long moment before she recognized what she held. The last thing she would ever have expected to see again—her pendant of petrified wood. "Malcolm! How in the world did you find it?" She'd lost count of the number of times she'd reached for it and been startled by its absence. Finding it felt like some sort of omen.

Soot covered the disk, and zigzags of silver crisscrossed both sides where the chain had melted onto its surface. But the pendant itself, fireproof stone, was intact.

"It was over there in what used to be the corner. Same area as a half dozen drawer handles."

"I left it on the dresser. Didn't grab it when I got dressed that morning." She gripped the pendant hard. *Stay tough* was the pendant's message. Well, she had done exactly that, even without the necklace to remind her.

The second meaning of her mother's gift was *don't believe in fairy tales*, but finding such a small and precious thing in the middle of all this destruction was pure magic. Perhaps faith in fairy tales wasn't always foolish.

Kat ran her thumb over the pendant the way she had hundreds of times in the past, but instead of gliding over the polished surface, her skin caught against lumps of melted chain. "Do you think a jeweler could get the clumps off?"

"If they melt the silver again, they can probably remove it," Sara said.

"But . . ." Malcolm's voice faded. "Do you really want it back the way it was?"

Yes, of course. Exactly like it used to be. Kat caught herself before she spoke the words out loud. *Exactly like it used to be*—but now, nothing was the same.

The pendant—changed but surviving. Malcolm—scarred but moving on despite it. The person she used to be. The stranger she was now.

This was the problem, the reason it was so difficult to know what to do. The fire had changed her. She turned toward the other two and tried to put her turmoil into words.

"Everyone tells me I saved two children. The nurses. The doctors. The story has spread." Her voice shook, and she rubbed the pendant again, hard, the raised barbs of silver piercingly sharp. "They say I'm a hero. Jennifer even thinks I deserve her prayers." She looked into Malcolm's calm eyes and Sara's puzzled ones, willing them to understand. "I remember every moment of that terrifying escape. But I'm having trouble believing it was really me who did all that."

Something fragile tore loose inside Kat's chest, as if her center of balance shifted. She had stood right here, on this spot, when she decided she owed it to the children to try and fight. Did she now owe it to herself? That moment of decision in the pond. Grabbing hold of the rope. She'd come to these mountains to resign herself to death, but in that moment in the pond, all she could think was *not yet, not yet.*

Images crowded in—Nirav clinging to the edge of the cliff, Lily hanging on to Tye in the leech-infested pond, Juni pinned under the fallen tree, but fighting anyway. None of them had given up. Unlike her nightmares, these memories were real, and they didn't end in tragedy. She had saved herself, saved the children, saved even the dogs. She had cheated fate.

"*The stars above us govern our conditions.*" The quote came, unbidden. It wasn't until she saw Malcolm shake his head in disagreement that she realized she had spoken out loud.

"The only line I memorized in high school is the opposite of yours. *It is not in the stars to hold our destiny, but in ourselves.*"

Kat tilted her head to look at him. "That implies I have the courage to write my own script."

"If you decide to keep fighting your cancer, it will be the woman who confronted that fire who's leading the charge. And I'll back you every step of the way, in whatever role you want and need. You're not facing this battle alone." In the look he gave her, Kat could see the staunch determination of the man who had led injured comrades out of frigid mountains. Someone she could rely on.

"Mom, it's what I've been saying all along." Sara's voice was shaking, but it carried all the love and commitment she'd shown during the past week in the hospital. "You can do this. Not for me. For yourself. Please."

Kat felt as if she stood onstage before an audience, struggling for the next line. She stared at the burned expanse. Gray on gray on black. Her eyes shifted, looking beyond the damaged mountainside. In the distance, the deep emerald green of untouched forest. White clouds embedded in a flawless sky.

Our destiny in ourselves. The long smooth line of the horizon beckoned, and with an unexpected sense of lightness, Kat saw an image of her future hovering there.

ACKNOWLEDGMENTS

No book is written in isolation, and that is particularly true of a debut novel. This story would not exist without the patient support of my amazing writing group, the Iron Clay Writers: Nancy Peacock, Agnieszka Stachura, Claire Hermann, and Barrie Trinkle. Dear friends, you've encouraged me through draft after draft. Chapter by chapter, your skill has ensured I didn't drift too far off course.

Heartfelt thanks go to those who've worked to transform my manuscript into an actual book. At Spencerhill Associates, Nalini Akolekar and Ali Herring. You believed in this story from the start, and your persistence in seeing it through to reality made me believe as well. At Crooked Lane Books, Chelsey Emmelhainz, Ashley Di Dio, and Jenny Chen. Chelsey's keen editorial eye made this story shine, and Ashley and Jenny helped fit all the pieces together.

Kathleen Furin, of Author Accelerator, helped ensure that Kat's emotional journey was firmly on the page. Tahra Seplowin's feedback pulled Malcolm forward into his proper place. Margie Lawson's voice lives always in my head, patiently insisting *you can do better.* Jessie Starr's feedback on an early draft shifted the whole tone of this book. Thank you all.

The Women's Fiction Writers Association has been an invaluable source of information, opportunities, and friendship over the years, and the North Carolina Writers' Network has provided workshops and valued connections to other local writers.

Thanks go to all the family, friends, and colleagues who've cheered my writing from the sidelines. Particular thanks go to Angie Morris, Amy Jones, Corny Motsinger, and Kimberly Hayden. Thirty years of firm friendship is a gift I do not take lightly.

For information on forest fires, I relied primarily on *Fire in the Forest*, by Peter A. Thomas and Robert S. McAlpine. Any mistakes that have made it into print are my own.

Last, but definitely not least, thanks go to my husband, George, and my sons, Austin, Daniel, and Carson. For decades, you have lived with someone who spends significant time creating fictional worlds. Your patience and support keep me properly anchored to the real one.